Holding on to Hope

A Novel

By R.B. Berry

Copyright

The author extends sincere appreciation to all those who shared their impressions and suggestions of this manuscript.

"If you bring forth that which is within you
that which is within you will save you."

The Gospel of Thomas

TO JOANNE, JOE AND ADAM

PROLOGUE

In 1967, before all hell broke loose from the Robert Kennedy and Martin Luther King, Jr. assassinations, the raucous Democratic Convention in Chicago, the escalating war in Vietnam, the tragic My lai massacre and unruly, growing student protests. This produced an American temperament that reflected a concoction of views, questions, doubts and fears about our nation's direction, leadership and moral standing.

From 1956 to 1975, more than 541,000 Americans served in the Vietnam War at a cost of $25 billion. To support the effort, more than a half million young men were drafted into military service. The War claimed more than 58,000 lives, 30 percent of whom were draftees. More than 300,000 were wounded, 75,000 were severely disabled and 1,626 were missing in action. Two million Vietnamese civilians were killed and atrocities were reported by all sides.

To avoid or postpone military service, draftees used college deferments, health conditions, physical limitations, essential employment designations, and religious restrictions. Some publicly burned their draft cards or moved to Canada or other foreign countries.

Many military and political leaders were determined to rein in on the spread of Communism in Southeast Asia. Many believed in the cause; a growing number considered it overreaching aggression.

Meanwhile, as troops were deployed or killed, injured or captured, back home thousands of other young men awaited the call. This is the story of how a small group of students from a Midwest college -- heralded as a premier party school -- were affected by the war as they awaited news of the fate of one of their own. This is the story about friendships and bonding. This is the story of how an unlikely leader emerged, mobilized others, and struggled to hold on to hope.

1967

At Grant State University, student unrest over the war had not reached the degree of provocation to disrupt plans for the next kegger. Demonstrations were few and far between and lacked the intensity, critical mass and threatening dimension necessary to incite. Marches seldom lasted longer than a lunch break and only attracted the scant number of do-gooders and troublemakers who never seemed to be taken seriously.

Life was still good at GSU: parties, mixers, traditions, pranks, streaking, and tubing along the rapids of a bubbling little river below the campus which was perched on a mighty limestone outcrop with a panoramic view of where four states come together. Through the GI Bill, surviving veterans enrolled in large numbers. Many were there to catch up on the good times they had missed. When *Esquire* magazine included GSU in its top 10 party schools, GSU's enrollment bumped from 4,200 to 5,400.

Despite the ubiquitous news coverage that percolated opposition to the war most everywhere else, activism had not registered with GSU's middle

1

Americans. Peace marches were for the major universities; the hippies on either coast; the small, liberal, liberal arts colleges. At GSU, the anti-war sentiment was muffled: too much of a reminder that draft deferments expired once boys were issued diplomas or flunked out; too much of a distraction from Greek mixers and theme parties and balling opportunistically; too incompatible with setting goals and making career plans after college. It was easier to paddle past the rippling reports of GSU alums who had been dropped into Da Nang or some buggy, sauna-like godforsaken jungle.

This rally was of a different bent. It featured scruffy, jaded army veterans who enrolled at Grant State when the GI Bill made the college scene more tolerable than drawn out days flagging traffic on some dusty construction site or suffering through night shifts on an oily assembly line. Little else awaited these guys. They were the undeployed who resented the public's indifference to their assignments, their plight, their demons. A few studied; most loitered. They had been torn by the war and were confused about how to stitch up a plan for whatever was next. Like

2

wisecracking construction workers, they showcased their crassness with shoutouts to the abundant young lassies on parade about campus.

Wearing scraps of camouflage, the vets paced on the sidewalk in front of the worn marble steps and imposing Doric columns of Peacock Hall, the administration building and oldest structure on campus. They lifted spray painted picket signs up and down in one hand, interrupted by swigs from quarts of beer disguised in brown bags in the other. Officials dismissed them and figured they were compensated like the vagrants the Salvation Army hired during the Christmas season to ring bells when not enough Kiwanians signed up.

"Forty-two! Sixteen! Hut-Hut!" To demonstrate their priorities, two flippant Pikes – the brothers of Pi Kappa Alpha – taunted the marchers by tossing a football back and forth over the scrimmage line and homemade placards. More brothers joined in, running unguarded post patterns and button hooks as if the protesters were an inept defensive line. All this was accompanied by the sarcastic folk-rock of Country Joe and the Fish, whose tunes emitted from an eight-track tape deck placed on a rattling metal chair along the sidewalk, left there alone as if it were a bomb that no one had the guts to disarm.

> *And it's one, two, three, what are we fighting for?*
> *Don't ask me I don't give a damn.*
> *Next stop is Vee-Yet-Nam.*
> *And it's five, six, seven*
> *open up the pearly gates.*
> *Ain't no time to wonder why*
> *whoopee we're all gonna die!*

Ellen Berman, an assistant librarian and one of a few campus Jews enduring this Bible Belt culture, joined in and brought the number of marchers to a dozen, not counting the Pikes who raided the demonstration. Professor Origen Cannon, an ancient eccentric from the religious studies department, joined in as did JaMar Brown, the cynical Black Power leader on campus. Even with these additions, the rally lacked rancor. It rolled along like a tire going flat. Yet the message from the veterans was obvious and understood: *We've been there; The war is a waste; Don't go; Tell the bastards in Washington to give it up.*

4

The Pikes parked their rusty antique fire truck in a nearby loading zone. This defining mechanical mascot offered terraced platforms from which to see and be seen. There they were, posing, a grandstand of brash collegiates watching the show, wising off, making room for a steady stream of impressionable coeds.

It was a Friday in April, and at GSU, another occasion to usher in a carefree, sweet-smell-of-honeysuckle weekend: tests and papers to defer until late Sunday night, girls in thinly draped halter tops signaling availability, a tapped keg, cranked up rock tunes with vibrating basses riding frayed, flapping curtains out of open dorm and frat house windows. Teasing. Covert flirting. Overt flirting. And aaah, the overarching adrenalin of the whole exhilarating scene.

Susan Strathmore had just come out of the GSU Foreign Studies Center located in one among a row of converted bungalows that framed the campus south side and housed the University Foundation, Newman Center, Student Volunteer Bureau and various underfunded fragile departments and services that shared space. On behalf of

5

Pauline Cody, Susan's perpetually horny roommate, she scoped out the hunk from Cyprus who worked at the foreign studies desk. His confident cocked smile, rugged darkness and quiet mystery left Susan and Pauline bumbling and yearning. Pauline's thoughts advanced to a scene in which she and Susan snuck the Cypriot into their room, turned up the stereo, and commenced to rip off his shirt. Susan giggled, knowing she would never have the audacity to do such a thing, although she wouldn't put it past Pauline. That thought set a chipper tone to their stride back to the Kappa Delta house, a roomy two-story brick box kept freshly painted and manicured by each new round of pledges. The brick was a bright white, accented by Kelly green shutters and decorative clovers. A pointed pediment framed the double-door entrance and the back-lit "KD" letters were mounted in the transom.

Scoping out hunks was more Pauline's style than Susan's. Pauline was full of mischief and risk taking, a stretch for sweet and self-conscious Susan. Hampered by a proper, affluent upbringing, Susan leaned on street-wise Pauline for social

6

courage. They were opposites that attracted. Petite and polite Susan tagging along with the robust and rambunctious Pauline.

To fulfill her duties as KD Social Chair, Pauline made a run to Baxter's Corner Market where she picked up a bag of oranges and a case of eggs to hard boil for the upcoming Cool Hand Luke theme party. To defy superstition, she stepped on every quake in the sidewalk and took a shortcut through the Faculty House where decades of tobacco smoke from the pipes of deans and faculty members was imbibed into the furniture and pine-paneled walls. Pauline spoke to everyone confidently as if her presence was authorized. She caught up with Susan and they headed back to the KD house by way of a path past a campus landmark – a small, charming plaza that featured a statue of Senator George Graham Vest and his devoted dog, Old Drum. Following a GSU good luck tradition, they patted Drum's bronze snout.

As they turned the corner on College Drive toward Peacock Hall, some sort of commotion came into focus. It was Vic again, in somebody's face.

Victor Devillez, a focused, volatile fourth year ROTC cadet from a working class Chicago neighborhood, on track to be the fourth generation Devillez to serve in combat, was unnerved by the grungy veteran turncoats who were demonstrating against the war in front of Peacock Hall. To Vic, honorable soldiers followed orders and chain of command and didn't question policy. The gig line of starched shirts was expected to line up with zipper cuffs. Hair was not to touch ears.

"What is it with you people?" Two Pikes pulled Vic back as he erupted with spasmodic swings at the vets. His pressed shirt became untucked. His inflamed forehead, darkening by the moment toward violet, brought forth a pulsating vertical vein that separated the emotional from the logical.

"Back off army man," said Luke James, a confident Vietnam veteran. He stepped out of the single file march to make peace. "Have a beer."

"You know..." Vic said while still yanking to free himself, "you're aiding and abetting the enemy." He could have

8

choked them all. He could have stabbed them.

"Oh come on, man. What enemy?" Luke said. "Are the VC knocking at your door, GI?"

Vic pushed toward Luke before being restrained again. "You're sending a message to the enemy that the American people aren't behind the war."

"They're *not* behind the war, man," said Luke.

"Yeah until they see the Communists get another foothold," Vic said.

"They're gonna do their own thing, man. We can't force Uncle Sam on the world," said Luke.

"China, Russia, southeast Asia, then what?" asked Vic. "It's the domino effect. The smaller countries won't have a chance."

"There's no such thing as stability over there, man. Hell, this country we're trying to save, they've had a half dozen governments in the last five years. Their elections are rigged. We're dying for that?" Luke asked.

Luke caught a pass thrown unexpectedly. The Pikes backed off and turned off the music.

"Let me share a secret with you, pal: The poor and pathetic Vietnamese people that I saw couldn't tell you or give a shit what kind of government they have."

Vic stood his ground. "We're not using our full force and military capacity. We're just playing around with the enemy."

"What do *you* know, man? You have no idea what our guys are up against in those jungles. What do you want to do, nuke thirty thousand people, or three hundred thousand? Hell, just make it three million. It's not military strategy; it's pure chaos over there. And endless. The more we kill, the more they keep coming – trillions, like a frenzy of ants spewing out of ant hills. We can't kill them all. Hell, we can't *find* them," Luke said.

"Our leadership, our tactics, our weaponry are all superior. We just lack resolve," Vic said.

Luke had pity on the kid, and sighed. "Guess that's what they teach you in the ROTC textbooks or when you march and salute in your cadet parade with your

10

shined shoes and polished brass belt. Training manuals won't mean much over there, kid. Basic training still eight weeks?"

"Yeah."

"Then you specialize, for eight more weeks, right?

"Right."

"Then you're dropped into some flooded rice paddy. Geez. Sitting ducks. When do you go to basic anyway?"

"Right after I graduate in May."

"Well, there you go. A future Lieutenant with a whole goddamn platoon to command. How long have you gone without a shower?"

"What's that got to do…"

"A couple two, three days – maybe on a Boy Scout camping trip or something?"

"What of it."

"Try six weeks. Or six months. You like dog meat? What'll you think when it's time for your bunk buddy to pull night guard duty and the next morning his head rolls into camp like a bowling ball with his dick in his mouth."

"Ever more reason to get the bastards."

Susan stepped in.

"YOU stay out of this," Vic said.

"C'mon, Vic. Now calm down," said Susan. "We're all on the same side here," she said as she tugged on his sleeve.

Pauline carried her eggs and kept her distance, mainly scoping out the Pikes who had taken off their shirts and worked up a sweat running their pass plays. She liked what she saw of the confident veteran who did most of the talking. She turned up the volume, but Vic had to get in the last word.

"All these fucking pussy peace freaks ...sorry ass examples of veterans." As others pulled him away he raised his voice: "America. Love it or fucking leave it, man!" As he left with Susan and Pauline, Vic grabbed a couple of eggs from Pauline's grocery bag and hurled them toward the Pike's fire truck. The first one missed and burst under a bumper. The other landed on the hood and left a slimy smear that no one noticed.

It took Vic well into the night before he put behind him the confrontation in front of Peacock Hall. While most everyone at the Cool Hand Luke theme party drank low-budgetly from the keg of Pabst, hooch with grain alcohol and Boone's Farm wine were also available. Vic – still fuming and ready to dive into anyone who smirked his way – had his own bottle of Glenlivet Scotch whisky to display at his table. He stood out with his standard issue buzz haircut. It was obvious that coeds favored the hairstyles of the latest British rock stars. Vic made up for his 5'6" height by developing a toned, v-shaped torso and a tough, disciplined disposition internalized through his family's military traditions and expectations.

Susan had been stuck with him for nearly two years. There were things about him that she valued and respected – in particular, that her parents liked him – but she never thought of him as *the one*. She knew he had big dreams for life in and beyond the military. He was principled and predictable, but to Vic, it was anything to win. Susan was his girl, and no one else dared ask her out because they'd have to deal with the hothead boyfriend. Susan was his catch, his possession. Given the horror of war he would soon be thrust into,

she hadn't had the courage to break up
with him.

The Cool Hand Luke theme party
and the hard-boiled egg-eating contest
attracted an overflow crowd. The movie,
with Paul Newman in the lead, included
classic scenes of the eating contest and
Newman, as Luke, stealing coins out of
parking meters. The movie was projected
reel-to-reel on to a concrete wall of the
Bluff City Jaycee Pavilion, a multi-purpose
building a block off the downtown square
that three fraternities and two sororities
jointly rented for the party. The scene in
the movie when the prison warden
delivered his infamous edict – *"What we
have here… is a failure… to communicate"*
– bumped up the rowdiness of the crowd,
some of whom wore hats and sunglasses to
mimic the prison guard who had it in for
Luke. The nasty egg eating contest
followed and as expected, failed to bring
forth a contender to challenge the eating
prowess of Barge Burlington, a 6'6" 280 lb.
tight end for the Grant State Grasshoppers,
who – after a pep talk and stomach
massage from boosters – chewed and
swallowed away eggs with remarkable

14

proficiency until, after his 32nd, he belched in two notes and spewed the goo and chunks until he was dry heaving, leaving drunken analysts to foolishly waste the rest of the night debating whether Paul Newman could have actually eaten the 50 eggs the movie depicted.

At GSU, the Kappa Delta sorority was a 62-member blue collar group whose sisters made up for their physical imperfections with rambunctious spontaneity and reputations for putting out. Many were of the first generation in their families to give it a go in college: daughters of machinists and boilermakers, store clerks and hairdressers and bus drivers. KD's tended to major in things like elementary education, office administration, dental hygiene and retail apparel merchandising – practical fields of study within the cultural reach of girls whose parents were not sold on college except as a means to marry up.

GSU's stuffy board of trustees were wary of its designation as a top party school, but appreciative of the enrollment and financial windfall. Celebrants strung a "Top Party School" banner (sponsored by

15

Sterling Beer) across Bluff Circle Drive, the prominent campus loop. GSU President Harlan Renwick looked the other way for a few days before ordering the banner down.

At GSU, tests and term papers were passed around handily, as were faculty ratings that scored teachers one-to-ten on their degree of difficulty. Pot was prevalent, but did not supplant the role of basic beer and cheap wine. Bars were open until 4 a.m. in Bluff City – about the time the nearby Huddle House opened for breakfast for local hunters.

No one was sure where the GSU "gooping" tradition came from, but when a coed was awarded a fraternity pin, her pussy whipped boyfriend was expected to be abducted by his "brothers" and tied to a tree – typically in a spot visible to neighbors and passing drivers who tended to honk and wave as if acknowledging that they once had their turn. Once fastened, the brothers commenced flinging every imaginable substance into and onto the victim's hair, face, and chest, under the arm pits, inside the ears and nose and shirt and crotch: chili, rotten sardines, ketchup and mustard, sour milk, molded baked

16

beans, piss, dog food, motor oil, catfish left in an unplugged refrigerator over the summer, sauerkraut, Limburger cheese – and many other undeterminable substances saved and stored for the next comparable berating.

But so as not to give the wrong impression, GSU Greek men enjoyed feigning sophistication in public settings. They took on the look with three-piece suits and pocket watches. They smoked pipes and strutted with canes like gentlemen, particularly when it was discovered that tubes of the hard stuff could be tucked inside the cane shaft and escape gate checks at Grasshopper football games.

For all practical purposes, weekends started on Thursday afternoons. Mixers, coed softball, flag football, Dizzy Miss Lizzy races, tug-a-war competitions, tubing and other social functions attracted scores more students than did political events, symposia, field trips and guest lectures. Even the dogs partied on: Gus, Lambda Chi's Saint Bernard mascot, could lap up a six-pack of cold beer from a Charles Chips can in 60 seconds.

Pauline could put away a half-case of beer and a lineup of stiff drinks that would knock many a drooling loser into a word-slurring unfashionable state. She had a knack for bouncing back from hangovers with a few Bloody Mary's and long steamy showers. And despite her image as one who would get down, mostly though, Pauline was more of a savvy tease than an easy lay, a one-step-ahead-of-you gal who could handle things and fend off the pricks and creeps.

She was also not above leading streaks across the quadrangle. These bold, rambunctious party girls would zip past the student union building and weave in and out of the columns of Peacock Hall before escaping from security guard whistles into the dark matter beyond the planetarium. Clemmy Fenner, the KD's sweet, naive House Mother, would observe the commotion but never catch on to what was going on.

Streaking was just another diversion from academics. Spending a warm, sunny afternoon floating down a river, grooving to music, kicking back with booze and buddies, was about as good as it got. Tubing was the pastime of choice once it warmed up and the water was high enough to lift inner tubes and rear ends above the sharp rocks that jutted up from the river bed. Possum Run River was at the base of the hill where the original Grant State buildings were perched. The river wrapped around the hill, defining the campus like a moat. It was a good quarter-mile hike through thick woods to the river from the campus. Atop the hill were several scenic stone overlooks and dramatic views of the campus and Bluff City beyond.

The trail from the campus led to a gathering spot known as Teddy's Landing. The first President Roosevelt was said to have made camp there in 1913. A century ago a flimsy sapling found a crevice in the stone slab there and brought forth a mighty birch tree that now stands guard. There are decades of etchings in that birch: "Sue loves Gary Wayne," "EAT ME," "for a BJ call..." or what was left of somebody's phone number.

Along the river, tree roots clung to steep banks, forming a canopy of limbs that, like large slow ceiling fans, powered an easy breeze that pushed the river along. The rapids could be so

19

rambunctious it was hard to hear one's own voice. Then there were times when the river calmed and, like a possum, held its breath and played dead before taking on obstructions of fallen limbs and tangled twigs the beavers left behind.

Teddy's Landing was where Pauline Cody and her pals gathered, where they snuck off and got wasted, where they learned enough about things to spout off opinions, and where they were free of parental oversight, university chaperones or matters governed by community standards of decency.

GSU tubers pretty much laid claim to the river that was too narrow, shallow and serpentine for speed boats, skiers or barges. When a floating convoy of tubers bobbed past a fisherman working a cove, the protocol was to hoist beers and greet in unison. Some fishermen would turn away and shake their heads in disgust of this boisterous generation; most would return the salute, grin and nod with envy.

The river appeared pure, pristine. Bass and blue gill burped along the surface, but fish populations were down from the factory discharges 15 or so miles upstream. Tubers never paused to think about chemicals in the river that might seep into their skin. By and large, GSU students in 1967 were oblivious to long-term effects of just about anything as guys braced for their notice via the draft board. But there was an upside: Lovely young coeds, the first generation on The Pill, were more inclined to leave boys with something to smile about before they were sent off to boot camp. As they awaited their fate, academics didn't seem important and they adopted the following theme song:

> *Don't know much about history*
> *Don't know much biology*
> *Don't know much about science*
books
> *Don't know much about the French I*
took
> *But I do know that I love you*
> *And I know that if you love me too*
> *What a wonderful world it would be*

To stretch out these good days at GSU, Pauline figured she would tell Hump that she was picking up another course over the summer. It didn't matter to him one way or another since it didn't come out of his pocket. Pauline had been ready to move out of the house since her sophomore year in high school when her dad married Rhonda, a Mary Kay representative. The name Hump was generally assumed to be connected somehow to his sexual propensities, when in fact it had been her dad's nickname from his chubby youth when his round face resembled Humpty Dumpty before his great fall. The Cody's lived in a Jim Walter prefabricated home in Bobcat, a southern Illinois town that held on to a 1950 census count of 452. Pauline was not ashamed of the house, a step up from their double-wide, but since Rhonda and her daughter moved in, the three tiny bedrooms were taken: one for the newlyweds; one with twin beds for Jesse and Lisa, Pauline's sister and new stepsister; and one filled with stacks of Rhonda's Mary Kay merchandise, promotional kits and sales charts spread about on easels. Hump convinced Pauline to give up her twin bed to Lisa as a gesture of good will under the circumstances. Since Rhonda claimed her room as an office, Pauline was relegated to sleep on the sticky vinyl living room sofa or the cold linoleum floor next to it when she had friends over.

Hump respectfully but strategically waited until Grace Mae, the girls' mother, died before he made a move on Rhonda, a flirtatious blonde who left her lazy husband and her job at the Heaven-Lee Hair Salon about the same time for the promise of multi-level marketing. It was a relief to Hump and the girls when their mom's multiple physical and emotional ailments finally took her down. She was in and out of institutions since the girls were born and lived a dreary life without pleasure – hymns by Tennessee Ernie Ford being about the only exception. Hump was glad that her tortured soul was finally at peace; the girls weren't as inclined to make excuses for her.

Grace Mae was a frail woman who once had a cute smile. Those memories and some eerie spiritual headlock kept Hump around. He was a big man with hair on his back who liked to grill out with friends. So often Grace Mae would go along with having people over, make the potato salad or slice some tomatoes and then excuse herself to the bedroom with another migraine or dark mood swings and a palm full of pills to deal with them.

She was consumed with the afterlife and browbeat scriptural lessons into her husband and children assiduously. She gave up on Hump believing at her level, but when it came to the girls, church and Sunday school were not worth feuding over. They were expected to recite chapter and verse, testify and evangelize. Hump didn't go for the heavy-handed indoctrination, but as large as he was, he wouldn't stand up to her.

While Grace Mae was still calling the shots in the Cody household, there were no cosmetics for the girls. Cheerleading was not an option because the skirts might blow upwardly and expose underpants. Pauline and Jesse couldn't wear shorts more than a couple of inches above the knee or accentuate cleavage. Going to the prom, in particular, was not a consideration, with all the drunkenness, oral sins and fornication that Grace Mae heard happened after the dance. Softball practices conflicted with Wednesday night services or summer Bible School, so God won out. Her resoluteness worked on daughter Jesse – who thoroughly turned her life over to Jesus when cleansed by the baptismal dunk – but Pauline was never persuaded when her mother harped on God's wrath.

The Cody's had not pushed schooling, since they had little and had gotten along. Grace Mae dropped out to have Pauline when she was 15. Hump quit school when he hired on at the seed and feed store there in Bobcat. He drove a forklift on the side. The extra money helped out but didn't get them through the eight years that Grace Mae was sick. Hump was stuck with the bills and it was tough going until Rhonda and Mary Kay brought order and cash flow into their lives.

Rhonda became a pal to her new husband's kids. She had her own religious eccentricities, but at least she took the girls shopping and helped them with their hair. Hump loosened up also, allowing the girls to participate in co-ed events. But high school was nearly over for Pauline and because of her dictatorial mother and capitulating ol' man, she missed out on the standard experiences, overblown as they were: boyfriends, Sadie Hawkins, Homecoming, the trip to Springfield for the mock legislature, pep club.

Throughout high school, Pauline babysat, scheduled appointments at Lloyd's Body Shop, and waited tables at the Pizzaria in Shawneetown. One night not unlike many others, she took the brunt of a cranky customer who fussed that a pickle was missing from his Stromboli Special. Pauline hustled to retrieve a long sliced dill from the kitchen, but rather than deliver it on a small plate, she carried the dripping pickle from one end like she had the tail of a dead mouse. "Heeere you go," she said without sarcasm, not having been briefed on the proper way to deal with the situation. The Pizzaria night manager saw it all from the kitchen, and when the last customer left and it was just the two of them, he called her an idiot for not putting the pickle on a plate and told her that he'd forget all about it if she was...well, nice. But when he latched on to her tank top she kicked him in the shin, and when he buckled over she brought her knee up against his jaw and sent him flapping into the salad bar.

When Pauline mentioned that she might not want to stay home and look for another numbing job, and instead see if she could get in the community college at

26

Rend Lake or SIU-Edwardsville or maybe Grant State over in Missouri, Hump told her she was not college material. He hadn't monitored her grades or ever met with a teacher, and he was well aware that he hadn't saved for any such thing as college. He wasn't about to go into more debt when he had a power saw and a clutch to replace first. But none of them liked their cramped quarters since Rhonda's family moved in; going off to college would improve that situation.

"When did you get to be such big stuff? What, you think you can be a doctor or lawyer or sumpn?"

"No, Hump. Don't really know what I'll do. Just gotta do *something*, you know? Nothing here in Bobcat."

Hump was privately proud of the initiative Pauline was demonstrating, but he didn't know where it was suddenly coming from. He knew that Grace Mae had gone overboard with the girls, particularly Pauline. Maybe it was time she got out of their obsolete town. She had her whole life to work a job and care for kids. Maybe his daughter was due some fun.

As if the whistle blew, Pauline took off in search of good times. College would be carefree. She would grab for gusto. She would scamper in the buff with a wild flock of streakers. She would buy a black light and some posters and a used stereo. She would be the one who was delivered to the front door of the sorority house in a wheel barrel. She would be the one in the middle of the dance floor riding on the shoulders of someone else's date.

Through the luck of the draw or intervening forces, Pauline and Susan were assigned as dorm roommates during freshman orientation and bonded instantly. Susan planned to enter sorority rush but she had to explain to Pauline how the Greek system worked. They both were offered bids from Kappa Delta. Pauline had but the one option, whereas Susan could have pledged with any of the snooty sororities. Susan convinced Pauline to join her and together they would leave their mark with the wilder KD bunch. As they bonded with their pledge class and tested their partying capacity, Pauline was the notorious leader of the pack.

The pledges semester included house duties, interviews with actives and quizzes on KD history. This led to a lovely little sisterhood ceremony followed by their own private pledge class blowout, dancing, jumping on beds in bras and panties, while singing Lulu's *To Sir with Love* into broomstick handles.

Susan ate conscientiously and in moderation; Pauline cleaned her plate. Susan had yet to develop a taste for alcohol; Pauline was not hard to please when booze was available. Susan was Episcopalian; Pauline had enough of religion after a dose of her mother's Pentecostal church and its heavy-breathing preacher. Susan was petite, elegant, guarded, soft-spoken with a lovely smile and golden skin; Pauline was big bone, heavy-breasted and freckly, loud, blunt and rude. Not quite Laurel and Hardy, but certainly an unlikely pair. Susan was a pleaser more than a confronter. She would give people the benefit of the doubt. Pauline was quick to measure you up, and if need be, defend you like a badger protecting its young. Without make-up and wearing sweat pants, Susan could turn heads; Pauline could look good when she had to, and she had a noticeable scar on one hand and forearm. Susan had blue twinkling eyes that were mounted glamorously on angled cheekbones like she could see sideways. She pulled back her shiny blonde hair with ribbons and bows; Pauline's brunette mop was long and uneven in the back with thick bangs in the front, accented only by a leather headband. She had a habit of blowing her bangs upward whenever she was aggravated or played the ditzy game. Susan sipped French Bordeaux; Pauline sucked down whatever was complimentary or whenever six packs were two-for-one. Susan easily made the dean's list, majoring in Literature; Pauline was content with her 2.2 GPA. She was pretty sure that she was majoring in Recreation.

Susan had the means to dress for any occasion; Pauline was limited to jeans and consigned mixes and matches. Susan drew on charge accounts without calculation; Pauline got by on loans, a $700 Civitan scholarship and, until the end of May, the $47.18 she netted every two weeks working at the GSU Student Center.

Susan breezed through courses toward a degree that need not advance her professionally or socially. Her parents already had her affairs laid out for her: a one-sixth interest in the family businesses, trust fund, and regular use of condos in New York and Boca. She was expected to marry well, so while they courteously acknowledged the drive of the Devillez boy, they were uneasy that their daughter may eventually cave in to his pursuits.

Pauline had more practical hopes. She was thinking that a GSU diploma might take her all the way to jobs in places like Cape Girardeau, Evansville, Paducah or smaller towns in between.

To gain an edge on his ROTC cohorts while earning extra ribbons and medals, Vic spent every other weekend at the Mt. Vernon armory learning advanced maneuvers and military strategy. Pauline was determined that Vic's routine absence would not withhold Susan from the social treats that awaited her underserved palate. So when Vic was away or just being a prick, Pauline would yank Susan out of the KD house to take part in the circuit of parties and special events that could be found every weekend and most nights in between on and off campus. Vic found Pauline's brash intervention hard to take, but he also had a sense of confidence that his girl would be in good hands with her confident and adept friend.

Consequently, Pauline, by way of her notoriety, and Susan, by tagging along, were reputed GSU party animals who caught the attention of young collegiates on the prowl. But the two were always one step ahead of the predators. They shared strategies and, unlike many KD colleagues, were not free with their favors. Susan knew well of her family standards and Pauline knew well what being 15 and knocked up had done to her mother.

Once at Susan's insistence, Pauline brought her roommate home with her for a weekend visit in Bobcat. Susan took the couch and Pauline slept on the cold, gummy linoleum. It was a good time to visit: Hump's marriage seemed to be going well as Rhonda launched new Mary Kay pyramids in Sikeston and Marion. Hump was doing less forklift work and more to help Rhonda set up her seminars and send out orders. He liked the way things were going: more money coming in than he was used to, a buxom bride who believed in pleasing her man, and who would have ever thought that he would have a kid in college.

Susan appeared to enjoy the Cody family. She never complained about Hump's bullshit or the wild game he would bring home from the woods nearby. Susan had never eaten squirrel, turtle or rabbit.

Since Grace Mae died, Hump's good ol' boy nature burst forth like his belches. He had developed a hard, stretched beer belly that couldn't be covered by his t-shirts. He chewed on Roi-Tan cigars. He trained his prize pointer, Sport, to ride like an ornament on the hood of his moving truck. Hump hunted, fished, played poker and cut his own logs. He was prone to gross generalizations while wasting away too much time drinking coffee and bullshitting with the fellows at the diner there in Bobcat. But since relieved of a manic-depressive wife and pills he couldn't afford, Hump was untied and more like the man he once was: a nicer fellow with a deep, contagious chuckle who made it a point to share with the neighbors the extra squash, tomatoes and other local produce that flourished from his garden.

Susan was not one to condescend. She appeared genuinely interested in the Cody's – their jobs and hobbies, and Grace Mae's Bible-based trinkets that Rhonda felt obligated to leave on the living room shelf. Susan listened attentively while Hump shared the history of the straight razor collection he inherited from his Pap who cut hair on the side in his musty cellar. She didn't challenge Hump's adamant speculations. His latest: "Them two sides o' that Gateway Arch they're buildin' up there in St. Louis? Ain't gonna match up at the top. Good lands. I hear they're off three-four feet. And they expect people to go up in that thang. Shit fire."

As Pauline watched Susan listen and nod and chat and smile gently with her simple family, it reinforced the notion that in her, she had a special friend, a lovely person who had it together and could make all sorts of folks feel at ease. If it was all an act, if she was really laughing at them from the inside, Pauline sure couldn't tell and never would have believed it. Pauline imagined her turn when she'd visit Susan's home to ride horses and sip lemonade on their roomy front porch. When asked about her family, Susan

34

downplayed her privileged circumstances. She had fallen in love with the GSU campus while participating in a mock legislature there in high school. She had been drawn by the setting, the old stone buildings, the cliffs and views and vistas, and the winding river at its base. She decided right then and there that Grant State would be where she would live out her best years yet.

Pauline had already thrown up twice and figured she was good as new. She and Susan made their way to the Huddle House for a Sunday morning recuperation breakfast following Saturday night's Sigma Epsilon kegger and scavenger hunt. They laughed out loud as they reviewed last night's highlights: Those who hopped up on the stage to play their air guitar with the band, the awkward unskilled dancing, the Pike pledges who *borrowed* the kiddy mechanical horse located at the entrance to the Big K store to win the scavenger hunt. They speculated on who went home with whom. All in all, they agreed, it had been a good night.

Suddenly the diner's cashier held up a transistor radio and turned up the volume to get everyone's attention:

We interrupt our regularly scheduled program for this KBLC news break: Will Yoder, Grant State University's most celebrated and beloved Grasshopper basketball player of all time, has been reported missing in action in Vietnam...

"What!" Pauline and Susan reacted instinctively, simultaneously.

Shocked and assuming the worst, they grabbed each other's hands tightly, then rushed out of their booth to get closer to the cashier holding the radio.

"Did I hear what I think you said?" Pauline was frantic. "Did they say when? Where? How many others were captured? Are they sending in troops to get them out?

"Turn that up," said Susan. "God!" It can't be," Susan said. "Not Will."

Pauline pounded her fist on the counter and spilled the coffee of the customer sitting next to the cash register. Pauline could feel her heart pounding. She was short of breath and felt like a heavy hand was holding her underwater.

Susan tried to calm Pauline as she smeared the tears off her cheeks.

"Missing means that he's alive," said Susan. "They'll see that he's a medic and he won't be a target."

"Oh sure," said Pauline. "As tall as he is, he'll be even more of a target. They don't play by the rules over there. Hell there ain't no rules."

Being a Sunday morning, the only other station the diner's radio could pick up carried preachers spreading the Good News and familiar hymns over the airwaves. Word spread quickly but no news was hardly good news. By early afternoon, hundreds of Will's fans gathered at the main gate of the GSU arena. Coach Shoals and President Renwick made an appearance, but they didn't have any new information. Renwick led the crowd in prayer. Pauline pushed a student who referred to Will as if he were already dead.

Susan and Pauline were there for one another, sharing in the shock. "Oh no," Susan said. "I knew this would happen."

"It can't be, dammit. It can't be," Pauline said.

37

Pauline and Susan were Will's special pals. For four semesters and two summer terms, Susan was his tutor and administrative aide (aka "Booster Buddy"). She was with him several times per week. Before his freshmen courses were selected for him, tests indicated that Will needed remedial work. Susan was to keep him eligible. Since junior high, Will had been on a vocational track to follow his father's plan for him to go into carpentry to supplement work on the farm, both earnest and humble ways of living that fit well into his northern Indiana Amish and Mennonite culture. But then came all the basketball distractions that showered upon him and clouded his future: reporters, feature writers, agents, financial advisors, fans, local and state dignitaries, faculty and staff, and fellow students who had courted and since then pampered the basketball icon. Susan prodded him to stay focused on course work, and just as important, she coached him on practical skills: how to greet dignitaries, which fork to use, media interviews, budgeting, how to pack for road games.

Pauline, on the other hand, noticed right off how the groupies moved in on

Will. "Star fuckers," she called them. As his basketball stats and skills gained national notoriety, Pauline knew that the coeds would be circling the wagon, yearning for a turn with the big guy. Some of his followers figured Will to be the marrying type, or at least generous with child support.

Concerned with the potential consequences of his naïveté, during his sophomore year, Pauline quietly introduced Will to intimacy the weekend that Susan went home to Kentucky for the Bluegrass Stakes at Keeneland. Once Will caught his breath after the first time he entered Pauline and came quickly, he just knew it was true and blessed and everlasting love, and he asked Pauline to marry him.

"You're sweet as the dickens, Big Red," Pauline said. "You don't need to screw everything in sight, but you best give it a go with a little more tail before deciding that I'm the best you can do."

"Huh?" he said as he panted.

"You heard me. And when they tell you they're on The Pill, don't believe them. Use your rubbers. Here." She tossed him a packet of condoms.

They had not been intimate; this was their one and only time together, a going away present seventy-two days ago, his last night on campus for his final furlough before he was back on base and then urgently deployed.

The official report indicated that Private First Class William O. Yoder was with an army infantry unit moving to secure areas north along the Saigon River toward Binh Long in War Zone C when U.S. troops came upon Viet Cong resistance. As a Mennonite, Will qualified for a conscientious objector religious exemption from military service. His parents, family and friends around him at Peaceful Springs Church in Minnow, Indiana did not approve of his participation, even as a medic, as that was an expression of justification for the killing that would go on around him. Mennonites were pacifists; they lived simply and rejected the things of this world, although unlike the Amish, they were allowed to drive automobiles.

After Will's senior season, before he graduated and just weeks from the NBA draft in which he was expected to be picked in an early round, he enlisted and

40

insisted on no special consideration. He figured he could still play ball after his hitch.

There had been a sense that as a medic Will would not be in the thick of things. If anyone would be invincible, if anyone would distinguish himself and come home with a legion of admirers, it would be Will. Now no one on campus escaped the grief. They were all stunned – students, faculty, alumni, athletic staff, administrators, office help, janitors, cooks in the cafeteria, lawn care crews, people from every walk of life in GSU's hometown of Bluff City. Folks were shattered, and they speculated, thinking the worst, that this terrific kid, this gifted honorable naïve kid, at six feet ten, "…was maybe just too big a target."

The same kind of bad news spread like fungus on the crops:

"He's surely dead."

"I knew it was gonna happen. I had a bad feeling about him signing up to go over there."

"Stupid idiot, trying to be a hero. He could've gotten out of it, you know. He would've just played exhibition games and put on camps."

"But that wasn't Will."

"He should have listened to his family, his tradition."

"Could've played ball at Goshen College and stayed near home."

"But he loved Grant State."

"Maybe, but what did he die for — huh? Tell me, then. Just what did he die for?"

"We don't know that he's dead. We don't know that -- at least for now we don't know that."

Street talk was pervasive. For weeks, months. Like the JFK assassination fresh on their minds just four years before, everyone connected with GSU would forevermore remember where they were when they heard the news about Will Yoder. Within minutes, Will's number 44 was suspended from windows and balconies around the campus and throughout Bluff City. Photos, banners, posters, basketballs, t-shirts and sweatshirts with messages, flowers, and personal recollections were all piled reverently at the front door of Grey Arena, where Will's talents were showcased and savored for four glorious seasons.

Mac Shoals, Grant State's lovable and — except for the Yoder years — habitually unsuccessful coach, emotional and atypically nervous as he yanked on his belt and snorted in the tears, read a statement and announced a prayer vigil planned that evening.

"Will Yoder was like a son to me. He was not just the best basketball player I ever coached; he was the finest young man I ever coached. They just don't get any better." He shared recollections with print, radio and television news reporters who had rushed in: "It was serendipity. Big Red was a gift from God to this old washed up coach. I got my first peak at him while on an off-season fishing trip to Oswego Lake in northern Indiana. I had made a quick stop in this tiny town of Minnow on the southwest cove of the lake. I bought some tackle and beer, and then I noticed a crowd roaring around a basketball court in the town's only public park by the lake. In 30 seconds, I knew I was looking at a future All-American."

Grant State had never even produced an all-conference player and Minnow, Indiana had never produced anyone at all with celebrity status beyond its county sphere. Minnow was among the small towns that catered to the sportsmen who fish the lakes that were scooped out of flat northeastern Indiana by glaciers ages ago. It was one of those places that old narrow state highways suddenly come upon, where local roads soften you and local laws slow you so that the people there can make a statement that things and lives do indeed go on there. The Lions Club posted its Tuesday noon meeting schedule on a slanted sign dimpled by BB pellets. There was a two-block row of stale storefronts that propped one another up like drunkards: buildings that housed Klaassen's general merchandise store where you could get a sliced bologna sandwich on white bread and a cold Coca Cola in frosty small bottles, a florist owned by the family with the funeral home in Warsaw, a county extension office, a realtor who rented lakeshore cabins and sold bait, a single screen movie theater showing *For a Few Dollars More*, Birdie's Hair Salon, Bud's single chair barber shop, and a drug store with a three-stool soda fountain. Oswego Bank and the post office were the only new buildings in town. The bank exploited the Amish culture of the

44

area insensitively with its horse-drawn carriage worked into its logo. Across Main Street was a farm implement store and a mighty grain elevator that hovered over the town. Its emissions left an oatmeal film on things when it rained and at times it smelled like cooking malt vinegar. From about anywhere you could see the lake and a dozen modest split-level homes and cabins with decks and docks to park fishing boats. Along an undeveloped section of the lake was Minnow's city park where the town found its notoriety and meaning through Will Yoder.

The park was named for Chesney Buck, Minnow's state representative from 1952-1960 who offered Will a new suit and $200 in knocking around money when he heard that Will visited Butler University, his alma mater. Will declined graciously and unassumingly. The Buck Park public swimming section was roped off and a make-shift beach was created by brown sand brought in from Lake Michigan's eastern shore. There were swings, see-saws, a May pole, monkey bars, and for the old folks, shuffle board and a dirt croquet court. A picnic shelter had a smoke-stained stone bar-b-q pit jutting out of one end. The premier landmark was the full-length asphalt basketball court with a crooked rim and chain nets where Will learned the rhythm of the game, where he quickened his pivots and doubled his vertical jump, where he took 1,000 practice shots a day, where he took elbows and toughened up to block out under the boards. As he kept growing and improving and dominating, the town council knew it had a once-in-a-lifetime prodigy in Will. They re-assessed property to generate the funds to install flood lights so Will could practice as late as he wanted. Boosters and prognosticators pulled alongside the court, sat in lawn chairs or on car hoods, and nodded at one another as they witnessed this genetically blessed seed sprout and blossom before their eyes.

It was hard for Will to be much more than a basketball player while growing up in Minnow. He was a gentle and soft-spoken young man, but no one asked him about school, family, church, or how a building project with his father might be coming along. He was aligned with the game and challenged to put Minnow on the map. When he had a chance to kick back, Will liked hanging out at Ivan Pogue's Barber Shop and, like his father, he enjoyed whittling on the porch at home when there was a nice breeze. But there was little time for loitering: Will had a rare capacity to play the game; he was expected to win, not to place or show.

Will's father, Abram, had a broad, 6'5" frame that Will passed in the eighth grade on his way to 6'10.""A special gift from God, being so tall," Abram would say. But the more that basketball encroached on their family priorities, the more the Yoders were not so sure.

Abram was stern, hard to convince of things. He believed in work, prudence and maintaining a perpetually prolific garden. He farmed 40 acres in corn and did carpentry and upholstery work on contract at a chair factory near Shipshewana.

Ruth was a loving mother and wife who seldom came up for air. She was a conscientious homemaker who found time to engage in random acts of kindness: knitting scarves or dropping off homemade peanut brittle to friends on no special occasion, or writing tender notes of sympathy to those who had lost a loved one.

The Yoders had lived through their share of loss. Their first child, Rachel, died after just three days. Paul, of pneumonia at six. Angie, 17, is engaged to a dairy farmer.

The frenetic sports and media culture that descended upon the Yoders was not welcomed or appreciated initially, but once they caught on to the rules of the game and saw how much joy it brought the boys on the team and how it made the people of Minnow so proud, Abram and Ruth Yoder got to as many games as they could and watched politely as best they could.

Despite his celebrity status that carried over into college, once on the GSU campus, Will could discover space to breathe in a library nook, under a tree along the quadrangle, or down the bluff beside Possum Run River. He liked the freedom he felt when he was off by himself, when no one knew where he was or had no way to contact him. But those were carefree college years, a safe haven before the war escalated and before he ever imagined being over there in it,

48

before his loved ones imagined him in some labor camp or dead and bloated and stiff and smelly in some gully on the other side of the world.

Underneath the image and public fascination, Will was an unworldly small town boy with an earthy conservative moral grounding. Will was always the first player to pull up an opponent who'd been knocked down, the first to say "nice shot" or "heck of a pass" to teammates or rivals. Will never said "no" to any charitable outreach, fund raiser or promotional role to help worthy causes and needy people. He refused to charge or take tips for his summer basketball camp. He visited old folks in nursing homes and delivered Christmas baskets to the orphanage in Fairfield. He stayed up all night to comfort a teammate whose mother was about to die. Being from northeast Indiana, Will hadn't been around many black people; however at GSU, they were teammates, classmates, roommates – family he'd go home with and invite up to his world of heavy snow, golden maples, deep-seated faith and slow routines of life, where fertile land was bought and sold in neat quadrants. Flat enough so that Will, some would say, could stretch his neck from Minnow and see the lights of Indianapolis from his sphere above.

Coach Mac didn't believe in Sunday workouts, so he scheduled study periods from 1:30 to 3:30 followed by skull sessions when he reviewed his players recurring mental mistakes and warnings about the next opponent. A half an hour of this came to be redundant and gave way to the coach's animated anecdotes from years gone by:

"Yeah at Anthoston, we played in this cracker box gym with ceilings so low you couldn't arch your shot higher than the backboard. The other team was banking in shots off the ceiling…"

"And them ol' boys at Larue Tech: They were waiting for us outside the locker room with brass knuckles and baseball bats. Hell there weren't no security at all. We had to sneak out the back through a basement window. They threw rocks and bottles at the bus as we was pulling out…"

"And God almighty, it was cold in '58, so cold at that game in Laporte that when the furnace blew out, fans were wrapped up in blankets and steam was coming off the sweaty bodies out on the court. We made a run to a Ben Franklin store and I had our boys out there playing basketball with gloves on..."

Coach Mac was better as a storyteller than with X's and O's. He could keep the team in stitches, despite his tendency to repeat his tales. While he told his stories, he held a basketball as if it were a sacred relic, petted it as if it were a trembling newborn puppy. He was increasingly reflective and unsure if his life in basketball had lived out his days in providence.

Will was the only top tier recruit that Coach Mac signed in his 38 years at GSU. From day one of their relationship, Will had a soft spot in his heart for the old fellow, and would remind folks that he was the first college coach to travel to Minnow to see him play, even though it was purely by accident while on a fishing trip. Coach Mac came to be a familiar fixture in Minnow; he put away more than his share of Klaasan's bologna sandwiches.

From his initial visit to Minnow, Coach Mac and Grant State had an edge in landing Will. His mother of few words, always in her modest cape dress and bonnet, didn't understand why Will could not enroll at Goshen College. "Goodness gracious after all, they have a ball team there, too. Your father and I just want your occupation to be pleasing in God's sight. You know that we are a humble people; we'll not stand for self-aggrandizement ," she said. "Besides (and then she would tear up) Goshen is closer and you would be among more of our kind." Will's father, however, whose conclusion overruled, heard enough advice from co-workers at the plant in Shipshewana and reasonable friends at Peaceful Springs Church – all tacit fans – that his son has a gift and that it would be a sin for it not to be manifested.

Will liked the idea of enrolling at a smaller school, a fare-thee-well underdog where he could pull some other top prospects with him and surprise naysayers with some wins, maybe a championship.

And they loved him for it. He signed his letter of intent the September before his senior high school season with unprecedented fanfare, and a month later, he was Grand Marshall of the GSU Homecoming parade, seven months before he was even a student there. It didn't take his fans and the media but a few exhibition games to award him with the name "Big Red."

He pulled other fine players off their major college track and plans to play for Louisville, DePaul and Memphis State respectively: Toby Hargett of Jeffersonville, Indiana; Shane Thornberry from Battle Creek, Michigan; and Dallas Charles from Memphis, Tennessee.

NCAA rules prohibited freshmen to play on the varsity, so the Yoder-led freshman team zipped through the season at 26-0, packing Grey Arena (5,600 capacity) consistently while the varsity games drew half that many through a typical 12-17 season. The freshman team won by an average of 31 points, a margin that would have been greater if it weren't for the stall tactics used by opponents to keep from being humiliated.

What the Will Yoder era would mean to Grant State was the talk of Bluff City and the source of giddy institutional pride. Devoted fans, boosters and know-it-all coffee drinkers at the diner were sure about one thing: it was finally their time.

Will got a kick out of GSU's crusty coach and wanted the team to live up to its expectations in this last stretch after which

the old man surely would retire. Coach
Mac was a funny buzzard, scatter brained,
full of baffling anecdotes. On the first day
of practice, it was "You boys line up there
alphabetically by height." He was also a
showman whose game prop was the 15
year-old scraggly net that had been
ripped off the rim following the 1952
conference championship at Vincennes –
GSU's last pre-Will successful season.
Coach Mac used the net creatively: he
wore it like a necklace; he waved it to
celebrate a good shot or a points run; he
slammed it on the floor when a player
dribbled off a foot or telegraphed a pass;
and the favorite — whenever he wanted to
risk a technical foul to incite the crowd or
vitalize his team — he turned his back to a
referee in a half squat and yanked the net
back and forth across his tush like it was a
towel drying his butt, lifting one leg, then
the other. The crowd loved it.

   After a season of his repetitive
platitudes, most players casually
dismissed him. He ran a predictable pick-
and-roll offense, a man-to-man defense,
and he liked his players to use the bounce
pass and the backboard more for bank
shots. He believed that his team needed to

look sharp to play sharp. For away games, they wore blue blazers, gray slacks and team neckties that featured tiny grasshopper mascots. Players had to hold on to a 2.0 grade point average, not a difficult task given the ample supply of cooperating faculty. But curfew was enforced, as was proper grooming, as interpreted by the coach.

Coach Mac considered himself an educator, and he was paid like one. He tried to keep basketball in its place as a game, a preview of life's lessons, a tool for helping young men grow up and use good judgment. When he reached 65, President Renwick and the board of regents considered phasing him out, but Mac's antics were entertaining and he was popular in the community, with alumni and the ephemeral athletic directors who impatiently resigned when budget after budget was inadequate. School officials were almost proud of their mediocre won-loss record, an indication that education and not athletics was the priority at GSU, even though there wasn't much else to back up that claim. Nonetheless, the talented bunch they had coming onto the varsity, led by the big red-headed fellow from Minnow, Indiana left them all wriggling with enthusiasm. And what that would do for the party scene at the ultimate party school.

Will didn't let anyone down during his three years of varsity ball, but the Yoder era did not result in the domination and national rankings that were predicted. Will more than held his own against Walt Frazier of Southern Illinois, Clem Haskins of Western Kentucky and Bob Netolicky of Drake – All-Americans and future NBA stars and the three toughest players Will faced in his years at Grant State. He had six clean rejections off shots taken by the 6'9" Netolicky; he outscored Clem the Gem 31 to 17; and he had 24 points and 12 assists to Walt Frazier's 15 and 4.

But before their sophomore season tipped off, Toby Hargett went down with a compound fracture and when he tried to return, lost his quick edge and confidence. Shane Thornberry flunked out but then found a technical college in Idaho that took him in before he landed a spot on an Italian team. And Dallas Charles quit the team when he concluded that his future was in the hospitality business after he knocked up the daughter of a Holiday Inn district manager.

With not much talent to work with, that meant Big Red had to bring the ball up the court, deal with double-teaming defenses, score, rebound and otherwise carry the team and keep up their spirits when they lost. Over his three varsity years, he averaged 28 points, 15 rebounds and eight assists. GSU went 15-12, 18-10 and 17-13 in that stretch – unprecedented for Grant State, but far from a transitional era or a new day of post-season play. When he lost his three support stars, Coach Mac missed out on several replacement recruits. He road it out and took the pressure off himself and his players. He loosened up the team's grooming standards: there were several afros, beards, mustaches, and Will's orange mop-top.

It leaked out of the selection committee that GSU was seriously considered for an NIT bid after Will's junior season, but they never got the call. Indeed, exposure for the school and its star came and went like a few fireflies lighting up a small backyard. Will and the Grant State Grasshoppers didn't gain much national exposure, but Will was still expected to go as high as the third round in the NBA draft before he withdrew his name, told his coach, then his folks, and went off to serve his country.

Will hadn't been through Basic Training but a couple of weeks when Pauline's nightmares started to haunt her. She worried that Will would be assigned to duties in the most intensive battle regions, facing an endless production of indoctrinated warriors and gorilla warfare on their home turf. This was proving to be confounding and the source of widespread angst back home.

Pauline had only received three letters from Will. His last one gave her a glimpse of the horrific experience of war and how his role as medic couldn't shield him from it.

Pauline diluted the pain with booze and blowouts. But when she would stumble home and lie in bed and see the ceiling spinning, she was increasingly aware that she needed to change -- especially when the nightmares kicked in:

Her eyes strained to see through the jungle fog and the thick, stout bamboo. She had just stepped out of a brown soupy creek that rose over her waist. Snakes wiggled and curled up her slippery legs until she snatched them and yanked off their heads. Wielding a machete, she sliced open a path to a clearing where there was a statue of Old Drum, the bronze dog from GSU's Vest Plaza, morphed into a growling creature when she rubbed its snout.

Muddy tears had dried on her cheeks. She could hear someone and she responded devotedly. "Big Red, is it you?" An image came into focus, dribbling, then spinning a basketball on his index finger. It was Will. He laughed like a madman and placed the ball under his shirt and told everyone he was pregnant with Pauline's baby. He recited a cheer and clapped with pom-poms. Pauline read orders from Westmorland: our mission: score points, kill more, win the war. It was all a game. All agreed that, if we could just take the hill ahead, that would settle it and afterwards we would all go home. They wacked their way through the denseness to a clearing where desperate Vietnamese girls were auctioned. Will picked at the scabs on his arms – infected sores of yellow puss.

59

"Will? Will? Give me a W, Will!"
Pauline   shouted. *"Give me a W!"*
Give me a W! -- W!
Give me an I! -- I!
Give me an L! -- L!
Give me another L! -- L!
What's that spell?
Will!
What's that spell?
What's that spell?

Susan was there, but her face was
pimply and her disheveled hair was caked
with green dirt. Will sat in Susan's lap. She
tutored him, slowly enunciating
Vietnamese words. He turned on her.
"How do you know their language, you
rich bitch? Do you just screw the all-stars."
Will showed no expression. His thin, pale,
sagging skin draped off his bones. Others
could smell his sickness and cringed when
he sprayed his repulsive cough. "I like it
here. Ivan gives me free haircuts," Will
said.

Pauline was there to break him out
of The Hole at the camp. But the hookers
charged and surrounded her with their
weapons. Snakes wrapped around her
neck and shoulders. Pauline raised her
machete but then buckled from an

impalement in her side. She felt the slicing burns of blades across her back, then deep into a hip. She crumbled and awaited the end, sweating and panting.

Pauline yelped as she shook herself loose from the dream. She retrieved her bearings. She knew this dream. She hated this dream.

The suspicions of Pauline and Susan — whether Will had been killed, wounded or separated from his unit — advanced through their psyche like a new strain of a jungle infection. They didn't think much about how Will might have wanted them to react to the circumstances. He might have preferred that they support the war, given his patriotic core. Despite the objections of his parents and pastor, he enlisted because he didn't think it fair for others to serve while he was excused because of a faith tradition he was born into. He rejected special privilege despite the risk and ostracism.

But Pauline knew these dreams had to mean something, had to be telling her to *do* something. So she opened herself to influence and the mounting array of Vietnam War opponents, from Mario Savio

and Martin Luther King, Jr. to John
Sherman Cooper and the Smother's
Brothers. Pauline and Susan were
newfound activists. They were sold on the
cause. It was simple. It was time to put an
end to the war and bring our troops home.
It was time to join the growing opposition
even though our GI's were increasingly
painted as the aggressors. Their public
cause was a broad policy goal; their
private cause was to get Will back —
whatever it took. Then maybe Pauline's
dreams would dissolve. Then maybe they
would not haunt her.

To gain credibility, Pauline and
Susan immersed themselves into current
events and social justice issues. They met
the leaders of the statewide chapter of the
Vietnam Veterans against the War who
were largely indignant and damaged by
the chaos and horror of what combat did
physically in some and emotionally in all.
Villages destroyed. Young Americans
doing things they could never imagine
themselves doing. These veterans, like so
many others, were bruised and scarred
and baked dark from jungle mud and
ammo that wouldn't wash out. Many were
without limbs, pugnacious, not to be

messed with, with no interest in continuing education except to max out their GI Bill allotment.

To experience the movement, a group of veterans talked Pauline and Susan into coming along to a march in Washington where, the chilly damp night before the rally in a pup tent along the mall, they fought off the bourbon-induced advances of Gator-man (from Florida) and the one they called Franco. They couldn't allow these strangers to have their way in Will's presence; placards featuring a picture of Will that they planned to wave during the march were propped up reverently in the corner as if Will were chaperoning.

Luke James, the savvy vet who stood up to Victor Devillez in the spiritless veteran's demonstration at GSU, kept a journal and took notes of the statistics that were shared from the podium. Susan found herself looking his way.

Early the next morning, Pauline woke first. She wrapped herself in a blanket to greet the morning vista and to get a better sense of this stunning spectacle. Susan joined her and offered steamy coffee. Their priorities were changing, internalizing. The former KD entries in wet t-shirt contests were becoming different, deeper. They took in confidence with every breath of the early fog. They took in inspiration as they scanned out over the multitude and the backdrop of monuments and landmarks and the sounds of Pete Seeger strumming and singing for peace and principles. They took in resolve as they read the pickets and banners and listened to the string of speakers: ex-marines, Dr. Benjamin Spock, Allen Ginsberg, a runner with a peace torch lit in Hiroshima.

It was unlike anything they had ever imagined — 100,000 people they heard someone say — with marchers from the Lincoln Memorial to the Pentagon. They met Ivy-leaguers packed in VW vans, hitchhikers, priests who defied their bishops, hippies who placed flowers in gun barrels of pensive soldiers along the barricade. Someone handed Pauline a soggy, tattered picket sign with a Cornell decal that said, "Hey, Hey LBJ — how many troops will you kill today?" It was a swarm of humanity guided only by impetuous instinct and audacious confidence.

As the day wound down — when people were weary or numb from the cold drizzle or still drunk or high or determined to disrupt — Pauline and Susan were close enough to see things get unruly. They saw protestors get clubbed for picking flowers in Lafayette Park and tear gassed for chanting, but they also saw marchers push over fences and sling garbage on the streets and spit on the soldiers. Jerry Rubin tried to levitate and exorcize the Pentagon. The mob pushed through on all sides.

Susan felt claustrophobic — a domino, but not lined up so as to play a part in something cleverly designed. She was unable to control her place or movement. It became a free-for-all, and the roar and smell of pot and alcohol and body odor hovered over the mob. She was scared and relied on Pauline's street smarts — to no avail.

More than 600 were arrested, and because of where they happened to be standing, Pauline and Susan were herded up with the perpetrators and honored with a noisy, chaotic night smashed in a cell with intellectual idealists and rowdy disrupters who saw this as another Mardi Gras. With this, their first criminal offense, the energized Pauline and Susan committed themselves to take on Westmoreland and any military official with a flat top. They brought back a harder edge and a sense of what it takes to provoke the establishment.

In no time, word got out about their DC adventure. They were interviewed by *The Hopper Herald*, the campus newspaper, as GSU's first students to be arrested in an anti-war march. Area network television stations picked up on it: radical Pauline Cody, a confounding thing for most to imagine, the hell-raising pistol from Bobcat. And troublemaker Susan Strathmore? Surely a mistake. When their mug shots were picked up by the wire services, instantly and ubiquitously, GSU had a new mantra as the Midwest center of activism.

Jennings Strathmore flew in with his lawyer, T. P. Heywood. Strathmore's face was broiled red and pressurized. He was livid as he confronted Susan, his heretofore sweet and saintly daughter. "I don't guess you ever thought about the family's reputation?" he said to her in a private dining room of the faculty house.

"There are consequences to things like this."

"I'm sorry, Daddy."

"I'd jerk you right out of here, but chances are that the schools up east are dealing with the same radical factions, perhaps even more so," Strathmore said. "What about Rhodes in Memphis? Or DePauw in Indiana?"

"Most every reputable school is dealing with this cultural phenomenon," Heywood responded. "And transferring at this point could complicate Susan's graduation, since it's just a year off. Credit transfers from GSU can be problematic."

"What the hell is Renwick doing anyway, letting things get out of hand like this? Grant State kids have never been troublemakers. Hell, they like to party and run around naked; they call it "streaking." That's a far cry from joining these radicals."

"We weren't doing anything wrong, Dad. The police just arrested everybody."

"It still will be on your record."

"Actually, sir, I think we can take care of that," said Heywood.

"Well whoever the hell is influencing you, you keep your distance.

We wouldn't be dealing with all this, hell the war would be over, if we had Goldwater in there. How'd you get to DC anyway? Don't tell me you hitchhiked."

"We went in a van with some veterans who are against the war."

"Good God. Don't tell your mother that you're shacking up with…"

"I didn't shack up with anybody. You know I have a boyfriend, Victor Devillez, who I might remind you, will graduate soon and be entering the service."

"Yeah, well that's another issue."

Hump heard that Pauline's name popped up in a wire service story that ran in the Carbondale newspaper. He couldn't find a copy in Bobcat so he phoned Pauline once he found her number.

"What the hell is this all about you being in trouble? What's goin' on?"

"It wasn't anything, Hump."

He didn't believe her. "Pauline?"

"They took a bunch of people down to the police station for a couple of hours – I think just to send us a message."

"About what? Where? What the hell you into?"

"Since we learned that Will Yoder is missing in action, we've just been trying to, you know, get involved, get him home."

"And how the hell do you think you can have anything to do with that?"

"By stopping the war. If he's alive, you know, there's a chance."

"Well la-de-fuckin'-da. College know-it-all. End the war, huh? Shiiit. You just need to get your schooling over with and get your ass home. You've been over there at that place too damn long anyway. You ain't gonna save no world. You just need to be getting you a decent job, that's all, and leave things to the generals."

He coughed into the phone and Pauline thought she could feel the damp spray through the receiver. "We've been talking about it. Even for college kids, ain't much in Bobcat for you. But Rhonda can set you up with a Mary Kay district over in Madisonville. Gal over there wants to go in with somebody, has a husband with black lung pretty bad, needs to stay home with him. You'll have to straighten up, though."

But the thing was: Pauline and Susan didn't feel like they *might* be needed; they *knew* they were needed. For different reasons and affecting their standing in different circles, both sets of parents wanted them, expected them, to pull back on the activism. Tell them to be practical. Let leaders lead. Party time's over.

But the cause had become their life. Pauline and Susan were innervated. They were not intimidated by parents, lawyers, family friends at cookouts or cocktail parties, or their own peers who made carousing their priority. Nonetheless, to gain credibility, they had a good bit of catching up to do on current affairs. They didn't know the Mekong Delta from a Norway fjord. The Six-Day War had slipped right past them. Until all this happened with Will, like so many KD's and GSU coeds, they had been preoccupied with things like Elvis's hasty marriage to a frightened girl who used far too much eye-shadow.

Now the two of them were writing letters to Joan Baez. Under their parent's radar, they expanded their cause to race relations, social justice and corporate power. They followed the riots in Detroit and spoke out against the fire hoses and police dogs in Alabama. And then, once again, the war came closer to home: two

70

former GSU students were missing in action in the Que Son Valley and another one was killed with a journalist in Dok To.

It was time to go forth, to add more disciples.

Pauline and Susan had been invited to say a few words to the Sigma Nu social outreach committee about their efforts to expand the peace movement at GSU. As they approached the frat house, they could feel the vibrations of Pink Floyd under the quaked sidewalk, and they should have guessed that the meeting had been adjourned early; after all, it was "Hell Week" when the hazing of pledges peaked. Pauline, in particular, was no stranger to the place; she had held her own with this crowd on many occasions -- finishing off kegs, winning in strip poker, learning the lyrics to *There Are No Sigma Nu's Down in Hell.*" They were greeted enthusiastically, handed beers, and asked by someone they didn't know, "So, you ladies ready to get down?"

They heard commotion on the upstairs landing. "Dor-sey! Dor-sey! Dor-sey!" was chanted from the crowd packed outside the bathroom. Pauline knew of

71

only one person by that name. She had heard about Dorsey Sugg and how the divot in his nose was caused by the exhaust fan in the girl's locker room. He had leaned in a little too closely to sneak a peek at the girls coming in and out of the showers. She was surprised to hear that Dorsey pledged Sigma Nu because they were generally seen as a frat that, as frats go, had it pretty much together. It was a stretch to imagine Dorsey as a Sigma Nu.

But in fact, Dorsey was a future legacy. His father was initiated into the University of Illinois Sigma Nu chapter in 1939, so Dorsey was expected to follow suit and become an active member in the Grant State chapter whether or not he was a good fit.

It was "Hell Week," the culmination of the pledgeship experience, the test to demonstrate one's worthiness to a lifetime active status. And there was Dorsey, no doubt worn down by a semester of verbal and emotional hazing, blindfolded and stripped to his saggy briefs, forced to crawl up the sticky, stale, beer-reeked hardwood stairs that had not been cleaned since... well, never, to the upstairs bathroom, where his hand had been plunged into the commode that featured a banana floating amid a few plies of toilet paper.

"Grab it worm! Bite into it, Sugg!" the brotherhood chanted among the rumble of overlapping stereo beats and jeering laughter.

"Stupid shithead! Eat it worm!"

"Dor-sey! Dor-sey! Dor-sey!" The belligerent crowd expected him to bite off a mouthful to prove his worth.

"Eat it, worm! Eat it all!"

"You suck, pledge, if you don't eat that shit!"

The brothers spewed their beer as they laughed and gave one another high fives while they remembered vividly how they had to endure the same prank. Pauline nudged Susan and gave a head signal that they needed to get out of there. The girls started to maneuver through the smothering crowd and cigarette smoke toward a way out when, suddenly, a defiant Dorsey rose, yanked off his blindfold, revealing a shaken, offended soul. When he saw that he was holding a banana, Dorsey shoved it into the mouth of the closest heckler, hopped aboard the stair rail in his underwear, and slid down past the crowd to a clean landing in the foyer. Without breaking stride, Dorsey was out the bay window and headed up the hill before any of the uncoordinated drunken brothers knew what was happening. His swinging limbs blended with the dark and his white briefs faded — a dot, bouncing into the night.

A week or so later, Pauline was behind Dorsey in the campus bookstore checkout line. She hoped he had not seen her that night at the Sigma Nu house. His blush and awkward avoidance suggested otherwise. He covered the wart removal ointment in his cart. She noticed the v-shaped scar on his nose.

"I tried to take your clothes to you."

"What?"

"'I'm Pauline Cody and this is Susan Strathmore. We grabbed your clothes at the Sigma Nu house that night when they played that awful trick on you – that night when, you know, you took off."

"Another shining moment for Mr. Cool."

"You were great. Quite an exit," Susan said.

"Well…"

"A memorable moment. Believe me."

Dorsey grinned. "I had to get the hell out of there fast."

"You're legendary. Folks will be talking about that for a long time."

"Well... guess I'm not cut out for the Greek life."

"Aw, you're destined for better things."

He picked up a travel-size bottle of *Brute* from a half-price table and placed it in his cart. "You're that girl, aren't you? Friend of Will Yoder. Went to that march. In Washington."

"That was us."

"Tough thing, going to jail, I guess."

"It was worth it."

Dorsey was awestruck. "Wow."

"I bowled with Will once in intramurals. He played in his sock feet because they didn't have any bowling shoes that fit him."

Pauline chuckled.

The clerk looked over Dorsey's student identification card and handed it back to him.

"That'll be $12.17."

"I, uh… I got a cousin in Nam. Marines," he added.

Susan grimaced.

"He touches base when he can. Says they drink a lot of beer over there. Yeah, they give it away so the GI's won't smoke so much pot."

"Not surprised," said Pauline.

"Reassuring," said Susan.

"Yeah, well, he told me not to go unless I had to."

Pauline squeezed his forearm and Dorsey noticed. "Tell you what. If you're not tied up Saturday night, why don't you join us at Vest Plaza — you know, at the statue of the Senator and his dog. We're having a vigil in honor of Will," Pauline said.

"Nothing fancy, just a few words from people who know him," Susan said.

Pauline added, "We'll light some candles, maybe build a little fire down by the river later. Play some music. Kick back. The kind of thing Will would have liked."

"Well… I don't know."

"Listen, you showed a lot of guts at that Sigma Nu party. Standing up to those jerks when they took their teasing too far.

We need you to be part of our peace effort. How about it?"

"Well...I'm no big man on campus or anything, you know. Nobody will follow *me*."

Pauline paused and blew up her bangs. She didn't like to be denied. "Oh, c'mon. Have some damn confidence. I told you we could use you." She pushed out a hip and perched a hand on it.

"Don't have to give any speeches or anything?"

"Hell no. C'mon."

"You know I'm not a big trouble maker or nothing."

"All I've ever done is party," admitted Pauline.

"You'll be fine," said Susan.

"Then we'll see you Saturday," said Pauline. "Now I mean it."

And so it was that Pauline and Susan's first recruit was Dorsey Sugg. While some saw a humiliated loser who was blackballed from a fraternity, a horny dork whose first peek at naked girls was through the flicker and the blowing rush of a large locker room fan, Pauline saw someone who'd been chewed up and spit out, someone with resilience and humility,

77

with skills untapped, someone who deserved a place where he'd be welcomed, baggage and all. She had her own share of it, and was learning to look past it in others. She would bring in all kinds of people now, to party on, with a purpose.

Jin Ae Kim had not enrolled at GSU for any reason except that it was less expensive than her other options and she could sink the difference into tax exempt bonds. She sought more than a finance-marketing double major from GSU; she needed practical networking and venture capital leads from the business department. She didn't get much of either from this faculty. They were comfortable instructors who rode out their careers without risk, innovation or extra effort, things that were second nature to Jin Ae.

To be aka Jimmie Kim was a business decision. To set aside Jin Ae for Jimmie would make her more marketable and accessible. She hated when she had to pronounce and spell her name after it came out so many wrong ways.

Jimmie was a young woman in a hurry: a driven capitalist, a non-apologetic, former most-likely-to-succeed high school senior superlative. At GSU, wisecracks about her Korean heritage were quelled with every new possession she flaunted that was out of reach for other students whose assets consisted of two pair of jeans, used textbooks and a few boxes of Ramon noodles. Jimmie was an anomaly: she owned an FM stereo and Super 8 movie camera outright and was making payments in layaway on a color TV. She was a materialistic hippie who wore round glasses, tie-dyed smocks and hemp hats. She fit in because she could buy in.

Jimmie was a fan of women who conveyed a tough-minded, independent spirit; Aretha Franklin and Lola Falana were sassy favorites. Photos of contemporary business women who overcame obscene odds, discrimination and the hard knocks of the workplace were pinned to the bulletin board of her West Hall dorm room: women who invented things like windshield wipers, flat-bottomed grocery bags, typewriter correction fluid, toll house cookies and Barbie dolls.

Jimmie had no real friends in which she could confide. There were students she tutored for cash upfront and employees she had to hire when projects got too big too quickly. She could delegate responsibility but not authority. She could assign projects but she was not good about acknowledging credit when things went well. She was one tough-ass boss.

She was mindful of her challenge: to not work so hard that she didn't work smart. She juggled 17 credit hours with the tutoring and two other jobs (a night shift in the library's reference section and an afternoon campus mail route) and two fledgling enterprises: a portable car wash service she took to workplace parking lots and a free campus literary tabloid that, unlike *The Hopper Herald*, accepted advertisements from liquor stores and brand-named alcohol products. And as if she had time to spare, Jimmie was promoting a business plan for *The Summer Games*, a board game whose release she wanted to coincide with the 1968 Olympics. She was waiting on a response from Parker Brothers.

She had file drawers full of notes and sketches and revenue projections. So many ideas, so little backing. Banks were impossible without collateral, her race and gender didn't help, and fat cat angel investors wanted documentation of demand and cash flow projections and a sense that this hot shot youngster knew what she was doing and wouldn't drop the ball after she found a guy to marry.

Dating at all, let alone the notion of marrying, had not occurred to Jimmie in her three years at GSU. She figured that once she made it and moved her headquarters to New York or Paris, there would be more Asian male options, and she was inclined to go that route. She didn't need the hassles and indignities of mixed race relationships. Besides, the Asians she knew were the smartest and studious of the lot, and she certainly wanted any offspring of hers to have a genetic edge.

Jimmie's tough disposition had a hard body to go with it. It was toned not from any workout regimen, but from the pace of her routines and her percolating metabolism. Her dark complexion was fine with her without makeup, as were her natural nails not colored to match. She was short and stocky

like a sawed-off tree trunk, and she didn't
think of herself as particularly enticing
when naked. Jimmie had a small mouth
and small teeth and a coy square smile that
didn't seem to fit her and so she seldom
used it. When she was irritated or needed
to put aside distractions and focus, she
would stand on her head against a wall in
her dorm room.

It was not coincidental that her times
at sex had been quick and unspectacular
before she or the boys had been totally
unclothed. Her few times with Lonnie
Youngman should have been better but
still didn't do it for her. She knew
afterwards that she had been one of his
conquests, and that his whispers about her
silky hair and beautiful skin were a means
to the end of nailing his first Asian. When
Lonnie said he'd like to keep seeing her
but that he was not yet prepared to tell his
wife, Cate, about them, Jimmie shut off his
allure like a spigot. But the spigot dripped
annoyingly.

She named her literary tabloid
Express Yourself, a name procured from
the hit tune of the Watts 103rd Street
Rhythm Band. Bundle drops were at both
ends of the student union building, the

portico of the administration building, dorms, bookstore, major classroom buildings, and at sports facilities on game days. *Express Yourself* more or less came out around the last week of every month when school was in session. When it was time to publish the April edition, Jimmie had to assume delivery duties after a student employee called in to say she had to attend an anti-war march for extra credit in Dr. Canon's class. Jimmie was used to picking up these kinds of pieces when employees called in; it pissed her off nonetheless.

The third drop-off point was next to the alumni center and financial aid office, near where some pesky ATO pledges dumped a box of *Tide* into the a fountain, erupting a river of soapy lava clear down to President Renwick's house. Jimmie pushed a dolly across the bubbly currents, teetering with bundles of her publication – - a heavy load that she could handle confidently. She yanked the dolly backward up a set of steps to a space for a covered cigarette vending machine, where she pulled out a pocket knife and snapped the strings loose. Jimmie's sleeves were rolled up and sweat had seeped through to outline her bra straps. A few students took a smoke as they sat on a short brick wall that framed the landing.

"Here you go, scholars. Hot off the press," Jimmie said.

One student swung around and picked up the edition without noticeable eagerness.

Jimmie was not the best salesperson. She could care less if anyone read *Express Yourself*. She found the poetry and short stories pretentious, flowery and a waste of time. But she guaranteed the advertisers that 3,000 complimentary copies would be distributed around campus.

"They're free. Have one, or two, or ten," Jimmie said.

The students shrugged as if to decline.

"It's student fiction. No editing. The writers can cuss and describe sex or drugs or anything they want," she said.

"Really? Hmm... Okay, then. Might as well. Thanks."

"Any album reviews?"

"Waiting for your submission," Jimmie said.

"Free, huh?"

"Yep, and there's some pretty good coupons in there for Boone's Farm wine. Tell our advertisers that you saw their ad. They might knock off a little more."

"Is this like some underground paper, man?"

"No, shithead," a friend teased. "Didn't you hear her: It's a literary publication. For the literate. Not dumb fucks like you."

The others laughed and picked up copies.

Pauline, Susan and Dorsey cut through, in a rush, carrying picket signs. Dorsey had on a long, sloppy t-shirt with a huge peace sign he had drawn on the front with a marker.

"Rally – front of Peacock! Half an hour! Speak out against the war!"

The students were uncertain, pensive.

"Sure. I'll, uh, I'll meet you there." Another one rolled his eyes.

"Yeah, but I uh... I've got class."

"Yeah, me too."

Pauline turned to Jimmie as she positioned a bundle more squarely on the dolly.

"How about you, when you finish your route? What time you get off?"

Jimmie resented the assumption that she must be somebody's delivery girl. "I'll, uh... I'll check with the boss."

"We gotta speak out, end this war," Dorsey said.

"We need you. We need everybody," Susan said.

Turning to the indifferent guys, Pauline challenged them: "And you there: skip class. This is more important."

"I, uh... I don't know. Got a test coming up."

"Well come if you can. If not, there'll be other rallies." Pauline noticed a quiet one with a religion textbook and a Bible. She thought of her mother for a moment. She figured it would be fun to put the religion student in his place, to challenge him to some biblical trivia because she knew it would all come back to her. But she had a more important thing to do, a more important place to be.

Jimmie bounced the empty dolly back down the steps, turned and raised her voice as the three hurried ahead.

"Hey, you're the ones... aren't you? ...didn't you go to jail? ...in D.C.! That you?" But the three were beyond earshot. As she approached Peacock Hall, Jimmie noticed the standing-room-only disturbance exuding from the president's office, and eased closer to observe.

"Just what is it you people want?" Dean Neville Ewing demanded sternly. His toady, Buddy Baxter, stood next to the flag.

"We want to stop this war," Dorsey said. "We want our troops home."

"Too many are dead, disabled — for what?" Pauline asked.

"And we're killing who knows how many innocent Vietnamese," Susan said boldly, uncharacteristically. This earned a stern look of surprise from Dean Ewing who knew who she was and the family she came from.

"We were told there would be a vigil on Vest Plaza," said the dean.

"Of course you can use it," said the dean.

"Good. But we'd like to meet with President Renwick too," said Pauline.

"Dr. Renwick is not a defense official. This is not the Pentagon," Ewing said.

"Students, faculty and administration from coast to coast are taking a stand," said Pauline.

Jimmie could hear the derisive crowd and see that it was too thick to pull her dolly through it. She heard Pauline taking on the dean.

"We're losing young boys with their whole life ahead of them," Pauline added.

"We have to trust in our president and military leaders. We sure don't want Communism to take hold over there," the dean said.

Jimmie, the newcomer, offered a shout out. "The key to peace is economic interdependence! Commerce can't take root until we stop blowing up the centers of commerce." Pauline realized she may have a live wire in this young publisher.

"Give peace a chance," Dorsey added.

Dean Ewing raised his voice: "We give you people some leeway and you're chuckling behind our back, missing classes and tests and you begin to think it's so funny and cool and *your right* to disrupt learning and order here at this institution. We are a small state school in mid-America; we have no influence on federal policy. I believe in standing by our great nation, our leaders. They have the inside information. We'll not have you burn buildings or throw rocks at police. We'll not stand by while you loot stores and spit on people who don't agree with you."

"You'll advance your cause through rule of law, not mob rule," Buddy said. The dean nodded; he could depend on Buddy.

A crusty mumble came forth from the rear of the room. The crowd went quiet as a path opened up for Coach Mac Shoals. He moved slowly to the front. "Sometimes when you need a little honey, you gotta kick over the beehive," he said. The crowd erupted in supportive cheers. The dean knew better than to disparage the revered legend.

President Renwick entered the room as if to observe.

"We're not condoning violence, Dr. Renwick. Just exercising our constitutional rights," Susan said.

"We want to hang a banner on Peacock Hall that keeps a running tally of the dead," Pauline said matter-of-factly.

"What? Absolutely not," said the dean.

"The people have a right to know," said Dorsey.

"What good would that do?" asked the dean.

"How can we honor the dead if we don't acknowledge them?" Pauline asked.

"Stand with us on this, Dr. Renwick," said Susan.

President Renwick removed his suit jacket. He opened a window blind and pulled out a pocket watch from his vest as if he could slow down time and the disruptive energy holding on to it. His presence calmed the crowd. He took off his glasses and looked out the window. Pauline held up her hands to quell the crowd so Renwick could be heard. He turned to face them.

"You don't think I agonized over the news about Will Yoder and the others from here at GSU who are now in harm's way, or those who may have already made the ultimate sacrifice? You don't think I hate this war as much as you do?"

He wiped off his glasses and put them back on.

"I was in a war. European theater, World War II. One of the most gruesome, unconscionable conflicts of that war, known now as Battle of the Bulge. I dare not convey my recollections." He looked down and ran a hand through his hair.

"I believe in hell, because I've been there. I've experienced it. I've contributed to it. And it haunts me... it haunts me, to this day."

The students were suddenly quiet.

"I have a nephew over there – in the central highlands, we've been told, on into Laos at times. My wife's sister's son. They live in Ohio. When he got his draft notice, he didn't hesitate. It was his duty, his turn, to serve with dignity and honor. You didn't see him dodging the draft or going off to Canada or suddenly proclaiming that he was a convert to some pacifist utopian commune."

Jimmie worked her way in and listened intently.

"Of course I *will not* let you hang such a banner. A well-researched position paper or letter to the editor in the *Herald* is one thing, but if I yield to you here you'll see it as a victory over the establishment. You'll do something bolder the next time. Agitators will come in here. They'll make it a media circus. More drug pushers will be here; mark my word. Class work will become less important to you. One incident and you'll force me to bring in the National Guard to maintain order. Someone will get hurt. My trustees will be up in arms. The governor will call, then our congressmen, then some general. Who knows where it would end," he said.

"In a democracy, the voice of the people matters," said Pauline. "So we pretend that the war is not happening?" she asked.

"No! No!" the students chanted.

"We don't belong over there!"

"Give it up, Renwick!"

The students started chanting. "HANG-THE-BAN-NER! HANG-THE BAN-NER!" A faint melody increased in volume from the vestibule outside the president's office. By the time it seeped inside, most everyone knew the lyrics well enough to join in:

And how many times must a man look up
before he can see the sky?
And how many ears must one man have
before he can hear people cry?
And how many deaths will it take till he knows

92

that too many people have died?

The crowd belted out the chorus:

The answer my friend is blowin' in the wind.

The answer is blowin' in the wind.

The Dylan tune miffed President Renwick even more. He'd had enough. Buddy and Dean Ewing pushed back the surging crowd and pressed the door shut. GSU had no security guards; it had never needed them. The students lifted their fists and roared. Jimmie was impressed with Pauline and could see herself getting involved, but she would need more help with her enterprises. Dorsey hugged Pauline and Susan and others joined in to form a circle as the singing continued. And Luke James, the jaded army veteran, hummed along as he watched from a distance.

Once the crowd dispersed, the aggravated dean stood atop the Peacock Hall steps. " ...such scholars, such scholars we attract to this institution. I'm sure they're headed back to the library."

Buddy and the dean remained in the president's office. Buddy sensed a chance to score points. "I didn't know that, Dr. Renwick, about your war experience."

"It's not something I talk about or like to remember," Renwick said.

"And your nephew?" the dean asked.

"Has absolutely no business being over there," Renwick admitted.

Buddy assured him: "Well your family has certainly stepped up to serve, sir."

Renwick turned to Dean Ewing. "Coach didn't help things, did he?"

"No sir," the dean said. "He and the Yoder kid were real close."

"This Cody girl – Pauline, is that right? – and her little following," Renwick said. "Keep a watchful eye, and make sure you have the number of your contact at the National Guard close at hand."

"The Mount Vernon unit is just an hour and fifteen minutes away," the dean said.

"I want them on alert status. And I want the best men in that unit, those who will be firm but keep their cool."

The vigil went well. It featured testimonials from veterans and challenges to fraternities and other groups to get involved. A rally was planned for the quadrangle. The buzz kicked in. Seeds of social activism sprouted about, mostly on welcomed soil, some still on rocky resistance. Students set aside their mainstream music to tune in to the cause. Faculty found courage. And like a pot of water heated on the stove, the voice of discontent bubbled here, then there, to a convulsive, uncontrollable, unpredictable boil.

The mail carrier brought a box of materials to the KD house lobby from the Students for a Democratic Society. Pauline, Susan and Dorsey identified prospective sympathizers — those connected with labor, the civil rights movement and intellectual circles. They read material. They corresponded. They piled into a friend's van and went to a training meeting at the University of Michigan.

In some circles, the peace movement went on sabbatical after Lyndon Johnson was elected in 1964 so as not to derail his Great Society programs. But when news trickled out that LBJ was deceptively expanding the war, there was news of brash — mainly young — leaders storming public buildings, burning draft cards and sabotaging factories where weapons were manufactured.

News of Will Yoder let the air out of GSU's party balloons. It was assumed that the Cody girl and this group of student troublemakers were responsible for the false alarm about a bomb in the ROTC building, but no evidence emerged. There were more peaceful assemblies, classroom discussions, stories and editorials in the *Hopper Herald* and more accusatory commentary that made its way into *Express Yourself*. Pauline and Susan had regular interviews on the campus radio station, WGSU. They were invited to speak to campus service and hobby clubs. Some of their sorority sisters – the party pals, tubers and streakers — initially resented the attention that Pauline and Susan received and thought all this activism was fleeting. But the more they observed of their dedication, the more they envied these sisters who had moved on, whose fate had lifted their lives and expanded their vista to a more principled plateau.

After the confrontation in the president's office, it was like Coach Mac had pulled off an upset and seen a bump in the polls. He was invigorated by this grass roots activism and was not intimidated to be part of it.

Then Jimmie Kim signed on. She discovered value beyond her enterprises. She listened to more Dylan. She circulated a petition drive promoting a conscientious objector status for draftees who opposed the war on moral grounds.

Luke James offered his carpentry skills to Pauline and her troupe. His vocational training had not earned him a deferment from the draft, so he did his duty in the infantry and claimed that he remembered little of Vietnam other than the sheer chaos. His hearing was gone now on one side and he couldn't quite disguise whatever injury caused him to limp.

At 28, he was older than the other student activists and worn down to look more like a 40-50 year-old man. Deplorable things had happened to him. He had an occasional twitch and his nightmares would end with a wail. He was thin as a jockey, and his strong hands and dark skin were leathery. Those who'd seen him without a shirt took note of the raised shrapnel scars on his shoulders and chest where hair could no longer grow.

But to Pauline, he would be a solid member of the team. Someone who could build platforms and displays. Someone who had been there, who could speak with experience about the hell we're creating in Southeast Asia, the fuel we're throwing on the fire.

Luke didn't intend to finish college at GSU or anywhere else. After some courses in design and drafting, he yearned for a quiet life where he might read Louis Lamour books and make cabinets, roll-top desks, maybe baseball bats.

As a registered Republican, Luke never had a chance to vote for Eugene McCarthy, his favorite candidate. He figured either Kennedy's money or Humphrey's speechmaking would get them the '68 Democratic nod. As for the Republicans – the party of his father and his father's father – Luke concluded that Nixon would be the one, but not the one to win it all. To Luke, the war was the only issue, and he held his ground with reason and principle and memories and what just felt right.

When Jimmie first saw *Suds and Buds,* her business instincts kicked in and she was pissed that she hadn't thought of the idea first. It was perfect for a college town: a have-a-beer-while-you-wait-for-your-clothes laundromat. She and her newfound friends walked past it on their way to *The Greek Shoppe*, both of which were in a small commercial strip two blocks from campus near *Long John Silvers*, a new restaurant chain and a big deal for Bluff City. Jimmie was already thinking how she could commercially tweak the hip laundry. She would add sandwiches, a juke box, some *Cliff Notes* on a rack. She would develop a jingle. Franchise it.

Next door to the laundry, the Beatles *All You Need is Love* spilled out into the colonnade in front of *The Greek Shoppe*. The store carried silk screened shirts, jackets and caps, engraved fraternity and sorority paddles, beer mugs, framed coats of arms and other memorabilia and party favors. Dorsey flapped open a folded sweatshirt but tossed it aside when he saw the Sigma Nu insignia.

"Hey, how you folks doing?" asked the lone clerk.

"We're all right, doin' all right."
Pauline said.

"Good concept you got here,"
Jimmie said, looking around.

"Thanks. Yeah, we seem to have a
corner on the college knickknack market."

"I'm Pauline. My friends Sally,
Dorsey and Jimmie."

"Dave, Dave Blazer."

The girls noticed the face right off.
The sweeping blonde Beach Boy hairdo.
The white shoes. An angled smile that
signaled he was up to something and that
he knew his looks would take him places.

Pauline brought them back to
business. "Need a banner there,
Faceman," she said.

"Pardon me?" the clerk said.

"That was a compliment," Susan
said.

"And a pulley so we can take it up
and down," Dorsey added.

Blazer was an Sigma Alpha Epsilon
(SAE) political science major who had
been picked as the fraternity's candidate
for USG (United Student Government)
vice-president followed by the presidency
next year. The SAE's always made sure

they had a controlling delegation in the USG.

Blazer also managed the shop that, unbeknownst to students, administration or the Greek community, was quietly owned by Dean Neville Ewing, an SAE alum who only hired superior, handsome brothers from the chapter. Ewing had used his connections on the local planning and zoning board to make things difficult for any enterprise that tried to move in on his little corner of the market.

"Well we can make you a banner. You may need to get your pulley from a hardware store. How big you looking at?" Blazer asked.

"Big as we can handle," Pauline said.

"Sounds like you're in a hurry. When you need it?"

"Saturday. For a peace march on Saturday," Pauline said.

"Oh I don't know." That triggered it: He recognized Pauline. "You're, uh... yeah, you're that bunch, trying to stir up things. Not that that's all bad."

Pauline reminded him why they got involved. "We may have lost a good friend to the war." "Guess you mean Will,"

Blazer said. "Will Yoder. Big Red. Yeah, I knew him, too. God, that's terrible. He's missing. They're not sure if he's dead – right?"

"He's not," Pauline said.

"He could be playing against Chamberlain and Russell in the NBA," Blazer said. "Could be making big bucks."

"Will didn't care about that," Pauline said.

"He was just trying to help out, you know, as a medic. He wouldn't fight. He's a Mennonite," Susan said. "They're like the Amish, only they can drive."

"Hard to believe. Damn draft. Every day, I hear of guys getting scooped up from schools like GSU," Blazer said.

"I'm headed for law school. Should extend my deferment until the war winds down," Blazer said.

"Whatever it takes, man," said Dorsey.

"So, I uh… I guess you're expecting a big crowd. These protests are going on all over," Blazer said.

"It's a revolution, man," Dorsey added.

"We're a little behind the movement here, but we're picking up support," Pauline said.

"You ought to come," Jimmie said.

"Saturday, eleven o'clock in the quadrangle. We'll have some music, speakers. We want to post the number killed in the war between the columns out front..." Pauline said.

"...until Renwick has his crew bring it down," Susan added.

"Hope you guys don't get in trouble over this, but I'm glad you're doing it. I support you all the way." Blazer said.

Pauline was not so sure she believed him.

Jimmie had wandered off to examine the store's merchandising scheme. She noticed a display case covered by a purple blanket with a gold GSU emblem on it. Blazer hustled over to make sure the blanket kept covered whatever was under it.

"What you got in there?" Jimmie asked.

"I, uh... I sell a few things on the side."

"That right?"

Blazer didn't feel threatened, so he pulled back the blanket and opened a box that included cigarette papers for folks that like to roll their own, a few herbal remedies, roach clips, bongs and more.

"You, uh... you move a little weed here?" Dorsey asked.

"No. "

They could tell he was lying.

"But I might be able to find you some if you're in the market," admitted Blazer.

"Good to know," Dorsey said. "Columbian?" Dorsey was trying to impress. He was ineffective.

"Maybe."

"Really?"

"Yeah. Maybe. Sometimes there's some Mexican floating around. And from other places. Some pretty good stuff is grown around here."

"No shit?" nodded Dorsey.

"That's right," Blazer said.

Blazer wasn't sure if he appreciated the "Faceman" label Pauline assigned to him. He already sized up the visitors as potential customers but he wasn't ready to make a sale. As they left the store, Blazer wrestled with whether it would look good

104

for him to be involved in these campus peace activities. His latest plan was to run for state representative in seven years once he's out of law school and after he knocks out his six months of active duty with the army reserves. Being connected with rebel rousers might alienate him from the older donor base, but he also couldn't ignore the obvious momentum against the war. He had no problem as a risk taker; he just needed to think through the right balance: Should he follow the light? Could he take the heat?

The following semester, to distance himself from the growing campus unrest, Blazer moved out of the dorm and into a mobile home with Odell Calhoun. The trailer was mounted on concrete blocks, it leaked and wasn't level. It was parked a mile or so from campus behind an out-of-business body shop. Since Blazer signed the lease, he claimed the choice bedroom. Odell was left with the bedroom that featured a built-in closet so small that the mattress filled the floor space and he had to stand on the bed to change his clothes.

Behind the body shop building and along the rear property line, high scrambled weeds and a barbwire fence blocked the view of Blazer's marijuana enterprise: a half-dozen rows of pot hiding between rows of feed corn.

He started out hoping the crop would cover the cost of his textbooks, but it grew to the point that it would make his car payments and application fees to law schools. The positive cash flow trumped his inner acknowledgment of the risk this posed to his political ambitions. Whereas Jimmie Kim was the idea person, the zealous entrepreneur, Dave Blazer was the subtle, slick dealmaker, traits that — like his looks — were expected to serve him well someday in public and private sectors.

Odell was a speech major from Mitchellsville who Blazer introduced as Brother Odell to acknowledge this up-and-coming man of the cloth and promising evangelical tent minister, "a future Rex Humbard," Blazer would say sarcastically. So powerful was Odell's calling that he felt no compulsion to enroll in theology classes. He had accepted Jesus at age ten and that had met his moral grounding as a literalist. He was more interested in style than substance and meeting the industry's expectations to pack the pews and lasso the sinners up front during altar calls.

Brother Odell's hair was long and high, held in place with a spray that dried into a sparkly web. He was tall and stickly, with sharp angled elbows and long fingers that held up The Book for all to see in its prominence. He buttoned his shirts to the top to disguise his thin neck, but his shirts sagged anyway. His face was kidney shaped and he seemed to have too many teeth which pushed them into an overbite. So he wasn't a handsome man, but he had a grin that was contagious and a soft sincerity that few of The Called conveyed. His audiences talked him up and he was already in growing demand for any Bible-based occasion on campus or for country church revivals.

Blazer considered Brother Odell an ideal roommate. Honest, trustworthy, quiet. He paid his rent early and did more than his share of chores without any need to keep score. Somewhere along the line, Odell got the notion that Dave Blazer followed the straight and narrow. He looked the other way and chose not to judge lest he be. Generally, Odell was asleep or pretended to be whenever

Blazer stumbled in drunk and tumbled over the coffee table, or when he lured a coed and shook the trailer with such obstreperous sex that it knocked picture frames off kilter, or when he took folks out back to admire this year's promising harvest.

All Brother Odell ever asked of his roommate was to listen to his sermons, his dry runs. Knowing how Odell put his heart and soul into his calling, Blazer played along, kicked back on the couch, popped open a beer, and allowed Brother Odell to turn it on automatic. Blazer spewed "amen" and "speak to me, Jesus" and "that's right, that's right" when Odell stressed points or used pauses. The naïve reverend took it as sincere, vital and constructive.

Odell's only real distraction from his calling was a deep-seated yearning for Yolanda Emerson, a bi-racial junior humanities major from Paducah. Yolanda was soft-spoken and sweet with a wide smile and large chalky teeth, tall and fit and well-defined, a Roman nose and a short dark afro that had a patch of premature gray in front. Were it not for her hair, she could have carried herself off as

108

white or as an exchange student from somewhere like Bali Ha'i, but she purposely redirected such notions with the colorful, beaded ceremonial African cloaks she wore about campus with elegance. Yolanda had long, contoured legs and a perfect bottom that Odell eyed temptingly and surreptitiously. He imagined her loosely draped in a translucent cloth and what her sigh might be like. He was drawn to her never ending tenderness, her flirtatious giggle, her broad thin back, how clothing adorned her, her moist hands. Really everything about her.

Odell prayed to no avail to be reprieved of this lust. He had never thought much about who he would take as a wife someday, certainly not a black or mulatto woman, even though he looked upon all people as his equal in God's eyes. He was not without career aspirations, and a life in the pulpit of a Midwest church would not lend itself to something so sociologically delicate.

Yolanda had run track in high school and was offered athletic scholarships to Southern Illinois, Austin Peay and Murray State, but she took less money and stuck to an academic strategy with an NAACP scholarship, GSU discounts for minorities and a student loan. The track coach invited her to walk-on, and even though she clearly would have earned the anchor leg on the relay team, she gave it up after one year to better prepare a future.

Yolanda was a do-gooder who Odell met at the Student Volunteer Bureau (SVB) Service Fair, an event held twice a year that matched students with government agencies and nonprofit groups for service learning experience and community service. The SVB saw a 30 percent bump in participation after the news about Will Yoder. Yolanda accepted an assignment as a reading tutor at Benjamin Curtis Elementary School. Twice a week, she walked the half-mile from campus and stayed about an hour, two if she could, to coach struggling fourth graders with their reading. Over time, she saw progress and found it gratifying to the point that she decided to complement her psychology-counseling degree with another major in elementary education.

The SVB placed Odell at the Curtis School also. He led wholesome games like

110

Red Rover or Kick Ball with the
kindergarten through third graders during
recess or after lunch, and then linked
lessons of sportsmanship and teamwork
into simple Biblical devotionals of the day.
Yolanda watched him through a classroom
window and felt his simple goodness to be
true, despite her sense that evangelizing
to students of this age was a bit much.

Odell spied on her repeatedly. He
was mesmerized to the point that
Yolanda's left-leaning ways were minor
details, set-asides. Her views about things
had weaved together from several
academic and social strands: a history
professor who aligned with Eisenhower
and the threat of the military-industrial
complex, JFK's assassination and Jim
Garrison's investigation from New Orleans
that she found tenable, the Birmingham
bombing that killed the four little girls and,
of course, The war. This horrific,
perplexing war. She knew a boy back
home in McCracken County who had been
killed, another who was AWOL and could
be anywhere. Yolanda was introduced to
spiritual matters and moral principles at
Mount Calvary AME (African-Methodist-
Episcopal) Church with her Caucasian

father and Negro mother, who were by and large shrugged off by the white side of the family and to a lesser extent by the black side.

It started innocently: One day when they were both leaving Curtis School, Odell pulled his car alongside Yolanda as she walked home.

"Give you a lift? Might rain," he said. "I like the rain. Cleans the air," said Yolanda.

It started to sprinkle right then.

"Let me walk you back?" he asked.

"That makes no sense. You're driving," she said.

He pushed open a car door and she jumped right in, sensing no danger.

A mixed race couple was new to GSU. It brought forth increasing, at times harsh, whispers and snoots. Over the days and weeks that followed, the two became one. They were inseparable, but Odell was too much a gentleman and too inexperienced in relationships to express his longings or venture into seduction. When they touched or when he could feel the breeze of her breath, his chest commenced pumping and his hardened crotch throbbed out of cadence. Certainly he was not ready to bring her to the trailer or suggest that he stay over at her dorm room. That would surely lead to, well... yearnings prohibited as he understood the seventh commandment.

So with innocence assured, they lightened up and laughed and teased one another. Yolanda showed him how to dress, lose the hairspray and part his hair down the middle. He looked hip, dapper, more sure of himself, independent and less locked into the cultural traditions that brought him along this far but could also set him back.

Since a growing number of ministers and seminarians were challenging the war and leaders in the civil rights movement were joining forces with peace groups, Brother Odell figured he could accompany Yolanda and a busload from the Missouri NAACP to a march in Nashville at Vanderbilt University. Vanderbilt had a reputation in the community as an island of intellectuals and liberals, while the country music industry, headlined by Roy Acuff and Merle Haggard, aligned with Barry Sandler, the singer-soldier who had a big hit with the *Ballad of the Green Beret.*

113

The crowd was not insignificant —
several hundred early, more than a
thousand toward the end. Marchers
gathered at Vandy by mid-morning and
preceded to the Parthenon in Centennial
Park where a larger crowd gathered to
hear speakers and entertainers
highlighted by Peter, Paul and Mary.
When Yolanda and Odell found their way
to a high point above the crowd, they saw
a cluster of GSU placards and inched their
way over to join forces.

When they saw Yolanda and Odell,
Pauline and company raised and pumped
their fists and shouted. "G-S-U! G-S-U!"
Most of the GSU group knew of the bi-
racial couple even if they didn't know
them personally. Pauline and Susan felt
rewarded: it was working, more converts.
Dorsey passed Odell a beer. He declined
politely.

"HEY EVERYBODY! MORE
DEVIANTS FROM THE BLUFF!" proclaimed
Dorsey. It was hard to hear. There were
more cheers, welcoming hugs.

"Quite a rally coming together,"
said Yolanda.

"It's a happening place," said Dorsey, still forcing it but picking up confidence.

"Yes! Yes!" Jimmie applauded the previous speaker who was effective, well-received, but unknown to her. His charge culminated with a responsive chant:

"Give me a P! Peeee! Give me an E! Eeeee! Give me an A! Aaaay! Give me a C! Ceeee! Give me an E! Eeeee!

"What's that spell! "

"PEACE! "

"What's that spell! "

"PEACE! " LOUDER!

"What's that spell! "

"PEACE!""

Dorsey raised his voice again to be heard over the roar. "SOMETHING, HUH? PEOPLE HERE FROM ALL OVER!" He snarled in a long draw when marijuana aroma wafted by. "THESE RALLIES (knnnk, knnnk) ARE HAPPENING EVERYWHERE! IT'S (knnnk) A REVOLUTION, MAN! WE'RE CHANGING..." He took in another sniff. "WE'RE CHANGING THE WORLD (knnnk),"

Pauline saw Luke James and waved him over. He wore a floppy hat labeled, "VETS AGAINST THE WAR." A guy with

115

one leg and a crutch was with him. Luke introduced him, "MY BUDDY, MARIO, FROM BROOKLYN. SAVED MY ASS."

Odell spied his roommate, probably not within earshot.

But then he heard, "David?" DAVE BLAZER!"

Blazer turned his way. "HEY, MY MAN, THE PREACHER MAN! HOW THE HELL DID YOU END UP DOWN HERE?

"I'M WONDERING THE SAME ABOUT YOU! YOLANDA AND I CAME DOWN ON THE NAACP BUS. I LEFT A NOTE ON THE KITCHEN TABLE."

Blazer knew he couldn't disguise being a little drunk. "Bring your little lady on over. Bring *all* your brothers and sisters on over. We're nondenominationally racially open, like, you know…ecumenically free to be you and me…" He chuckled as he stumbled over words.

Without thinking through the risk or implications, Blazer had responded to Pauline's invitation early that morning to join them. "We'll have a blast, Faceman," she said, selling him as if this were just another KD bash.

116

"PAULINE, JIMMIE, LUKE, EVERYBODY... WANT YOU TO MEET MY ROOMMATE, BROTHER ODELL CALHOUN, THE NEXT ORAL ROBERTS," Blazer said.

The mighty stack of speakers on either side of the stage emitted a painful squeal,

Blazer turned to Yolanda. He had to shout to be heard: "HEY YOU KNOW YOU'RE ALL BROTHER ODELL TALKS ABOUT. HE'S GOT IT BAD FOR YOU, GIRL. BUT DON'T YOU WORRY; I CAN'T CORRUPT BROTHER ODELL. HE'S PURE AS CLEAN SHEETS."

An NAACP delegation made its way through the crowd, and the races mixed, and they learned one another's songs, and they drank from the same bottle, and they kissed strangers on the lips, and they shared in resolve, and they felt part of something beyond what they had ever felt before.

The Nashville rally was an energizing, defining experience, capped off by Barry McGuire's raspy voice:

Tell me...

Over and over and over again my friend.

I do believe

we're on the eve
of destruction.

They soaked in the day, shared food and wrapped one another in blankets and plastic ponchos, dampened by the day's drizzle. The lights in the Parthenon eased on to accentuate its statuary. Vendors came by again, hawking tie dyed t-shirts, drugs, incense, flowers, bumper stickers, trinkets that could display a peace sign. A police officer guarding the perimeter indiscreetly bobbled his head to the beat of *So Happy Together* by the Turtles. There were harsh songs of protest and catchy tunes for sing-alongs, sincere social changers and two-faced opportunists, a sense of peace amid an atmosphere of explosiveness.

They returned to GSU with an added something between them, the sense that they were part of a greater mission with an obligation to pull together: the party girl torn by news that her dear friend and clandestine lover is probably dead on the other side of the world; her wealthy roommate stuck in a relationship with a possessive, volatile future military man; a trampled-on victim of humiliation and bullying; a foreign student driven by

118

American opportunity; a savvy drug dealer and rising star student leader; a skilled army veteran mysteriously injured by the war; a naïve fundamentalist preacher following a call and the bi-racial liberal he adores. Not nearly enough, not exactly fishers of men. But an impressive launch into community organizing and social activism from young people who heretofore focused on whether or not the latest tunes featured on American Bandstand had a good beat and were easy to dance to.

Pauline did not feel anointed. She had not orchestrated a movement. The fact that she could devise a good hooch recipe or theme party, run buck naked in the middle of the night, chug beers with the guys while floating down a bubbly river, and manage to graduate from college without remembering what major she had declared. This didn't mean she was comfortable speaking in front of people or skilled enough to influence public policy. She knew little about Vietnam, but she knew that Will would not be where he is now if our leaders hadn't taken on the cause of this futile war in the first place. In

119

honor of him, Pauline had an obligation to do something, to challenge herself, to be someone different — to listen and learn, to go places, to show folks back home that she could do things — important things — and not just stay put in Bobcat to serve Stromboli sandwiches at the Pizzaria.

Courage. More than anything, Pauline figured she needed people with guts. Jimmie had the gumption to take a plunge into a business world controlled by white men. Dorsey showed spunk by smashing the banana into the Sigma Nu's forehead and to escape frat house hazing in his underwear. Blazer had the guts to risk law school and his political aspirations for a nice tax-free crop of pot. Luke James was willing to speak out against a war that had left him scarred. Odell and Yolanda were an item despite the social ramifications. All had shown courage, except for Susan, who — given that Vic would soon be shipped off to Vietnam — couldn't find a time and place that felt right to break it off with him. She didn't have the courage now, and she wondered if she ever would.

JaMar Brown was the preeminent militant on campus. Five feet ten inches tall, six-four with his afro. Dark shades worn outdoors or indoors — to mystify and intimidate. Solid black clothing set off a gold chain around his neck from which a large ornament must have meant something. Taciturn. Serious. He sat alone against a window in the cafeteria, reading, sipping soup.

"Did I see you, in Nashville, at the peace march? With the NAACP?" Pauline asked. He looked up and then went about eating.

"Anybody sitting here?" asked Pauline. He didn't respond and she realized it was a stupid question. "Can I...?"

He spoke slowly with precise articulation. "Do you see where restrictions are posted?"

"What?"

"You risk alienation from your so-ro-ri-ty sisters."

"I can handle myself." She stuck her hand out and sat down. "I'm Pauline Cody."

He didn't extend his hand. "I know who you are."

121

"Sounds like you've already come to judgment."

"Is it safe to assume that if it were a black man who was missing in action rather than whitey superstar Will "Big Red" Yoder, there would have been little, if any, public outcry?"

"Well, uh… maybe, yeah, no, probably not." She liked his afro but not the way he hid behind his glasses.

He leaned up in his chair, anchored himself on his elbows and spoke through clasped hands. "I went home (East St. Louis) to visit my grandmother over the Christmas break. Took her shopping across the Mississippi to downtown. We went into Schubach's Department Store. Granny picked out a hat, a feathery pill box kind of thing. She liked it, but then she found another one that was a better match to the color of her dress. The clerk made her buy the first one."

"What? Why?"

"Store policy."

"Policy?"

"That's right. We Negroes have to purchase any hat we try on. Did you know that? No respectful white woman could ever be expected to wear a hat defiled by

122

the greasy nappy head of a nigger woman."

"That's terrible."

"You have no clue, do you, so-ro-ri-ty girl? We deal with this *every single* day. Now when I graduate next year, I'll be forced to fight for a nation and alongside people who set us back hundreds of years and still treat my black brothers and sisters and my granny as second-class citizens. Why should I go? Why should *any* black man go?

"The war sucks. The draft sucks. You got a raw deal. If I was your grandma I'd be pissed too. You gotta move on. What are you majoring in?"

"What's that?"

"Then just tell me what you're interested in? I'm just trying to make some conversation here. Give me a break."

"I guess you think I'm a running back, probably a P.E. major."

"I didn't say that."

"Yeah, uh-huh. Well, there *are* uncoordinated black people, black people who are slow, who can't dance, black people who don't like watermelon and fried chicken, black people with tiny dicks." He eased out a grin.

123

"Ah, a breakthrough. You *do* have a lighter side." Pauline liked this guy. "We need you involved in our peace group here at GSU."

"This is a party school. No place for an uprising."

"No, not yet, at least not here at GSU."

"Civil disobedience has its merits. I like economic sanctions better.

Go after Lockheed, the war machine, the capitalists. More effective."

"You're an economics major."

"Hell no."

"Sociology?" He didn't respond.

"What, then."

"I bring forth from within, on to the canvas."

"An artist? Groovy. Really? An art major. What kind of stuff do you do?"

"Portraits."

"Cool."

"Is indeed."

"What… or, uh, who do you like to draw?"

"I capture the pain. In my brothers and sisters. Political prisoners. Those on the streets. I give them value."

Pauline nodded. She tried to peer through his dark glasses to his eyes.

"It's Brown. JaMar Brown," he said.

She extended her hand and this time he took it.

"Not easy to make a living at that — art, I mean, when you graduate," she said.

"The white man holds back the black man anyway. Money is power. He who's got it hangs onto it. Why study high finance when the loan committee's just gonna turn you down later on?" he said.

"Look, you've been screwed, but don't make yourself miserable."

"So you want me to turn to the old Negro spirituals for inspiration, or maybe just play along, *yessa massa*?"

They both noticed a group at a nearby table watching them, wondering. Blacks and whites got along fine enough at GSU. They just kept their distance. It was unusual for them to have lunch together.

"Well, I don't have the answers," Pauline said. "I'm new to all this. Just trying to get some good things going around here. Could use you."

"I was out there before you were, when the veterans marched. Added some color to their pallet."

"See. I knew you cared. You were marching before it was cool. I was just a party girl then."

He didn't respond as she stood up to leave. He opened his book again: *Voices of Resistance*, by Angela Davis. He sipped his soup and pushed it away when he realized it was cold.

As attendance increased, vigils for Will Yoder and marches to proclaim the growing number of dead and missing Americans in Vietnam were moved to the quadrangle. As an opening act, body count banners were suspended from dorm rooms overlooking the quadrangle and rolled up before officials could confiscate them. As the number of dead increased, more converts joined the fold: students, Will's former teammates, instructors, staff — from registrars to the kitchen help, dorm monitors to groundskeepers. Before the spring semester adjourned, 500, 800, 1000 or more were coming together to listen, speak out and take part in this latest campus craze. At GSU, it had become hip to be an activist.

Susan slammed the door of their room so hard that the needle trailed off the album that was playing. "I heard you again this morning. It wasn't just another hangover, was it?"

"What are you talking about?" Pauline said.

"Throwing up. Again."

"Yeah, it was the rum."

"Bullshit. How long did you think you could keep it from me? Did you think I wouldn't notice, figure it out? The morning sickness, your pooch." Susan tapped Pauline's tummy. "Your puffy face. The weird cravings. You're pregnant, aren't you?"

Pauline stared ahead.

"What, were you gonna get rid of it before anybody found out? Maybe you're still planning to do that. That way, you wouldn't have to let anybody know — not your ol' man, not your followers, not your *best friend*!" Susan was angry, hurt.

"Sue, I was going to tell you. Of course I was. I've been putting it off until I was showing. I'm gonna keep it, but the doctor said I might be prone to miscarriage. Thought in the meantime I

127

could hide it, you know, with big flowery print dresses like Mama Cass wears."

"You know I'm probably not the only one who is suspicious," Susan said. "You need to come clean, fess up. Who's the father, anyway? Do you even know? It's that swimmer, isn't it? Or the guy from Cyprus. I thought you were on The Pill."

Tough as nails Pauline couldn't hold back the tears as she sat down on the bed with her head in her hands. Susan wrapped her arms around her friend.

"I'm so sorry. I've needed somebody to talk to and I was afraid to tell you. I thought you would lose respect and confidence in me. I don't know what I should do."

"You know I'm always here for you," Susan said.

Pauline confessed: "It was Will."

Susan pulled back. "What?"

"Will. Will's the father," Pauline said.

"Oh my God. When? Where? Does he know?

"No, he doesn't. There was that time, you know, about three months ago, you went home for your grandmother's birthday. It was that weekend that, I, uh... I helped Will through, you know, his maiden voyage."

"His first time?" Susan asked.

"Yeah." said Pauline.

"You been screwing him since then?"

"No. I was willing, but it's the Mennonite in him. You know how religious he is."

"It's just that after Will enlisted and had been through basic training, I knew he'd be thrown into the worst possible hell hole and I was afraid I'd never see him again. He was giving up so much — the money, the fame. I wanted to comfort him anyway I could, say goodbye. I wanted to give him me. I wanted to give me as a going away present," Pauline said.

Susan reached out and grabbed Pauline's hand.

"I had taken a break from The Pill and he used a condom. I don't know what happened. I was surprised that this was his first time; dozens of GSU girls would have jumped at the chance to be with him," Pauline said.

"You're right about that," Susan said.

"You're supposed to be my best friend. Best friends don't keep things from their best friends," said Susan.

"You can't tell me that you haven't held onto some secrets. How many times have you and Vic done it? asked Pauline.

"Oh...six, maybe six times." Susan said. "

"With Vic?"

"Yes."

"Sure that's it?

"Well... there was one other time. But it was... uh, with a girl. Does that count? Susan asked. "Happened at a summer camp. Before my Junior year of high school. Never saw her again."

"Well aren't we full of surprises today? Then are you bi-sexual?" Pauline asked.

"No, no... I don't... I don't think so. She came onto me and I didn't fight it," Susan said.

"Takes two to tango... but I don't want the details," said Pauline.

"How about you?" Besides Will, any others?"

"Nope. Closest would be that time I went skinny dipping down at the landing with a Lambda Chi. And then I had an

130

uncle feel me under my bra, but Hump walked in on us and that was the end of that.

I'm not the experienced, hot-mamma free-love kind of gal that most people think. I can party with the best of them, but when it comes to going all the way, I've been a master at ways to slip out of reach."

"Well you need to change your ways now, honey. You've got a kid in your belly. No smoking. No drinking. No dope. Fresh food. Prenatal checkups. I'll keep up with the paperwork, and I'll be watching. We should get the word to Will. He would want to know. Knowing he has a kid back home will keep him going, give him something to live for."

"You forget."

"What?"

"He's missing. No way to reach him."

Over the summer months, depending on the speakers, music and the latest reports, each rally took on its own personality, guided by Pauline's ad hoc inner circle. Chores and roles were shared: Jimmie printed and circulated fliers; Odell gave the benedictions; Yolanda read poems for peace written by fourth graders; Dorsey led the chants with a megaphone; Luke built the speaker platforms and portable displays for booths at rallies and shopping malls; JaMar came on board and assured the black students that these were allies, not adversaries; Susan assisted administratively and paid for things quietly; Blazer took care of the permits and reached an understanding with security. He also managed to sneak along enough pot as one would expect for such occasions.

Once Vic started basic training, he wrote Susan every day, picking at her scab of ambivalence that had not quite healed, that was not quite ready to flick off her skin. Vic's intentions had a sweet spot, but his hovering nature brought on a haze of suspicion so smothering that Susan couldn't breathe. She prayed for his safety, but she didn't look forward to his return.

As the campus rallies grew and took on brash confidence and a more daring tone, as threats became more of a possibility, President Renwick and Dean Ewing focused on ways to put down the unrest without betraying student rights of free speech. They considered a new campus ordinance, curfews, noise policies, a "Support America" counter demonstration, all of which threatened to backfire and make things worse. Renwick was irked by the body count banner but stood by his decision to disallow it. That only fueled the wildfire, advancing the cause despite efforts to contain it.

Pauline, unconventionally pregnant by an unrevealed partner, was building an effective team, but she knew that things could always could go wrong and set off confusion that might escalate into chaos and ignite a threat and a soldier's flinch that could fire a rifle. A rock could be thrown from behind a parked car. Molotov cocktails were easy to make. A loyal veteran may resent a wisecrack and pull out a knife. The crowd could surge. Lots of bad things could happen.

If things ever got out of hand, the administration was prepared to send out its posse to round up the protesters, bring them in for a hearing or challenge their right to exist. Some protestors were sure that suspension or expulsion awaited them. In the meantime, they could escape below the bluffs, beyond the campus

133

boundary. They could gather at their little spot by the river.

The Grant State campus was built atop layered bluffs overlooking a spacious valley and serpentine river. Beyond the valley were cascading misty hills of cedars in subtle hues of green and blue. The campus stood alone atop the town, closer to the sun than the settlement of Bluff City that wrapped around it. A low limestone wall framed Peacock Hall's front lawn, forming an overlook that, through the years, has been used to carry out suicides - six students and one faculty member over the past decade.

To hastily accommodate the infusion of pleasure-seeking students brought on by the *Esquire* ranking of party schools, GSU's board of regents had been forced to compromise the Greek Revival architectural vocabulary of the campus for cheap modular buildings that could go up quickly. The older sections of campus were characterized by stately buildings with porticos along the front supported by columns that had heavy, fluted lower ends without bases. Most of the buildings were symmetrical, featured gabled roofs and

134

were built with area limestone or otherwise painted to match. The 1891 plaque in the vestibule of Peacock Hall paid tribute to the builders, architects, regents, senior management and patrons of the day: people with first names like Hiram, Increase, Thaddeus, Horace, Vachel, Titus, Uriah, Wentworth, Winfield and Rube.

Peacock Hall had enough dark, undefined spaces that ghostly explanations evolved from generation to generation. Storytellers posited how many scandalized deans or suicidal paramours lingered there in another realm. A stroll through the corridors brought forth an echo as if spirits teased those who found the space creepy.

Tree-lined streets, grassy commons, limestone outcrops and flowing water enhanced the stately architecture of the campus with a sense of permanency. And sculptures of Grant, Peacock and Missouri leaders Marie Watkins Oliver, Dred Scott and Senator George Graham Vest were sprinkled about as if they had been assigned a section of campus to chaperone.

The expanded south campus was flat, surplus land where the regents added freshmen dorms and found a few adaptable buildings for berated programs. Houses in the neighborhood were used up. The new campus parking lots were graveled and in need of shade trees. Trailers worked as makeshift classroom space.

The campus site was selected and purchased by George Parson Peacock in 1888 for a teacher's college, and later absorbed by the state of Missouri in the hard times of the 1930's. The deal was devised by Woodford Grant, a leading corn grower from central Illinois who had a string of successful patents on drip irrigation systems.

In 1938, Grant offered $150,000 to add an agriculture curriculum if the state would take over the fragile college and bring it up to university status. During The Great Depression, he endured crop prices that dropped 60 percent and international markets by two-thirds. Grant bet that technology and international commerce would bring stability to farmers and agribusiness, and he wanted Grant State to lead the way. He had no interest in having the college named for him. That was done posthumously to extract additional gifts from his widow, Eleanor Lea Albright Grant, who liked the idea of an enduring legacy.

The subsequent annuities and bequests from Mrs. Grant enabled the School of Agriculture to establish a $600,000 endowment that grew to $5.3 million by the mid-60's. This didn't make farming any less difficult in the stony soil around GSU, but over time, it introduced machines and chemicals and hybrids that increased the bounty of some already prolific agricultural land, among the best in the Midwest, just a few hours to the north, including the river bottoms of Iroquois County where Lonnie Youngman had been expected to farm.

Lonnie was allergic to pollen and he had an aversion to sweat. He was a night person; he rolled over when the cock crowed and was not dependable for the morning milking. His idea of life on the edge was more than the drama over gilt prices and chances of rain. He wanted to control his outcomes, make his own forecast. About the time he was old enough to drop out of high school, he

137

figured that making music had to beat scratching out a living pushing a plow. He might sing about the farm, but he wasn't going back to it.

He knew enough chords to get by strumming a guitar. His act was his smooth style, his soft clear voice, his shoulder length hair, the way he would introduce a song and end it with "Sweet. Thank you, good people. Let's remember the wisdom in those words." His way had an affect on teenyboppers who, after a few glasses of spiked punch, fell in lust with something about him. In gig after gig, Lonnie would work his way to the edge of the stage, scope beyond the hanging lights and send a tacit eye-to-eye seductive invitation to the receptacles at the other end. He relished in this teasing, exuding a sense that he was available, as much as anything to aggravate Cate, who had been drawn to him in the same way for the same reason.

They married in 1963, when she was 19 and he was 24. Since then, they lived a life on the road, playing mainly at pubs, peace rallies and folk festivals. Her parents disapproved and hardly welcomed them home for anything. His parents were never mentioned. When they closed out their busiest festival season ever, Lonnie and Cate stayed put in Bluff City so that Cate could enroll in a course at GSU. She thought anthropology would be fun, but she dropped out within three weeks. They had a few nice gigs and too many late nights to make it work.

Their best weeknight gig was at Dooley's, a bar named for the Kingston Trio's murderous character. It was located a mile or so off campus in a converted seed and feed store. On weekends, they were regular opening acts at larger anti-war assemblies at SIU, Missouri's main campus in Columbia, the branch at Rolla, schools in St. Louis and beyond. Most were open mike formats whereby anyone could take on LBJ, McNamara, Rusk, Westmorland, corporate America, Bull Connor and the Alabama police — symbols of injustice anywhere.

Cate and Lonnie went by The Drifting Duo. They blended popular tunes with folk songs that had a social message: *Windy* and *Brown-Eyed Girl* with *Green Green*, *If I had a Hammer, Blowin' in the Wind* — sing-alongs that went well with beer served by the pitcher. Lonnie sat on a stool and played the guitar; Cate stood

139

next to him and provided high range harmony while slapping her hip with a tambourine. She had long auburn hair and wore beaded buck skin elk tooth dresses of the plains Indians. She had the better voice of the two, but she let Lonnie take center stage.

Lonnie seldom put his heart into playing at Dooley's because he had to compete with pool tables, fooseball and pinball machines. About the time he and Cate performed their *I Got You Babe* finale, he figured out who the Asian girl in the back of the room was. *Ah yeah, the waterbed*.

He thought it was maybe in Springfield. Perhaps Urbana. He remembered how the gray light from a window framed her silhouette. He remembered how she wanted to get down to business and how her strong legs almost cut off his circulation. Her name didn't come back to him. She sat alone in Dooley's against a back wall where poets gathered on slow nights,

He thought he had been with her just the one time. He never had a chance to know much about her other than she seemed ambitious and preoccupied.

140

Lonnie and Cate were always back on the road; he never thought much about keeping in touch.

After an encore of *Both Sides Now*, Lonnie packed his guitar in his case, grabbed a check from the club manager and stepped off the stage beyond the lights so he could see into the crowd. Two underage girls were already waiting there with that look.

Jimmie. He remembered now. She had an Asian name but went by Jimmie. He looked for her as the bar and game room started to empty. Cate could see that he was scoping out prospects but she shrugged it off as his normal womanizing. Maybe it wasn't Jimmie after all, he thought. He returned to Cate and was unscathed that he may have been snubbed, confident as ever that there would be occasions for many a playful romp yet ahead.

After the last set at Dooley's, without a whiff of liquor on her breath, pregnant and conscientious, Pauline led her followers down the bluff off GSU property to Teddy's Landing, their ideal spot to get wasted, unwind, debrief, scheme, spout off and escape the volatile times.

On most nights, they would build a fire and set out kerosene lamps on logs set end-to-end to form benches in a semi-circle surrounding the fire. Luke built a shed where they stored the lamps, tossed empty beer cans, inner tubes and belongings left behind. JaMar painted the shed with psychedelic patterns, a large peace sign and images of Dr. King, Medgar Evers and the Kennedy brothers.

Like a possum, the river could be still and play dead and, at other times, come at you with roaring rapids that bounced over settled rocks long scrubbed by the currents. Fireflies blinked like scouts reporting that more intruders were on the way. The regulars kicked back and were singing along with *The Times They are a-Changin'*. Luke strummed a guitar gently as if he was playing on a front porch alone. The fire in the pit absorbed the river's chill.

Some of the Pikes dropped in after their cheap wine tasting. The event showcased *Mad Dog 20-20*, *Boone's Farm* and *Reunite*. These connoisseurs of rotgut were welcomed but would not contribute much to the evening's conversation.

"Good group there at Dooley's tonight," said Pauline. "How many you figure we have on our mailing list?"

"More than half," Susan said.

"Not bad."

Pauline's pregnancy was another symbol of rebellion against the rule makers who took us to war and kowtowed to corporate interests. She dressed informally: bellbottom jeans; a flowered blouse tied above her swollen belly; and a fringed brown suede vest accented by her signature headband. She sipped on a quart of lemonade, once approved by Susan's sniff.

The two were always ready to jump into plans for the next rally or other ways they could make a political statement. Their followers were not always so dedicated. After a long night, many were still buzzed and available, seeking skin.

JaMar had an eye on Jimmie and Susan liked the looks of Luke. Odell was always glad to see Yolanda. Jimmie liked what she saw in Dave Blazer, the Faceman.

Pauline got everyone's attention: "You know... if you're like me, a few weeks ago, I didn't know the Gulf of Tonkin from the Gulf of Mexico."

"Now we have the brilliant Tonkin Resolution and we can just move our troops right in there," Luke said.

"Who needs a declaration of war?" Jimmie was cynical.

"LBJ calls all the shots," Luke said. "Ah, but it's just a conventional military."

"What the hell's a *conventional* military anyway?" Blazer asked.

"Maybe anything that involves an *operation*," Pauline said. "They love those *operations*: Operation Jungle Fever. Operation Snakehead."

"Operation Blow-Up Every Fucking Village in Sight," Luke said.

"You know, the way the Pentagon keeps a daily body count scorecard, you'd think it was a board game or something," Pauline said.

"How many points does it take for us to win?" Susan asked.

"The black man is more worried about the Birmingham police than the Viet Cong," JaMar said.

"We damn near have a half million troops over there now," Blazer said.

"And we're closing in on 20,000 U.S. dead or missing. Who knows how many wounded and disabled," Luke said.

Pauline looked to Odell. "Tell me, reverend...

They knew the words and joined in.
"War... What is it good for?"
"Absolutely nothing."
"Say it again, Hey, war -- good God now"
"Huh, what is it good for?"
"Absolutely nothing."
They repeated the chorus.

"They love that word: deploy. Deploy this and deploy that," JaMar said.

"I got their deployment hangin'," Luke said.

"The whitey big shots sure as hell see to it that *their* sons ain't sent over there," said JaMar.

"Bound to be a bunch of folks getting rich selling bombs and planes and rifles and grenades," said Jimmie.

"Generals are chomping at the bit. They've been waiting their whole career for a chance to get in the game," said Luke.

"But it's not a game," said Susan.

"You don't see *their* big asses starving to death in prison camps," said JaMar.

145

"They roll out their big maps and little pieces like they're playing chess: tiny tanks and   platoons and air fleets," Blazer said.

"Here comes the napalm," Dorsey said. He held up a small piece of wood as if it were a toy airplane. He zoomed up and down, in and out, making more sound effects. But they'd had enough laughter.

"But it's not a game," said Susan.

"Susan's right. Everybody's right." Pauline paused. "And then there's Will, our own Will Yoder. Big Red."

"Hate to think what he's going through," said Dorsey.

"If he's still hanging on," said Blazer.

"We miss you, Will," a shout came from the dark lane that led to the landing. As the light from the fire brought their flickering images into focus, they could see it was Lonnie with his arm around Cate and a guitar mounted on his back. He always seemed to draw attention to himself.

Pauline was skeptical when it came to Lonnie and his cellophane character. She heard that after basic training he sweet-talked the daughter of his company

146

commander to approve Lonnie's transfer to Ft. Knox where he sang background music at the officer's club. The thought aggravated her because she knew that Will could have had easy duty if he had exploited his fame.

Pauline welcomed them nonetheless: "Let's hear it for Lonnie and Cate Youngman, The Drifting Duo! Straight from Dooley's." Everyone except Jimmie turned and clapped for the couple-act some had seen that night and most had at some point or another. Jimmie scooted a few inches behind Odell and Yolanda to block Lonnie's line of sight.

Lonnie figured they wanted a statement since he thought of himself as a celebrity: "It could have been any of us, man. Will's a good and decent friend to all of us." Pauline wrinkled her forehead; she wasn't sure that Lonnie actually knew Will. He went on: "Just went over there to help and not hurt anybody, and well..." Lonnie held up a beer. "Here's to you, big guy."

"Big Red, we hope you're okay wherever you are, man." Blazer said.

"Let's remember to also lift our thoughts to all the Vietnamese people

147

caught in the crossfire. They didn't ask for all this." Yolanda said.

Susan interrupted. "And then there's Vic, Victor Devillez. He's in basic training at Fort Dix."

"Aw shit, man," said JaMar. "Dude *supports* the war, couldn't wait to get over there."

Susan was awkwardly protective. "He believes we're helping an oppressed people. That's a good thing, to help oppressed people, don't you think? Besides, he had lots of family tradition and issues to deal with, too."

Pauline called on Odell, who had his hand raised. "May I offer up a word of prayer, please?" Odell was an anomaly: he had a way of looking past the booze and the weed and the cursing and the sex that was pretty much common practice and to focus on the good in people. He had not been introduced to anything other than the tenets of his faith through which truth had been revealed. No one was in the mood for a preacher and a few eyes rolled, but Odell was too likeable to belittle.

"May every head be bowed and every eye be closed. Lord Father and ever living God. Help us Lord. Show us the way."

Odell squeezed his eyes shut and gripped Yolanda's hand on one side and his roommate's on the other which made Blazer uncomfortable.

"Help us, Father, to stand up to evil, and to help people wherever and whenever we can. But help us to know when there are limits to what we can do and when we might be making things worse. Be with us and, Lord, help us to trust in your words — blessed are the peacemakers and thou shalt not kill. Help us to bring home safely our men and women in uniform. We especially pray for our dear friend and classmate, Will Yoder. If Big Red is still alive, Lord, we pray for his health and safety. If he has been taken from us, we hope and pray that he is already in your loving presence. And then there's Victor Devillez. We pray that..."

"Thank you, Brother Calhoun! Thank you! That's some first rate prayin." Blazer was compelled to cut him off. "That's Brother Odell Calhoun, ladies and gentlemen! Remember that name. If he can't save the world, nobody can. Let's give the preacher man – and my favorite roommate — a big round of applause." A few scattered claps followed.

"Okay then." Pauline got things going again. "Any thoughts on advancing the cause of peace and putting an end to this stupid-ass war?"

"Fuckin' aye," said Dorsey. "We need to get out of there, man."

"They got our number in those jungles, man," Blazer said.

"I hate that fuckin' Westmoreland. You don't see his ass out there in the line of fire," Luke said.

"And what's his name, the guy who slicks his hair back, wears those little specks…" Dorsey asked.

"McNamara," Luke said.

"Yeah, what a dork," Dorsey said.

"Smart motherfucker, though," Blazer said.

"Maybe. Whatever," Dorsey said.

"It's like the most important thing is for the U.S. to save face. Let's just get the hell out of there," Susan said.

"Shit yeah. How about if they gave a war and nobody came?" Yolanda asked.

"I can dig that all right," JaMar said.

Lonnie sighted Jimmie and Cate noticed that he had.

"What if everybody stood up to the generals, laid down their guns," Yolanda said.

"Right on," JaMar said.

"Ah shit, man. If we'd done that 25 years ago we'd all be speaking German," Luke said.

"And Japanese," Blazer said.

"Not if their soldiers laid down their arms too? Not if they refused to follow orders. Not if the whole damn world gave up on war," Yolanda said. "Sorry, honey," she apologized to Odell for cursing. He patted her hand.

"Like that time soldiers on both sides called a time out on Christmas Eve to sing carols and play soccer," Susan said.

"Yeah, we just needed to do that times several hundred battles for it to do any good," Blazer said.

"It did some good for them," Susan said.

"Until they started blowing up one another again the next morning," Luke said.

"Hell, the Germans and Japanese — they brainwashed their military. Drip water on foreheads, yank out finger nails and shit. Japs have some crazy-ass warriors," Blazer said.

"Their Kamikazes *wanted* to die," Dorsey said.

"We couldn't reason with their leaders. God, they wouldn't even surrender after we dropped the first bomb, man," Blazer said.

"Why couldn't we have dropped the bomb out in the countryside or something," Yolanda asked.

"Had to prove we had the guts to do it. Had to scare the Russians," Luke said.

"But just imagine, wouldn't it be something if people everywhere stood up to their military and leaders and said we've had enough of this shit," Blazer said.

"Ain't gonna study war no more," Odell said.

"Yeah, right. And just hand everything over to the next Hitler," Luke said.

"He was different. He was a monster," Susan said.

"If his army had refused to serve, he wouldn't have had any power either," Yolanda said.

"That's so naïve," Blazer said.

"Afraid he's right, man," Luke said.

152

The slurry worded banter was going nowhere, aggravated by too much beer on top of the wine and the weed wafting about. Pauline tried to steer her followers in a discussion of local action steps when she was interrupted by commotion above and the sight of Dorsey and two buck naked girls — goose pimply in the light of the moon — rushing out of the shrubs from a bluff maybe twenty feet above the gathering.

"WHOOOAH!" With their running start, they soared off the bank of the river, Dorsey clasping a rope tied to a tree and the girls clasping Dorsey's shoulders like two Janes hanging on to Tarzan. They swung across the river to the opposite side. Dorsey pushed off again and on the return glide, he let go and they broke free of one another and dropped into the deep pool as their fans cheered below. The girls, stiff as ladders, sliced through the water without making a bubble. Dorsey clasped his knees to his chest and executed a robust cannonball that erupted enough of a splash that a four-inch blue gill was scooped up, landed on somebody's blanket, and flipped about in hysteria.

Pauline's misfits were called lots of things, but they adopted the name STudent Alliance for a Nonviolent Democracy (STAND). STAND counted among its own anyone who attended rallies, signed petitions or claimed to be part of the movement. There were no membership dues, no obligations. But to organize the events, Pauline turned to her unofficial inner circle of helpers and advisors: Susan, Jimmie, Dorsey, Blazer, JaMar, Luke, Odell, Yolanda and occasionally Coach Shoals. She needed more help, but was careful to invite only dependable, savvy or thick-skinned volunteers for the important tasks. Cate and Lonnie offered to lend a hand, and Pauline was likely to take them in, even though Cate had second thoughts when she overheard someone say that Jimmie Kim used to roll in the hay with her husband.

Pauline had other prospects in mind, but it turned out that Arnie Latham, a slow but reliable fixture on the GSU campus lawn crew, would become one of her favorites, a nice offset to the young and brash. He was a chubby hulk of a fellow who wore a St. Louis Cardinals cap and pulled his britches up to his rib cage with

154

suspenders. Pauline guessed he was about 60. He was soft as a Teddy Bear, and he had a deep, mellow chuckle, there to set the pace like a steady bass of a jazz combo.

Arnie loved to fish, and he carried on a conversation with the one that always seemed to get away. His favorite spot was off the far side of the river within eyeshot of Teddy's Landing. Once Pauline invited him over for a beer, they couldn't get rid of him. He was teased by the guys and the gals thought he was precious.

More than anything, he was a devoted Will Yoder fan and was distraught at the news that he was missing in action. During Will's years at GSU, Arnie was the volunteer stationed under the basket to wipe up sweat after players slipped or were knocked to the hardwood. "I wish Will Yoder had not gone to the army. I liked to watch him put it in the baskets," Arnie would say slowly.

Arnie didn't say much when they gathered at the landing, although his freewheeling chuckle was his way of confirming that he was where he wanted to be. For the others, it was not just a place to kick back; it was where they let off steam, reflected on their efforts, learned and argued and got high and figured out what to do next. It was also an intimate place, a place to befriend, a place to bond. Time together there tended to go on well through the night; at times they'd talk and laugh and dream until the morning sun soaked up the moist river haze and the fire simmered and the cicadas stopped snoring and the birds chirped the news that humans were still in their midst.

Dean Ewing and President Renwick each had their agents monitoring things. They were to report potential trouble and troublemakers, instigators and blow pots. Compared to what their colleagues from other schools were telling them at conferences and through scuttlebutt, things were still mild at GSU. They knew from Buddy Baxter how the Cody girl and the yahoos that hung with her had been slipping off campus below the bluff at Teddy's Landing to drink and smoke pot and be more unrestrained with their anti-war rhetoric. At this point at least, officials had not seen the need to aggravate things worse by interfering or catching STAND in the act of something illegal off-campus.

Plus, donating a few cases of beer and a little weed was all it took for the Bluff City police to look the other way.

Despite the subtle efforts of authorities to discredit them, STAND increased its visibility with their booths and displays in the student union building, fliers on the counter at the library and by the cafeteria cashier. Their credibility was advanced through The *Hopper Herald's* editorial support, and their notoriety through the full use of Jimmie Kim's *Express Yourself* alternative tabloid. Their events were listed on the monthly calendar and promoted free of charge on WGSU, the campus radio station. All of this exposure aggravated President Renwick and Dean Ewing. They knew that any form of censorship would make things worse, attract national media and all hell could breakout. Ewing had Buddy spread some hearsay about Pauline's pregnancy — perhaps suggesting that she was knocked up by a black man or a cousin back in Bobcat — but with every effort to exploit, Pauline seemed to gain stronger and broader support.

She was seen as the one with the vision, confidence and skills that found homes in leaders. Few knew of the misgivings that gnawed on her. Unlike her New Testament namesake, she had never been knocked off a horse or challenged by a vision. To propagate her cause, she had to mobilize others. She relied on her disciples, and the dependable steady assistance of her pal Susan who kept the checkbook and calendar and composure.

There weren't many clear and pleasant Saturday mornings when Arnie wouldn't be off fishing, but he had a hard time turning down Pauline for favors, particularly after she treated the big, simple fellow with a clear angle on her inflated cleavage and bra-less top when she bent down to pick up a box of leaflets for him. Just a quick innocent peek to accompany the request made his day. Arnie got a kick out of these spunky youngsters and they took him in as their own. He was their mascot.

Saturdays in Bluff City meant downtown sidewalk sales, so Pauline stationed Arnie in front of J. J. Newberry's on Second and Chestnut Streets in the heart the town's three-block commercial core. He had been distributing leaflets about the mounting death count and anti-war activities planned in the region over the coming months when he noticed a dressed-up lady in a midnight blue Chevy Impala about to give up on maneuvering into a tight parallel parking space. He set aside his literature to steer her with hand motions and nods.

The driver was Barb Renwick, the GSU President's wife. Striking and made-up, she pivoted out of the car, thanked Arnie, glanced at the kitchenware close-out sale table and a rack along the sidewalk of 50 percent-off stay press ladies slacks normally priced at $4.95. She took the pamphlet from Arnie and was drawn to a magazine cover photo of a terrified naked Vietnamese girl running in the streets of a village. Then she noticed a sidewalk newsstand and another magazine cover with a composite of the 79 U.S. servicemen killed in just one week in Vietnam.

Barb was not indifferent. She lifted prayerful hands to cover her opened mouth. She thought of her sister, and what she must be going through, and her sister's son, who had been thrust into that hell.

159

"War's bad, ma'am," Arnie said. He knew who she was, but she didn't make it a point to get to know people like Arnie who handled the manual labor around campus.

"It's awful. Just awful," she said. "I have a nephew over there."

"*Dey* say 20,000 of our GI's have been killed."

"I know. I know." Holding up the photo of the screaming, terrified little girl: "That poor little thing. That's just awful."

"Wonder why we can't just get along, ma'am." Arnie asked.

"Yeah...wonder why." She could tell he was limited.

"Ma'am, you wanna sign my paper here and tell President Lyndon Baines Johnson that he should bring our boys home?"

"Oh, I don't know."

"You know Will Yoder's over dere."

"Yes, I know."

"He may be dead, or he may be alive. They don't know. They cannot find him. They say he is missing. We call him Big Red. He was my friend."

"You don't understand. I'm... My husband is... I'm in an awkward position."

"Well, you fink about it." He didn't feel he should let on that he knew who she was. Arnie knew of his limitations and wouldn't ever think that he had much influence on people.

She nodded and a tear welled up as she took his leaflet and went toward the store. Arnie held the door open. A bell tinkled and the old floor squeaked, drawing attention to the entrance. A courteous clerk nodded a welcome. Mrs. Renwick faded into housewares. Arnie stayed past his shift through a drizzle, figuring the nice lady might need some help getting out of the tight parking space when she was ready to leave. But then at some point later when he remembered that he was going to do that, he noticed that her car was already gone and that she must not have needed his help.

Early into the next week, while Arnie was humming *Puff the Magic Dragon* and raking freshly mowed grass on the GSU library lawn, a car abruptly stopped at the curb. There was a honk followed by a woman's arm waving out the window. Arnie looked around for someone she may be calling. Seeing none, he shuffled closer and the woman's face was there.

"Ma'am?"

"Hello, Arnie. I'm Barb Renwick. Dr. Harlan Renwick, the university president, is my husband. We spoke in front of the Newberry store on Saturday. I have a little something for you."

"Ma'am?"

"A contribution, for your peace organization. You have expenses, I'm sure. Maybe this will help a little."

"Well my gosh. Fank you, ma'am. I, uh... don't know what to... you, uh... you were in a blue car on Saturday."

"Yes, I was. You're very observant, Arnie. Gotta go. You and your friends are doing important work."

"Fank you."

"Well, I'm due at the guild meeting at 10:30. Got to go."

"Actually ma'am it's 10:18."

She handed him a wad of bills, then he grinned and stuffed the cash in his shirt pocket below his name on his uniform. Arnie was speechless and waved as Mrs. Renwick drove off.

The Bubba Factor was alive and well in Bluff City. Folks who didn't hunt or know much about carburetors couldn't

162

contribute much to the conversation. You knew a real man by the kind of soap he used, and *Lava* was the standard issue. Basic Bible was instilled through the Bluff City public schools and open prayer was not challenged. Teachers kept paddles by their desks and were not reluctant to wield them. Black people were served at the diner, but the stares were so threatening that they generally picked up orders to go.

Dances at the American Legion post were the classiest social events of the year. The dance hall was wrapped in thin pine paneling with neon blinking signs of a half dozen beer brands, photos of past post commanders, and mounted bucks showcasing the art of taxidermy. When on Legion grounds, one was expected to be allegiant to the American Way and not complain about the runny pork and beans.

Around Bluff City, gossip spread like feathers from a ripped pillow caught up in the open wind: the peace freaks were sacrilegious socialists spreading syphilis; agitators had been brought in from California; sissy British haircuts signaled you were queer. At the diner, regulars who hung around and fueled up on the Sunrise Special of fried squirrel and over easy eggs and unlimited coffee refills were quick to circulate what they'd heard about pot and LSD and sex out in the open and how the rabble-rousers were about to sabotage the Fourth of July parade and ruin it for everybody.

Yet Bluff City folks couldn't very well abandon GSU because of its few rotten apples. The town relied on its purchasing power. Local contractors had enough pals in the right places that they almost always submitted a just-low-enough bid to be awarded the next campus construction contract. Faculty and administrators had no problem buying homes and cars, clothing and groceries. Students had little discretionary income to spend, but sales added up and were worth the complications of bad checks and property damage that went along with renting cheap apartments to kids taking their first sips of rum and independence. Stores couldn't keep enough Ramon noodles and hot plates in stock. Pizza deliveries picked up after 11:00 p.m. seven nights a week. And unlike the illegal stuff, beer, wine and the harder liquor were at least taxed to offset some of the social costs that went along with its prevalence.

Even in summer when enrollment was down and some of Pauline's entourage didn't stay in Bluff City, STAND stood its ground and strengthened its position. There were rallies to attend, articles and petitions to circulate, body counts to update and tally on banners that hung defiantly from dorm and fraternity house window ledges. When confiscated, banners would reappear by students and supportive faculty who were increasingly furtive and brash.

The campus demonstrations did not disrupt GSU's graduation or get in the way of the town's Independence Day parade. However, STAND's growing trouble-making reputation and a phone call from Dr. Renwick to Susan's father forced her to renege on the invitation for Pauline to join her during the summer at their Kentucky horse farm. Being unmarried and five-months pregnant did not help things.

So over the summer: Susan was ordered home by her father and was assigned the care of a well-bred foal. Jimmie Kim drove to Salem, Massachusetts and waited seven hours in the lobby of

Parker Brothers until somebody would see her and dismiss her Olympic board game idea. Luke James built some cabinets for a neighbor and picked out some Pennsylvania white ash to shave down into baseball bats. Dorsey Sugg got on at the new *Long John Silvers* and was the brunt of more wisecracks from reeking of fried fish all summer. Dean Ewing had not learned of Dave Blazer's involvement with the peace group, so the Faceman held on to his job at the Greek Shoppe and harvested another dandy crop of weed behind his mobile home. Odell Calhoun gained evangelical notoriety for his altar call tallies at summer tent revivals. Yolanda Emerson tutored and put together an art show to showcase JaMar Brown's portraits. Lonnie and Cate Youngman performed at folk festivals and county fairs. Lonnie struck out when he came on to Jimmie and suggested that they pick up things where they had left them once upon a time. Arnie Latham fished his favorite spot across from Teddy's Landing and passed out more literature in front of JC Penny and the downtown Kresge store. Coach Mac Shoals recruited Grasshopper fans to write notes to Big Red that would be delivered once their hero was located. Barb Renwick was alone much of the summer while her husband played golf in a half dozen states with major donor prospects. But she did manage to spend several weeks in suburban Cincinnati to comfort her sister whose son awaited his next military deployment. And whether on campus or back at her old Kentucky home, Susan couldn't escape worrying about Vic even though she was relieved of the pressure he induced when he was around. She didn't expect him to be on campus again until his furlough was issued just before he would leave for Vietnam – his requested assignment.

STAND's activities in the summer of '67 were inconsequential compared to events of the day: the 43 killed, 7,200 injured, and 1,400 buildings burned in the Detroit riots; China's hydrogen bomb test; the appointment of the first African American Supreme Court Justice, Thurgood Marshall. All the while, the marines moved into Que Son Valley. And there was still no news about Will Yoder.

Some of the area newspapers, TV or radio stations could be picked up back in

167

Pauline's hometown of Bobcat, but the dominant media presence was KMOX out of St. Louis – especially when it came to Cardinal baseball games described by the popular, eccentric Harry Caray, a fixture there for more than 20 years. It had been a good year for the Redbirds with the likes of Bob Gibson, Orlando Cepeda and Curt Flood. The war was not so horrible that it pulled people away from a tight pennant race.

It seemed to never fail that something about Pauline would be on the air about the time Hump put meat on the grill when friends were over. Hump didn't appreciate having discussions about sports or engines diverted to social issues. He figured that Pauline was on her own now, beyond his scolding or advice, beyond any grip he may have had on her. Just the same, it was tough for him to be critical of a daughter who put herself through school and had become a feisty young tigress who fights for what she believes in. She was Bobcat's first celebrity, although many in town thought her activism was taking her down a booby trapped path of a traitor.

Despite Rhonda's thriving Mary Kay enterprise and Hump's role in it, there had not been, nor would there be, help from home for Pauline. So to remain eligible for the job and expanded hours in the campus cafeteria, she enrolled in a fall term graduate night class: Gender, Crime and Justice (Sociology 546). In between she led meetings, recruited volunteers, spoke to civic clubs and, with Susan's help, submitted op-ed pieces. She talked Luke into corresponding with Eugene McCarthy, the principled senator from Minnesota who was a long shot as a presidential anti-war candidate in the fall. McCarthy's hand-written response was something Luke framed and would always cherish.

Her pregnancy notwithstanding, Pauline's reputation grew and with it came responsibility and leadership expectations that she quietly found intimidating. A few months ago she was the little pistol from Bobcat and the person who came up with the next theme for a KD mixer and the creative punch concoction to go with it. Now she was looked upon as an authority on troop strategy and war casualties. The pace of her activism had been more than a social distraction. When the pressure and expectations peaked, she was soothed by nips of *Jim Beam* until Susan discovered it.

The outcrop of rock that formed Teddy's Landing baked all day and stayed warm through the summer nights. Beer tasted better after a summer sweat, but overdoing it affected coordination and senses and communication and good judgment. When STAND came together socially over the summer, jumps from the cliffs were clumsy, loud music and camaraderie overwhelmed the sounds of nature, deep discussions about public policy were convoluted.

By the third week of August, the GSU campus buzzed in anticipation of a new wave of students. Dorm assignments, class registration, facelifts to fraternity and sorority houses in preparation for rush, the invigorating beat of the marching band practicing every bit as hard as the football team. The chaotic campus beehive signaled the adventure of leaving home, special times ahead, new friends, sexual opportunities and freedom subsidized from home or through grants and loans. Newcomers came to know the campus celebrities: key players in sports, student

170

government, the student newspaper, fraternities and sororities. When it came to the counterculture of activism, Pauline was the queen bee.

In just a few months, GSU had been transformed from a stale regional university not known for much of anything other than a great place to get wasted to a center of activism now tracked by university officials, politicians, FBI agents, the National Guard and right wing institutes. Like a balloon expanding with every puff to a hard and fragile thin layer on the brink of bursting, at every peace rally there were those who cringed waiting for something to pop.

The fall semester registration was chaotic as ever. Faculty and staff manned booths that filled the floor and ramps leading into Grey Arena. There were dozens of displays for fraternities and sororities, clubs, service organizations, tutoring, foreign study and other groups offering pizza coupons and campus shuttle tokens. It took several hours for most students to find the right stations and learn if the classes they were told they needed were already full. Courses taught by the easy-grading

171

professors filled up quickly, generally by the Greek chapters that kept files on instructors, papers and exams.

Parents weren't typically as distraught over their children enrolling at GSU as those who went off to the private schools or the larger, more prestigious universities. GSU was close to home for most students, relatively homogenous, academically sufficient, and it was cheap – only $225 per semester for full time enrollment (15 credit hours or more), maybe fifty bucks for used books. The affordable price attracted veterans on the GI Bill, small town high school athletes, and a good number of young men who weren't sure they were college material but took this route to avoid or at least postpone the draft.

The start of the fall semester meant fraternity and sorority rush and scores of naïve, enthusiastic pledges busy with their ice-breaker activities. The GSU fraternities didn't go to much trouble; they would just tap a few kegs and see who shows up. However, for the dolled up sorority girls, there were lovely spreads of finger foods, unspiked punch, songs, poems, skits, and descriptions of why their sorority is

172

special. The KD ladies gained distinction
as the only sorority with a six-month
pregnant member welcoming prospects at
the front door.

The Greek Shoppe attracted a
steady stream of customers; on this
weeknight, near closing time, a new one –
the only one left – lingered.

"Excuse me, aren't you Mrs.
Renwick?" Blazer asked.

"Yes."

"Nice to have you in the shop,
ma'am," Blazer said."

"Well, thank you."

"I'm Dave, Dave Blazer.

"You have a unique inventory."

"We cater to the GSU fraternities
and sororities, sports, customized gifts."

"I can see. I trust these fraternity
paddles are for decoration only."

"We only beat our pledges once a
year."

"What a Faceman", Pauline thought.

"Thanks. My husband thinks highly
of you."

" I'll be working closely with your
husband once I'm elected USG vice
president."

"Is that so? Are you unopposed?"

"Just confident."

"I see. You usually get what you want?"

"Not always, but..." He raised an eyebrow suggestively. "Did you find what you're looking for?"

"Not yet," she said. "A gift, for my husband to give a student member of his staff, for his birthday."

"We can iron Greek letters onto jerseys or t-shirts. Mugs are always appreciated," he said.

"I don't think he drinks." Mrs. Renwick said. She was speaking of Buddy Baxter. Mrs. Renwick was awkwardly struck by Blazer's chiseled face and wind-blown blonde hair, sort of a Beach Boy look.

"Dr. Renwick has been here now for, what, five years?" asked Blazer.

"Soon be seven."

"That right?"

"Yes. He's on the road a lot these days. Alumni parties. Fund raisers."

"I see," Blazer said. He told himself to be careful and not be obvious that there were vibrations between them. "Stay as long as you like. I'm in no hurry to lock

174

up." He was confident that he could lock the door and take her to the back of the store and have a round that neither would forget.

Mrs. Renwick noticed a poster on a bulletin board.

"I see you're promoting activities of the peace group," she said.

"Well, I uh... consider that to be public space. Anybody or any group can put up whatever they want on the bulletin board," he said.

"Fine by me. Hope it helps to get the word out. Might be what this school and little town needs. Wouldn't hurt to shake things up a bit, challenge the status quo."

"I not sure I expected that from you. Does your husband agree?"

"We don't talk about things that matter. But I've heard him grumble through some late night phone calls. I suppose it's about the following that the peace group has attracted, and how it appears to be growing."

"Really?"

"Yes, since we lost the basketball ballplayer, it's been..."

175

"He's missing. We don't know that Will is dead," he clarified. "May still be alive somewhere."

"Right. Let's hope so."

A different tone characterized life at GSU during the '67 fall semester. Everyday body counts increased the tally, now on display at locations for the administration to track and remove. Students, faculty, and administrators knew graduates from the May ceremony who were already "in country." In September, 114 Americans died in the Que Son Valley, but not to be dispirited, military spokesmen bragged of the 376 Viet Cong that were killed in the battle. Secretary of State Dean Rusk concluded that escalation must continue since peace initiatives were futile. Hundreds were arrested across the country and there were more international protests from Japan to Western Europe.

Factions were not giving in. A push against the establishment was reflected in Jim Morrison's defiance of Ed Sullivan's censorship of the lyrics *"girl we couldn't get much higher"* from the band's hit tune, *Light My Fire*. A month later, Joan Baez was arrested for blocking a military induction center, and *Hair* opened on Broadway.

But the music of '67 had a lot of catching up to do. Songs like *Come on Down to My Boat Baby* and *Snoopy Versus the Red Baron* and tunes by the Monkees and Strawberry Alarm Clock sold better than Woody Guthrie or Pete Seeger. And, of course, baseball became a priority of autumn when St. Louis Cardinals ace Bob Gibson pitched three complete games and held the Boston Red Sox to 14 hits in 27 innings to take the World Series.

By and large, male students at GSU planned to hold on to their deferments and stay in school as long as possible, except for those who had reason to think they would flunk the physical or skip out for Canada. Some enlisted thinking it would improve their chances for an easy gig in Europe or on some U.S. base, but the strategy seldom worked. Not much persuaded the draft board to make exceptions.

Among the girls, Pauline and Susan included, there was less talk of job prospects and ground floor opportunities and more about moving into socially sensitive careers or frontline activism.

177

Pauline was brash enough to suggest they round up a group and go to Vietnam to find Will, but with a baby on the way – *his* baby on the way – she set that aside and did what she could given her circumstances.

While the weather and water level in Possum Run River were just right, there were still students who made riding the rapids their preferred use of time. There were still streakers, binge drinkers and theme parties, but they were less and less likely to include Pauline and her followers.

Pauline heard from Susan that the Cypriot who worked at the foreign studies desk had been accepted to the University of Chicago architecture school. Before Pauline was showing, she and Susan had been tempted to reel him in, but Susan felt threatened by Vic even when he was away at basic training, and it was hard for Pauline to have any fun or focus much on anything as long as there was no news about Will. She would always remember her time with him: his innocence, tenderness, and as much cuteness as could be imbedded in a speckled pup. Susan couldn't hide her crush on the Cypriot, and Pauline teased her about blushing in his

178

presence and how she should not give a shit if Vic's spies noticed.

Buddy Baxter doubled as an in-house spy who self-servingly reported to his superior, Dean Neville Ewing. Together they explored ways in which STAND could be discredited, but the protestors had all the momentum, all the cool factor, and all the First Amendment axioms on their side.

Susan noticed that she was bumping into Buddy more often, but brushed it off as coincidental. "Sign our petition?" Susan asked him while handing out STAND information outside the student union building. She knew that Buddy was aligned with the administration and that he knew of her father's influence.

"I'll take your literature, look over it," he said. "Nice bracelet."

Susan was not used to compliments; Vic was not one to issue them. Buddy had a hidden crush on Susan, but he never felt the feeling was mutual. Whenever Vic was around, he knew better than to move in on her. She could sense his advances, but she knew he wouldn't fit in. He dressed too much like an adult: He wore a coat and tie when jeans and a t-shirt would do, and

179

someone needed to convince him to let go of his self-promotion -- things like campaigning for Mr. Sophomore (a popularity contest) or buying his way into the "Who's Who" directory (an honor designed for a friend or colleague to submit).

"So, uh...what's your major? Susan asked.

"Plastics," Buddy said.

"Plastics?"

"It's a joke. Don't guess you've seen the movie."

"Guess not."

"The Graduate."

"Oh. No. Heard about it."

"Great movie. You need to go. Soundtrack's by Simon and Garfunkel."

"I don't get to many movies. My boyfriend's not here, at GSU, and he won't let me go out with anybody else."

"Won't *let* you?"

"He's at boot camp at Ft. Dix, hopes to be in Vietnam after paratrooper training."

"Geez."

"Yeah, he was in ROTC, so he's starting out as a lieutenant."

"I'm sure you're proud of him."

180

"Yeah. Sure. But I'm still against the war."

"So your boyfriend enlists, and you're back home protesting the war?"

"Vic would like for it to be over as much as anybody. He just believes in military service."

"Well more power to him. But does he know that you're telling folks the cause is not justified; here with all this propaganda and your rallies and marches and all?"

"There's more to it than that. Vic's family — father, grandfather, uncles — they've seen action, earned medals. And it's not propaganda just because people like you don't want to face up to the mistake of this war. Pauline, Pauline Cody, my roommate, we weren't political or anything. We got into this after the news came out about Will."

"Yeah. Good man, that Will Yoder. Best b-ball player to ever come out of GSU. Hate to think what he's been through over there."

"Well we believe he's still alive," Ruth said.

Pauline arrived and pinned a poster on a bulletin board. Buddy turned to her.

181

"Don't cover up the Box Tops promo. You know we're bringing them in for Homecoming."

"You don't mean it," Pauline said sarcastically.

"I'm the student representative on the Cultural Enrichment Events Committee."

"Well ain't you sump'n," Pauline said.

"Looks good on a resume," Buddy said.

"That's what counts, I reckon," Pauline said.

Susan added, "These days, most guys around here aren't thinking much about their resumes."

"I know. I lucked out. Dean Ewing wrote me a letter, managed to get my job as his assistant classified by the military as an 'essential civilian occupation.' "

"An essential civilian occupation?" Pauline said."

"That's right," admitted Buddy. "People who do important work can get deferments."

Homecoming '67 offered STAND more of an opportunity to make a statement than a typical demonstration or rally. GSU's football team was a perennial loser, but the university went all out for the annual celebration, as did Bluff City merchants and motel owners who reaped the windfall of the buying power of thousands of alumni who converged annually on their alma mater. Over three days, there would be a public tour of campus improvements, a trustee invitation-only reception at President Renwick's house, the Harvest Day Sing competition in Peacock Hall, a donor's brunch, the Greek house decoration awards presentation, the faculty tug of war, a dance with music from the 40s and 50s, the Box Tops concert, and a long parade featuring GSU's ROTC honor guard, Bluff City Brownie troops, Shriner clowns, an Uncle Sam on stilts, horses and riders from the Bit and Bridle Club, floats sponsored by the French Club and the honor societies and the Baptist Student Union, the forensic team, and four blaring area high school bands joining GSU's own Marching Grasshoppers.

The football team was, once again, among the weakest in the conference. This year's homecoming contest with SIU

Edwardsville would be the only game on the schedule in which Lou Bates Stadium would for the most part be full. The 6,500-seat facility was named for a rugged record-breaking linebacker from the time of leather helmets without face masks.

The theme for this year's festivities was "May Patriotism Prevail." This was to be reflected in the parade floats and music, the tunes selected for Harvest Day Sing, campus decorations and the like. Student groups were encouraged to enter floats in the parade – with one expected exception. During media interviews, President Renwick's inference to STAND was obvious: "Homecoming is a time to rejoice, recollect, and re-connect. It is *not* a time to agitate."

Increasingly to Renwick, agitators were like mid-continent twisters darting down from the sky: damaging, unpredictable, with no redeeming value but to demonstrate their purposeless power and the consequences of their puffery. But unlike twisters, he was determined to lasso them, to tame them.

News from the war was wearing down both the hawks and the doves, leaving subliminal impressions on some and debilitating symptoms on others. Heightened TV news coverage. Graphic cover stories. Veterans sharing their gruesome experiences. Leaders obviously misleading.

There was only so much that officials could do to tie down the antics and rhetoric that swung like vines from one campus building to another. But they took precautions. The president convened his deans, his closest confidants from the faculty and administration, and compliant Buddy Baxter, of course, who had gained their trust. The National Guard would station a platoon nearby — off-campus and on-call. Areas for demonstrating would be limited and clearly marked. Campus security would search for alcohol and pot to thin out and intimidate the renegades. President Renwick and Dean Ewing did not expect there to be a need for guard dogs, cattle prods or fire hoses, but supplies had been stashed.

The student party crowd, however sensitive to social issues and the war, was wound up about Homecoming, always the blowout of the year. Classes let out by noon on Thursday. Festivities, music, and dolled-up babes. Drumbeats of the rehearsing band. Pep rallies that stirred up hope for an upset at a school where sports really didn't matter — that is, before the Will Yoder era.

While administrators and student groups reviewed the Homecoming plans and assignments for the upcoming weekend, STAND wrestled with its options within its nonviolent parameters: A march in the designated area? A clandestine float that invades the parade? A smoke bomb in the ROTC building? Flag or draft card burnings? Something that sends a simple message or something that will be talked about for years? Something that would get them a slap on the wrist or land them in jail?

Dave Blazer was comfortably elected USG vice president at the beginning of the fall term. The Faceman was carried by his Beach Boy good looks prominently featured on posters and advertisements in the *Hopper Herald* and Jimmie Kim's *Express Yourself* alternative publication.

Dean Neville Ewing owed Blazer a congratulatory visit. He dropped by the

Greek Shoppe. Blazer turned down the store's stereo.

"David, you, uh, you have plenty of inventory for Homecoming, I presume."

"Yes, sir. And I checked it against Homecoming sales over the last three years."

"Good. Makes sense. Anything particularly promising this year?"

"Tie-dyed t-shirts are moving pretty well. Mugs and pledge paddles are fairly predictable."

"You think we could sell some jeans if we rearranged or added on?"

"Bellbottoms for sure. Maybe Dingo boots."

"You do a good job staying on top of trends, David."

"Thank you."

"Congratulations on your election."

"Thanks."

"You better watch your step, though, young man."

"Sir?"

"You assured me that this would not get out."

"I'm real careful about who can buy..."

"Don't blow it, now. We've have a good thing going."

"There are plenty of other people moving a little pot."

"But they're not student government leaders, or people with a bright future in the corporate world, even politics. Just be discreet. Be careful. Know who you are selling to. Don't be cavalier."

"I hear you."

"Are you sure everything is well-hidden there behind the body shop?"

"Absolutely."

"And what is it with this peace group? I told you I could get you a deferment through law school."

"It's a good group, sir. I like them."

"Well an arrest won't look good on your record and it won't help me get you any special consideration."

"Maybe I don't want any special consideration."

"See, you're not using good judgment."

"I'm not bailing out on my friends."

A bell rung as a customer came through the door.

Ewing leaned into Blazer and left him with a firm whisper, "Don't you people do anything stupid during Homecoming weekend. Hear me now?"

Lumbering about with Will's growing seed gave Pauline a heightened sense of confidence and strength and helped her hold her own when she spoke to crowds or needed to put an opponent in their place. But her Bobcat twang and indifference to grammar did not connote an impressive rising star. Her purpose was not to elevate herself or network; it was not strategic or vocational. As long as Will was away, GSU felt like the right place for her, a place better than where she was from, a place where the big bushy red-headed fellow's presence hovered like a puffy cloud that moved with the wind. But her direction was as hazy as the early morning view from the top of the hill. She worried about what she and a baby would do next – stay there in Bluff City or move on to some other place where she and newfound friends would find a way to get along. Before long she expected to get this activism out of her system. But surely she could do better than take the bait cast out by stepmom Rhonda and be reeled back to Bobcat for the opportunities in Mary Kay cosmetics.

It was odd but true: The longer Will was away, the longer Pauline felt his presence. The longer he was away, the more she held on to a sense that the two of them were destined to be together. For now, she was in need of solace, topped off with a shot of bourbon. She figured there was no downside in praying for Will to receive special consideration from The Almighty. Based on what she saw on news clips and the increasing body counts on both sides, it didn't seem like God was intervening.

Most of the Americans captured near the North Vietnamese Dirty Bird Camp were pilots who had been injured from an ejection or forced landing, but Will Yoder and other remnants of the 5th Regiment ended up there after having been besieged at Con Thien a few miles south of the Demilitarized Zone. Unable to connect with their unit — and not knowing if there was anything left of their unit — a dozen of them hiked and hid for six days before being overwhelmed by the enemy.

190

Will had stayed back in a greasy scorched gulley with a marine named Sweeney who was in shock and facing a leg amputation as another barrage of artillery strikes shook their earth, took their hearing and sprayed shrapnel all around them. Will placed his large body atop Sweeney's, while a covey of enemy soldiers suddenly encircled them, frantic, ready to gun down or impale. The IV and bandages that Will applied to Sweeney's wounds signaled to the enemy that Will had medical skills that could be useful. One of them shouted out an order, and then it took several of them to yank Will up and out of the gulley, where they shot Sweeney promptly and indifferently. Will was forced to go with them, his hands locked by his fingers atop his head.

They hiked through a meandering muddy soup, home of long snakes that wiggled alongside them. The creek rose to Will's waist but all the way to the chins of the shorter enemy. To take advantage of Will's height and strength, they mounted several supply packs on his back and shoulders. The muddy creek bottom held on to Will's boots and sucked on them as he yanked out every step. Bloated bodies and parts of bodies littered the banks. It was hard to distinguish one side over another. He didn't recognize the stench, but it made him gag, then vomit, then he dropped the backpacks and was poked by a short guard with a bayonet who ordered him to do something as if Will was supposed to understand what he was saying.

They reached the make-shift base, and Will was loaded onto a truck with other quiet U.S. troops for a ride to another unknown destination. He learned later that the Dirty Bird Camp was near the Hanoi Thermal Power Plant, and that the U.S. prisoners were placed nearby to shield the facility from bombing. Within a few weeks, Will was removed to the Hoa Lo (Hanoi Hilton) camp, then to a clinic in the Pu Loung Valley near an underground tunnel system where he refused to treat the North Vietnamese unless he was also allowed to help the other injured or sick troops and villagers. He took some hard blows and threats for that insistent stand, but given his valuable role, the camp commandant barked out an order for his people to pull off the one with the medicines.

Just before sunset, a golden streak slit through a cloud and spotlighted the contrast of this place: the shacks of cardboard and tin, the machines of war that had scraped bare a once plush valley into a black dusty camp without anything alive and green. The destruction was up against a stunning backdrop of steep mountain ascents, misty waterfalls, and home of marvelous, colorful unknown tropical plants and animals. Like the others, though, Will grew indifferent to the views and vistas and all that was so marvelous beyond the camp when he heard the pitiful screams from the interrogation cells, the beatings, and cellmates holding on to secrets they pretended to have.

They chose starvation over the stench of rotten fish soup, food and water contaminated with human and animal feces. Lengthy stays in solitary confinement. Buddies lined up, spit upon, then executed. Deprived of sleep, bound in ropes and irons. Until Will came along, broken and dislocated bones were left untreated.

Beyond the punishment, the enemy aimed to break the will of the American prisoners, to extract written or recorded statements to support their propaganda campaign. They knew that every man had his breaking point, and once that happened, the Americans would praise how they were treated, and denounce U.S. practices and policies.

Because of his medical knowledge, however limited, the enemy needed Will. He had introduced them to the use of green papaya and ginger as a treatment for infection, herbal remedies for snake bites and malaria, and super glue as a surprising way to stop bleeding. Despite the meager supplies, Will removed shrapnel and sutured wounds, treated burns and seizures, performed tracheotomies, improvised splints, and did what he could for those going mad.

But understanding what Will needed and getting medicines and supplies to him were very different things. The enemy was surprisingly responsive to him, not because of Will's medical tricks as much as their superstitions. They were fiercely frightened by the ace of spades, the fear of the wandering soul and the evil eyes painted on the front of Sea Knight helicopters, all of which were systematically used by the U.S. to intimidate and terrify. The enemy was also tentative about Will: they had never seen a man so tall; they had never seen red hair.

Unlike the policy during World War II and the Korean War, U.S. medics in the Vietnam War were no longer identified with special helmets and arm bands. Despite his intent to serve and remain a pacifist, Will had been issued weapons, but he had never used them.

The gaunt, colorless, despondent faces of the prisoners wore on Will like it did on the others. Depression was contagious at the camp, and they fought it with old jokes and stories of Saigon whores. They mocked and impersonated their keepers, and when they took it too far — charging a guard or ignoring an order or mumbling indifferently — they were yanked out to the yard, forced to kneel and beg and given the option of a bullet to the temple or more time in the hole. Most chose the bullet; their bodies left for the trenches and the buzzards.

Will could not seal his senses to the horror that leaked into his pores. His very being ached in dismay. He had lost his smile. He always assumed that he was grouped with the good, but he had seen enough and heard enough to know that enemy soldiers were not the only ones capable of atrocities. He knew that the war brought out the worst on both sides. He pushed back the tendency to judge and learned to let it go. He couldn't let go of regret, though. He regretted his impetuous decision to enlist which offended his parents and his Mennonite community who had long embraced the pacifist way. Being a medic was not enough. In their judgment, he supported the war, defended it and justified it, just by participating in it. Will would always cherish his home, family and faith community, but he knew they might not ever take him back.

Perhaps Pauline would. Perhaps she thought of him as he thought of her. Perhaps she would wait for him. But with every fellow prisoner thrown in the hole, or every one that reached the breaking point, Will could not escape the sense that he might be next. He might be blamed for not being able to stop the bleeding or revive a heart. He might be charged with giving extra attention to Americans, allies, refugees or villagers. He might refuse to submit, and let whatever is to happen, happen.

In six months, everything had changed. The party school had re-defined itself. Pauline Cody, the hick from Bobcat, Illinois, once the ultimate carouser and now very pregnant with somebody's child, was accepted as leader and spokesperson. Students, dropouts, some gutsy faculty and staff, and even a few residents of Bluff City had followed Pauline and brought in others. They had learned and challenged authority and surprised themselves.

But there were consequences. Pauline and her best pal Susan had fallen out with their parents and family. Susan's monthly allotment was cut off. Pauline was let go in the cafeteria without cause or explanation. Dean Ewing threatened Dave Blazer in The Greek Shoppe and directed Buddy Baxter to uncover scoop that could be useful. Jimmie's *Express Yourself* editions were confiscated from distribution sites. GSU's athletic director, Gil Westerfield, was advised by President Renwick to make it clear to Coach Shoals and his simple sidekick, Arnie Latham, that they were both on thin ice. Pastors of the Bluff City Protestant churches convened to determine how they might blackball the hotshot young preacher, Odell Calhoun, and his mulatto girlfriend. Luke was suddenly having complications in drawing down checks from his GI Bill allotment. Cate and Lonnie had their stuff stolen from the dressing room at Dooley's, and the mirror was marked up with messages: "Hippies and Pussies Go Home," "Commie Freaks!" and "Canada Can Have You!" Dorsey had his hours cut at Long John Silvers. And JaMar woke to a burning cross in the front yard of his off-campus apartment.

Easter was long gone, but this was their Maundy Thursday. The 12 convened at Teddy's Landing on what would be one last time. Pauline found it particularly gratifying that her closest and most dependable followers came together for what could be a defining day in their peace movement experience: Dorsey, her awkward first recruit; Jimmie, the ambitious one; Blazer, the slick and savvy and good-looking one; JaMar, the hardened young black man; the unlikely couple, Odell and Yolanda; Cate and Lonnie, who provided the music that everyone needed; Luke, the experienced, confident veteran; lovable Arnie; crusty old Coach Shoals and, of course, Pauline's closest friend, Susan.

Pauline went over the plan one more time.

"We're all set then, right, Luke?"

"Got it."

"Dorse?"

"We're ready. Gone over it a dozen times."

"Remember: Right after the Shriner clowns in front of the band. They'll have to slow everything down to make that tight turn by the alumni building."

Pauline answered a few more questions before reflecting on how far they had come since they heard the news about Will. "Ya'll know I'm not one to get mushy, but you dipshits are aaal right," she said. "We've come a long way, and each of you... well, you've been great, and I couldn't have done any of this without you. It started with the news that our hero Will was reported missing. But it's become much more than that now as we've learned about the misguided nature of this war.

199

We've stood together and been part of a greater movement. I feel a special bond with you people."

Pauline sat in front of the old birch tree on the limestone outcrop down the bluff from the campus. Teddy's Landing was slightly elevated above the water level and worn smooth by wind and water when the river was higher and rushed through there. This had come to be a place of reverence through the stories of hunters, gatherers, runaway slaves, and adventurers like Teddy Roosevelt who was said to have camped here. A steady fire burned in the middle of the gathering, popping with expectation. Susan and Pauline shared a blanket; everyone else sat on logs in a semi-circle around them. Dorsey showed up with a bucket of fried fish and hush puppies from Long John Silvers. He was surprised that they could feed so many with such small servings.

"Pauline, if we've finished our official business, I'd like to suggest a special activity tonight. Up for it?" asked Yolanda.

Pauline shrugged and welcomed Yolanda's participation. "What do you say, folks?" There were a few nods and thumbs-up.

"Pauline raised her arms: "There being no opposition -- Yo, you have our undivided. You're the one with the psych minor. You gonna hypnotize us or something?"

"Have you barking like a dog," Yolanda said.

"No way," Jimmie said.

"Do me!" said Dorsey.

"Just a little exercise. We'll see how it goes," Yolanda said.

"Well have at it," Blazer said.

"Tunes? I got some Archie Bell and the Drells." Luke pulled an 8-track tape out of his pack.

"No, this is not a Hootenanny," Yolanda said. "This is about bonding, the beauty of bonding."

"I could do some serious bonding: James Bonding. That's one beautiful man," Cate said, to remind Lonnie that she could be on the lookout too.

"Uh hmm," Pauline agreed.

"The floor is yours, kind lady." Jimmie said to move things along.

Yolanda explained: "Honesty, vulnerability, trusting one another. This is an exercise called Johari, and it really can take our friendships and relationships to another level. We think we're close, we think we know one another, but we really... we really don't. In a few weeks or another semester or maybe after this weekend," she added as if warning, "many of us will be leaving this place. We may not see one another again, or maybe we won't until there's a reunion down the road. Some of you may have to go into the military. Others may start a new life in Canada or another country. Some may go to law school or go on to get a master's. When we go our separate ways, who knows when we'll connect again. This exercise, if you'll give it half a chance, will leave us all with some special things about one another to hold on to, to remember and cherish."

"So what's the game plan? You've got our attention, Dr. Joyce Brothers," Pauline said. "We've gotta stick together, now more than ever. Do your magic, Yo," Pauline said.

They passed around more beers and shared in the hits on a joint that Blazer offered them. Yolanda broke off a twig from the big birch and drew a large box in

202

the dirt in front of the fire pit. Then she drew a line down the middle followed by a perpendicular line within the box to form four contiguous rectangles. She put Roman Numerals I and II in the two rectangles across the top, III and IV inside the rectangles on the bottom.

"Imagine this as four windows," Yolanda said. "Window number one represents the things that you know about yourself that everyone else also knows."

"Like, uh...that Dorsey smells like fried fish," said Lonnie. Dorsey, still in his Long John Silvers uniform, fired a hush puppy at Lonnie.

"Suck my big one, Lonnie," he said.

Yolanda steered them back: "We can do better than that, now. Something that you know about yourself that everyone else knows."

"That Arnie is just a really, really great guy. Everybody knows that," said Blazer.

"I'll buy that," said Coach Shoals.

Arnie grinned. "I like dis game."

"Okay. You get the idea," said Yolanda. "Now, window number two represents the things that other people know about you that you don't know."

203

There was silence. "C'mon, you can do this," said Yolanda.

Jimmie tried to interpret: "How about...like if, say, a boss doesn't realize that he or she is showing favoritism to an employee."

"Right. Good," Yolanda said. "Everybody get that okay? That's window number two."

Lonnie glanced at Jimmie, and Jimmie could feel his eyes staring. She put her hand on her thigh, slid it down to the underside of her leg so that Lonnie was the only one who could see it. She slowly curled up all but her middle finger.

Yolanda continued: "Jumping over to window number four: that represents things about yourself that you don't know and nobody else knows either."

"Is that even possible?" asked Luke.

"The Lord knows all," said Odell.

"Maybe you got the flu but you don't yet have a fever," Coach Shoals said. "You don't know it and nobody else does either until you start puking all over the place."

"Now you got it," Yolanda said.

"Or maybe you have a phobia or something..." Dorsey said. "Or.... uh, a

204

skill — maybe you *could* be a concert pianist but you've never had a lesson or access to a piano to bring out the talent," said Susan.

"We're getting there," Yolanda said.

"So... you, uh... you skipped one," JaMar said.

"Yeah, that brings us to this one." She tapped on window number three with the twig. "When we open our third window to others, to those we care about and trust, we connect in a special way, we reveal what we know about ourselves that no one else knows. It's all about sharing things you've held back from one another. When you trust a friend this much and share these intimate things about yourself, a very special bond takes place," Yolanda said.

Several nod. Some are uneasy and squirm.

"It's not easy, and it takes courage. Is everyone on board? Who wants to start?" Yolanda asked.

No one volunteered.

"C'mon, now. Who'd like to start?" Yolanda asked again.

"Why don't you begin, Mr. Blazer -- Mr. Faceman. How about if you let a breeze come through your third window.

What can you share about yourself that no one else knows?" asked Yolanda.

Blazer had had plenty to drink and he'd smoked a few joints. He shuffled in his seat and flung back his Beach Boy hair. "I, uh... I don't know. Nothing comes to mind."

"I didn't mean to put you on the spot," Yolanda said. "Maybe we can come back to..."

"I have a bum knee. How's that? I don't go around whining about it. I doubt if anybody knows about *that*," Blazer said as if he wanted to get through this little game in a hurry.

Dorsey spoke again without thinking: "You could tell everybody about the noises old lady Renwick makes when you two..."

"Ass hole," said Blazer with a hint of a grin. He actually didn't mind that a rumor had circulated about his fling with the president's wife even though there wasn't anything to it. "Tell you what, though, I was once offered $300 from a woman about her age... if I would, you know, *satisfy* her."

"You're shittin' me," said Dorsey.

"Nope, it's true."

"Well you *are* a Faceman after all," said Pauline.

"Pretty good gig!" said Luke.

"I'd be available at half price." Dorsey said.

"Buy one bang, get another one free!" said Lonnie.

"You guys are fuuunny," Arnie said.

"Can we do a little better here people?" Yolanda asked.

"I'll go next," said Odell, feeling a need to support his girlfriend. He turned to Yolanda. "I've never even told you about this, shoog. I worried that you'd think I was some kind of fanatic or something." A few in the group cleared their throats.

"It's okay. Go ahead," Yolanda said.

"Well, you see…the uh… the Lord spoke to me once."

Some of the group showed interest and attentiveness; others rubbed their chin or looked down and scratched their head.

"Really?" asked Coach.

"Wow," said Arnie.

"No shit, Rev.?" said Dorsey.

"Go ahead, hon," Yolanda said affectionately.

"I never told anybody about this, but it's true; it really happened."

"He never lies," said Blazer.

"We, uh...about 8, 10 years ago, a group from church, you see, a high school group... we were just messing around on a rope swing along the riverbank down by Cave in Rock after a hike and cookout. Well I wandered off a bit, was by myself, when I decided to swim from Willow Island across a little channel to the Illinois side when I guess I got caught up in the current or something. I knew how to swim — pretty good, actually — and I was doing fine, then I noticed that I was peddling and stroking and kicking and just wasn't going anywhere. I had a sweatshirt on and it got soaked and was real heavy and started pulling me down. The harder I worked the worse it got. Then I started to panic and I started swallowing water and just wore myself out. The harder I worked the worse it got and I thought, 'Well, Lord, I guess this is it.' I imagined the coroner finding me in a few days, washed up on the bank a few miles down river, olive green and swollen. I imagined people saying, 'Well, that's what he gets for messin' around in that river.' And then I heard a little whisper. I did. I swear I did."

Odell spoke softly as he remembered it, "The voice said, 'Relax. Relax, Odell. Easy does it, don't fight it.' I eased up and slowed down and then just floated a minute until I got my breath back, and it was like the current let go of me or something and I worked my way free."

Odell looked at the still and quiet and expressionless faces around him.

"I believe that was the Lord whispering to me that day. Nobody in our group even knew I was struggling out there in that river, and I never told anybody about it. Maybe it was my imagination... but no, by golly, I don't believe it was. It was real. It was the hand of God."

The tone of the group dialogue changed. It was tender, contemplative.

"That's bad, Rev." said JaMar. "A bad ass story."

"Not your time, man," said Luke.

"So when you hear me say that I've been saved, you'll know there's a little more to the story for me." Odell said as he smiled.

Yolanda took Odell's hand. She waited a moment before calling on the next participant. They could hear the trickle of the water moving nearby, but that was all.

"Thank you, sweetie," Yolanda said. "Proud of you for sharing."

"Who's next?" she asked. "You're getting it. See how special this can be?"

Susan pulled off the blanket she shared with Pauline and held up her hand. Yolanda nodded her permission to proceed.

"I was a Woodford County 4H winner when I was 13," Susan said with all the poise and perkiness of young debutante. "Had my own cow."

"Bet nobody knew that!" "All right!" said several of her friends simultaneously.

"Bet you won Miss Congeniality, too," said the Faceman.

"Figures," Jimmie said.

"You're getting off too easy," said Cate.

"Remember. No one else is supposed to know this about you," said Yolanda. "Think hard. You can come up with something… more personal. Something you know about yourself, or something that you did or that happened to you that nobody else knows about."

"C'mon, beauty queen," said Dorsey. "Play the game."

Susan folded her arms across her chest and brought forth another memory. "Here's something. I believe I was in the fourth grade, walking home from Richland Trace Elementary School with Angela Vaughn. The principal — his name was Littlepage. Yeah, I remember. Mr. Littlepage, a stocky fellow who always kept a pencil tucked behind his ear. He always wore bow ties. Well, anyway, one day he let us out early because of the snow. Angela and I got off the bus at Bernie Greenwell's store like we always did. Well, we sort of took the long way home and then Angela veered off to her lane and went on home and I was just taking my time, kicking the new snow as I walked along State Road 58 where we lived, a narrow and winding road in the rolling bluegrass countryside. At a distance before they went inside the stable, I could see Angela playing with a foal that was prancing around in the snow. The flakes were huge that day, perfect for snowballs. The snowfall was so thick; you couldn't see ten feet in front of you. I took my time, just meandered, you know, made some angel's wings in the snow and stuff. Well, I had made this really terrific snowball, you see, and I was just carrying it, packing it down as I walked, when I heard an engine right there next to me, just poking along. Without really thinking and not intending to do anything harmful, I fired a snowball that burst on the windshield in front of the driver. It was all really very innocent."

"Uh oh," said Yolanda. "There must be more to this story."

Susan had everyone's attention. "The driver of the car slammed on the brakes and then I could see that the words Woodford County Sheriff were painted on the side of the car. Well wouldn't you know, the sheriff's department was leading a funeral procession! The sheriff's car slid to a stop and then the driver of the limousine behind him slammed on his brakes but couldn't stop and plowed right into the back of the sheriff's car. And then the next limousine swerved to miss the one in front of it, hit a slick spot and brushed an old stone wall and rolled backwards off the road and down into a gulley. Well, as you can imagine, I was one scared to death little kid, so I was out of there, running faster and longer than I had ever run in my life. As I ran I heard several more crashes on through the procession of cars. I looked back and I could see a group of drivers standing outside their cars slamming their hats on the hoods of their cars in disgust and pointing toward me. I can still hear that driver:... YOU GET BACK HERE YOU LITTLE SHIT... GET YOUR ASS...

"The weekly *Woodford County Examiner* came out a few days later and this made the lead story on the front page. That's when I learned that the limousine that slid down into the gulley was the one with the casket in it, and how the pallbearers, who were mostly elderly men, had such a time getting it back up to the road and actually slipped and dropped the casket several times. The paper also reported that the sheriff's department was searching for a youngster for questioning."

It took a few minutes before everyone stopped laughing. "I never told a soul until now," said Susan. "Not my parents or friends or anybody."

213

"Well I sure didn't know that we had a fugitive from justice in our midst," said Blazer.

"Wonderful story, Susan," said Yolanda. "If Woodford County High ever had a senior superlative award for the 'Least Likely to Ever Get Into Trouble,' you'd have won it, hands down."

"But now we know your little secret," said Luke.

"How much you pay me to keep quiet?" Lonnie asked.

"It's safe with us — right guys?" Yolanda said.

"I think you need to turn yourself in! Definitely, come clean." It was Victor Devillez, in his starched pressed khakis strutting down the lane to the landing, home on furlough before his first deployment to Vietnam. He lifted Susan from behind.

"Welcome Vic," said Pauline, out of deference to her best friend. Pauline never liked Vic and Vic could always tell. Luke signaled a greeting to his nemesis, just a slight, confident nod. He was always ready to match his experience and savvy to Vic's blind allegiance to his superiors like he

214

did in front of Peacock Hall back in the spring.

"Let's continue, then. Coach? Coach Mac Shoals, got anything for us? Bet there are lots of things you could share with us, things you've held onto through the years?" asked Yolanda.

"Well, I reckon so, although my memory's not what it used to be. I, uh… I don't believe I ever told anybody, but I once stood in line with Fred MacMurray at O'Hare Airport – you know, there in Chicago. You know he's from Kankakee — MacMurray, that is. You know, the father on *My Three Sons*. Coach started right in on the theme song, trying to sound like a clarinet: Prr prr prr prrrrr… Prr prr prr prrrrr…

Yolanda correctly concluded that this was about the best they were going to get from the lovable old Coach, so she didn't press for more.

"Okay, who's next? JaMar? JaMar Brown. What do you say?"

He bowed reverently, stood slowly and stoically, turned to face everyone, and adjusted his sunglasses. His comb was parked in his afro. "I find it safe to assume that none of you are aware of the fact that my brother, my one and only biological brother, is serving time in the state reformatory at Eddyville, Kentucky. His name is Jonas. He was named for a white man, Jonas Salk, who — I assume you are aware — developed the polio vaccine. The polio virus crippled my sister, Leticia. Jonas was an A-minus student at McCracken County High School, president of the sophomore class. He's served three years of a fifteen year sentence for breaking and entering. Eligible for parole in 1969."

Yolanda was taken aback. JaMar had gotten right to the point and had not minced words.

"Uh... okay. Thank you, JaMar," Yolanda said, "for sharing that."

"Did he do it, JaMar?" asked Blazer.

"Let me just say that it's safe to assume that, had a white man been charged with a comparable crime with the same circumstantial evidence, the case most surely would not have gone to trial," JaMar added.

"Shit man," said Lonnie.

"Bummer," said Dorsey.

"God, anything we can do?" Cate and Susan asked.

216

JaMar didn't answer and walked to the back where he remained standing. Yolanda looked around to see if anyone was willing to share next. None were apparent, but she wanted to keep it going. "Jimmie?" Kim? Would you like to be next?" Jimmie pivoted on her log seat to face them and remained seated. Lonnie noticed how she filled out her jeans.

"This is not my kind of thing," Jimmie said.

"It's okay. Good to open up sometimes," Yolanda said assuredly.

Jimmie picked up a handful of dust and thought about whether she would participate, then she tossed down the dust forcefully.

"This will be difficult for me," she said.

"That's the idea. Take your time," Yolanda said.

Jimmie took a deep breath. "My father... my father was... a loser. He brought disgrace to our family. He struggled with financial problems all his life. Banks cut him off. The county impounded his car. Collection agents with pistols on their hip parked in front of our house and waited for him. The pressure --

you could sense it — got to be too much. He hanged himself in the garage."

"Oh my God," said Yolanda.

"You know the simple difference between winners and losers? Winners do things that other people are not willing to do to succeed," Jimmie said. "My father was a quitter. A coward."

"Surely he had some positives…" Susan said.

"At first, he was an inspiration. He started as a tailor. Couldn't speak English. He provided great service, built a strong customer base, added an apparel store, expanded to St. Louis and six locations in the suburbs. But then came the chain stores and a manager who stole from him and the shopping centers and malls with all that parking where you could shop and stroll in a climate-controlled, festive place. His wholesale costs were higher than the retail charges of his competitors. He caved in. He quit. His dream, his belief in the American Way: it took his customers, his business, his self worth."

The fire pit popped and no one moved. No one sipped from their beer or drew from their joint.

"That's not the worst of it. My mother, devastated, would not accept the fact that her husband took his life. She was disgraced. She just could not face up to it. No, to my mother, he died of a heart attack, stress from working so hard. And that's what it said in the obituary. And that's what we told friends and family who came by our house or to the funeral. The undertaker and the coroner let it pass. We lied to... well, everyone — family, friends, bankers, customers — to the point where we even believed it. My mother went to her grave hiding the truth."

Yolanda hugged Jimmie and called for a break. A breeze picked up as if spirits were looming. The guys pissed against tree trunks beyond the light of the fire and the gals used the make-shift potty buffered by blackberry bushes. Cate passed around a pan of *special* brownies. Coach Mac didn't think twice, "Have kind of a bitter taste, but they're plenty good." Susan and Pauline shared a grin.

While the guys relieved themselves and wriggled, they weren't sure what to make of Yolanda's little game.

"Shit's getting deep around here," said Dorsey.

"God, yes," said Lonnie.

"Touchy-feely bullshit," said Luke.

"Oh, you fellas ease up now," said Coach Shoals. "Something about Jimmie's story though."

"Poor soul," said Odell.

"I see where she gets all that drive," Blazer said. "Jimmie wants to finish what her ol' man couldn't."

"She's putting a lot of pressure on herself," said Luke.

"Yeah, man," said Dorsey.

They re-assembled, hugged Jimmie in passing, and Yolanda called on their leader.

"Pauline? You're up. Now don't tell us you won the Little Miss Bobcat contest," Yolanda said.

"Yeah, you got it." Pauline said. She knew she would have a turn.

Susan pulled her up off the log. Pauline, cautiously pregnant, waddled to get in place. "C'mon now."

"Okay, okay. Let me think."

"Let me guess. You're with child."

"Arnie's the dad," Blazer said.

"You guys…" Arnie said.

Pauline paused as if she had a bank of stories from which to draw. She rolled up her left sleeve. "Some of you, I'm sure, some of you noticed this scar here." She pointed to it and tugged on it. It was fleshy and pink and ran the length of her forearm. "Sue, you know about it. Maybe others of you have seen it. Kinda gross."

Several cringed as if it were a fungus, or leprosy.

"I haven't wanted to talk about it, but when I've been pressed for more of an explanation, I've just said it was a burn. And that's true. It was a burn, but I've never told anybody how it happened."

"When... how long ago?" Dorsey asked.

"I was in the eighth, ninth grade, just a teenager. Thirteen, fourteen. Momma, was... well, she was a sick woman. She'd be down. She'd be up. She'd be ... just plum crazy sometimes. She was scared to death that we were all gonna get struck down if we didn't repent and get saved and all. Life was hell for her on earth so she put all her hope in the hereafter."

"Well, the Cody girls – me and my sister Jesse – were expected to recite a complete list of the 66 books of the King James Bible while holding a lit match as a painful reminder of what was in store if we veered off the straight-and-narrow. I usually did pretty well, but I had trouble saying Habakkuk and sometimes I'd skip Haggai. Well, one day I was helping Hump, my ol' man, shellac a wicker rocking chair. I'd spilled some of the shellac on my sleeve when Mama came up on us all of a sudden and had me and Jesse rattle off the books – kind of a pop quiz I guess you could say – but first she gave us a match to light. Well I started off all right, and then I just went blank after Zephaniah. I was determined to hold onto that match, by God; I'd studied and studied and knew those damn books and I knew the names would come back to me. Jesse cried and ran away, but I held on to that fuckin' match. But you know you can't very well stop a natural reaction: when you get burned, you flinch. And when I flinched, I burnt my fingers and shook my hand, but then the match fell inside my sleeve and just like that my whole arm and shirt was on fire. I flipped out and started running instead of rolling in the grass. By the time Hump caught me I was burned pretty bad. Mama saw it as a sign. The doctors at our little county hospital wrapped it up and gave me some salve to use. We couldn't afford all that fancy plastic surgery, so I've just been living with it."

"Geez," said Susan.

"I've never really noticed it all that much." Cate lied.

"Yeah, I've kind a gotten used to it," said Pauline.

Lonnie pulled out his guitar and strummed Simon and Garfunkel's "*A Dangling Conversation*." Cate sang a verse, softly.

The brownies had kicked in.

"Shit, Pauline," Dorsey said. "Sorry you had to go through all that."

"Oh, I don't think about it much anymore. Gotta move on," Pauline said.

Yolanda nodded and looked around for the next participant. "Luke? How about you? Can we ask you to share what might blow through your third window?"

"I'll pass."

Yolanda angled her head and shifted it back and forth like a puppy trying to understand an order from its master.

"I'll pass. Some things are better just to stay with you to the grave," he added.

223

"All right. Maybe later."

"I doubt it."

"You'll always be one of us, Luke."

Vic sighed and Pauline gave him a sneer. Yolanda looked around to see who was left.

"Dorsey. Dorsey Sugg. What say you?"

Dorsey had been thinking about what he might say when his turn was up. "Uh, nobody... nobody probably knows that my ol' man was my mother's second husband. Her first husband – the love of her life, she often reminded me – died young from a disease nobody had heard of, and she remarried as soon as she could find someone to support her. They're still together, but she never really cared much about my dad. Name's Tom. Tom Sugg. He never matched up to Ellis Rideout, mom's first husband. Ellis was a pilot who could do anything apparently. He designed and built their house all by himself. He started a business and developed some patents. He was active in the Chamber of Commerce – you know, one of those pillars of the community. Could do anything. A young man who was going places."

"My dad... well, he's a good fellow but he's pretty ordinary. He works at Sears and mainly watches his favorite TV shows and does chores around the house. The only other thing I've seen the two of them do is play Yatzee with the neighbors down the street. Mom still tells me 'If you were Ellis's son and had his genes and not Tom's, you'd be handsome and popular and smart.' "

It was easier now to get a sense of Dorsey's self-consciousness.

"But didn't your pop go to college? Weren't you looking to be his Sigma Nu legacy?" asked Susan.

"Oh I stretched that a little bit. Mom's first husband was the Sigma Nu, went to Kansas State. My ol' man went to SIU for a year was all."

"Okay then. Thank you, Mr. Dorsey Sugg." Yolanda put another log on the fire. "We sure are bringing out some personal... You guys have really been holding in a lot of stuff for a long time."

Susan brushed back Vic after he whispered something in her ear.

Yolanda continued. "That brings us to good ol' Arnie. We love you Arnie.

You're very special to us. Anything you'd like to share?"

"Oh, I haven't done all the stuff dat you guys have done."

"That's all right. We'd like to hear from you just the same," Yolanda said.

"Well, okay. Fing's about myself dat nobody knows?"

"That's right," said Yolanda.

"Well you may wonder why I always wear my St. Louis Cardinals ball cap."

"Yes, you *do* like that hat," she said.

"Well dats cause I have a receiving hair line."

"You mean a *receding* hair line."

"Uh huh, a receiving hair line."

"That's fine, Arnie. You're a fine looking man with or without that cap. Is that all you have to share with us?"

"Well, da main fing about me dat's kinda weird is dat I always know da time."

"How's that?"

"I always know da time."

"Well, you *are* pretty good about never being late. I've noticed that."

"No."

"So, what, you always carry a watch with you so you know the time?"

"No, I don't have a watch. I don't need a watch. I always know da time."

"So what time is it now?" asked Lonnie skeptically.

"It's one-firty-seven A.M. in the morning," Arnie said confidently.

Luke looks at his watch. "Son-of-a bitch, that's right."

"I got 1:35," said Lonnie.

"Your watch is slow by two minutes," said Arnie.

"He's got a watch stashed in his pocket," Dorsey said.

"No I do not. I promise," Arnie said.

"He looked on somebody else's watch," said Jimmie.

"I didn't look at nobody's watch."

"He heard a DJ or a radio newsman tell the time," said Luke.

"No radios are on that I can hear."

"Somebody here is working with you. Somebody gave you some kind of signal," Cate said.

Arnie laughed. "Don't you see. Dis is why I never tell nobody. Nobody believes me," he explained.

"Hell, that's amazing. I've never heard of anybody who could do that," Dorsey said.

227

"What weird kind of syndrome is that?" asked Yolanda.

You're a fuckin' freak of nature, Arn," said Blazer.

"He ought to go on TV or something," said Jimmie.

"Hell they'll want to study you at some institute or something," Dorsey said.

"Well I've been around and I've never heard of such a thing," said Lonnie.

"I don't want to go to an institute, or on tv." Arnie said.

"You really know the time, all the time?" Yolanda asked again.

"I do. I don't know how, but I do," said Arnie.

"Wow," said Yolanda. "That's amazing. You people... I tell you... Who's next? Who hasn't gone?"

"*You* haven't gone, oh great Kum-Ba-Ya leader. When do we pull out the knives, cut our palms and become blood brothers?" Luke asked as he pulled out a large knife.

"Cute. But I'm leading this discussion, and I say Lonnie is next."

Scattered applause for Lonnie. He lifted his guitar strap on his back, did an Elvis hip move, slung his guitar to his front

228

and jumped into a hard-driving Chuck Berry instrumental lick that he ended abruptly. Lonnie held his hands up as if the cheers were for real. He entered into his pocket and pulled out his wallet, and then he yanked out a card from it that he held high. He passed it on to Yolanda.

"Whatcha got there, Yo?" Pauline asked.

Jimmie stretched her neck to see.

Yolanda looked at it more closely. "Looks like an organ donor card. Well how about that. You surprise me. That's a good thing you're doing, Lonnie. You don't seem like the kind of guy who'd do such a thing, but I'm proud of you. Never knew you were so considerate. This is a little secret you've kept to yourself, huh?" asked Yolanda.

Cate squirmed in her seat and hated when Lonnie showed off.

"Read, uh… read a little closer there," Lonnie suggested to Yolanda.

Yolanda read it more carefully, then threw down the card as if she'd been out-bluffed in poker.

"You're awful, you know that?" She handed the card to Dorsey to share with everybody, but he started chuckling and could hardly finish a phrase.

"Says here that Lonnie is donating the following organs to science for purposes of transplant: kidney, liver, heart, eyes, and…" He chuckled even more. "… and his genitalia! That's right folks, Lonnie's dick will live on attached to another to satisfy and be satisfied," Dorsey said.

Lonnie added with an unconvincing grin: "My only motivation, you understand, is to allow someone who's lost their member in some sort of tragic accident or malignancy to have a proven gadget so they can get back in the game. I've made it clear that I'll not be part of any penile transplants purely for cosmetic reasons."

No one could not chuckle at that one. The group had come to appreciate Lonnie's sarcasm and cleverness, and Cate hid her giggle behind her hands cupped over her mouth. She knew, for all his faults, that Lonnie would always be able to make her laugh. Blazer lit a fresh joint and it lapped around. There wasn't much left of it by the time it made its way back to Blazer.

"Cate, is there anything you would like to share that you've always kept behind your third window?" Yolanda asked.

"Gosh... " She took a sip of Jim Beam and coughed. "I'm afraid mine's not very entertaining or for the faint of heart." Cate said.

"That's okay. If it's important to you, that's what counts," said Yolanda.

Cate looked at Lonnie. "Remember that time when we opened for the Rooftop Singers at that little folk festival in Rolla?"

"Yeah, believe so." He remembered their hit and started singing:
"Walk right in, sit right down
Baby let your hair hang down..."

Lonnie added: "You blew 'em away with *The Lion Sleeps Tonight*. That was our finale. You nailed those high notes. I remember."

"And you bumped into Monkfish, your buddy from Baton Rouge, and you all went out after the show."

"I remember. I think. Sort of. Been a while."

"Well that night while you were gone, I...I, uh..." Cate paused and had a hard time getting it out. "I needed to wind down a bit so I went for a swim there at the Motel 6 in Rolla. They had a small indoor pool. It was late and I was alone. Or I thought I was. After I dried off and as I was about to go back to the room, I was jumped and dragged behind a dumpster by the air conditioners."

Lonnie was instantly sober. "You never told me."

"What was there to tell? There were two of them. They were big. They were strong. They stunk. They held me down. They took turns. They put a gun to my throat and would have used it if I screamed."

"Oh my God," said Lonnie.

Yolanda put her arm around Cate and could see the stunned looks all around. It upset Arnie to see others get emotional.

"Did you go to the police? Did you tell anybody? Did you need to go to the hospital?" asked Dorsey.

"I just wanted to go to my room, lock the door, get in the shower and scrub myself. I wanted to turn myself inside out and dunk myself in antiseptic and scrub myself raw."

"Were they ever found?" Lonnie asked. "Lucky you didn't end up pregnant," he added without convincing sympathy.

"I never reported it. I wasn't about to relive it all by ending up in court and called a whore."

"God. I wish you had told me," Lonnie said.

"Right. You didn't even get in that night. And you didn't even notice my bruises or scratches. You were so caught up in yourself," Cate said.

"JaMar, they weren't black, in case you're wondering." She needed to tell him. JaMar nodded appreciatively.

"But I'll tell you what. I will *never* forget them. They may turn gray or bald or get fat or grow a beard, but I will never forget those mother fuckers. And if I ever see them, I will get my pay back. I don't care what the consequences may be."

Pauline motioned for everyone to huddle close and hug. They were tired and drained from the evening's emotional roller coaster that no one had expected. They could hear a pack of coyotes in the woods encircling what was probably a doe. It reminded them that they were in the wild, that maybe they were more vulnerable in this place than they thought,

233

but that the support and companionship they shared with one another was real and lasting.

Yolanda said, "Well, I can't very well ask you to spill your guts without me doing it, too. I hadn't planned on getting into this, like some of you. And Odell, I knew I would have to break it to you at some point."

"Can't be that bad, my lady," he said.

"I'm sorry." She walked over to him and held his hands as he stayed seated. He thought all of a sudden that someone had died or was moving away. "I'm sorry, Odell, but we're more different than you think. More different than our skin color or cultural traditions. And it's something more difficult to overcome than anything else that might keep us apart. I should have told you sooner but I didn't want to give up on your company. You are such a tender, virtuous person. But Odell honey, I'm just not with you on all this Jesus Saves stuff. I've never told anybody this, but... well, I just don't believe. I'm an atheist. I don't believe in God. I'm sorry, but I just don't."

Odell leaned back on his log and landed in JaMar's lap.

"What? What do you mean you don't believe? You went to revivals with me. You heard me preach and pray and bring people to the Lord at altar calls."

"I'm sorry, hon."

"Don't call me hon. You're making me out to be some kind of fool. I don't know how many ministers of the gospel warned me that I crossed over the line when I started being seen with a black girl. I stood up to them because I, uh...I knew we were right for each other."

"I'm sorry Odell, but I just don't buy it. To me God is a man-made concoction to help us cope with our fears."

As they volleyed theology and biblical interpretation, Vic got up and walked to the birch tree, traced his finger along a message that had been carved in the bark and turned to face the others. "While the reverend and the heathen have at it — I know I'm not in your little club here — but earlier tonight my girl over there told all of you something that she hadn't shared with anybody, so if I'm to bond with her, I need to unload on you folks too, I guess."

235

"That's right. Please...share, Vic." said Susan.

"So... what can I come up with? Let's see, something about myself that nobody else knows."

Luke sighed and slumped down indifferently. Vic didn't have many fans in the group.

"You wouldn't know this, of course, but in a former life, I was Alexander the Great."

"Vic," said Susan. "You really don't have to participate."

"Yes I do. Yes I do." He rubbed his chin to bring back a memory. "How about this: I was in high school, and our scout troop was camping near Buckhorn Lake," Vic said. "Every night we'd hear this racket out by the garbage cans and we'd go outside and the cans would be turned over and shit would be strung out everywhere. One night after everybody else was asleep, I heard it again and it kept me awake and I'd had enough. I rushed outside and there were three raccoons just having a big ol' time in our trash. I took off after them; two escaped into the woods but I had one by the tail. It swung around and scratched me and then

236

it bit me and that really pissed me off. Well I didn't have my knife so I just grabbed that little son of a bitch around its neck and I saw that scared look in its eyes and I choked it with my own fucking bare hands until it let go of its last breath, then I slung it out into the woods. I didn't brag about it. I just kept it to myself. I thought maybe the scoutmaster would hear about it and jump in my shit. But I taught that little fucking raccoon a lesson, huh?"

"Oh yeah," Lonnie said.

"What a hero," said Luke. "You have the guts it takes to kill. A mighty big man, you are."

"Saved everyone from a monster all right," Lonnie said.

"God, what a tough guy. You're sure ready for 'Nam, man," Lonnie said.

"Up yours, ass hole," Vic said.

"Cool it guys," said Yolanda.

Vic's audience was not as robust as it had been for the others throughout the evening. Some were worn out, some were still hoping to get screwed, some were wasted from too much booze and pot, and all were anxious about where all this was taking them.

"What time you got, Arnie?"

"Sebanteen minutes before free o'clock," he reported without hesitation.

Blazer peeked at his watch, "On the money."

It was way past Coach Mac's bedtime. Vic had intruded. Arnie needed to get back by 6:30 to unload chairs for the reviewing section along the parade route. Jimmie left the distribution of her latest *Express Yourself* edition to her assistant, for the first time delegating authority with responsibility.

All of Pauline's inner circle was there or would meet up. No one wanted to leave Teddy's Landing or be away from one another. These were friends, they just knew, that would be lifelong. It felt right to be among them and all that comprised this place, to be anointed with its morning dew.

Friday morning: The ripples of Possum Run River were more agitated than usual, a wake-up call as the morning sun blinked through the hovering trees at the bodies curled atop and around one another. The fire pit sustained a few simmering logs. The sketch of the four windows could still be seen in the dust.

238

Some in the group huddled under blankets and offered warmth to others as they regained their bearings after a long night. Most reeked of alcohol and pot. Like penitents, they scooped up holy water from the river to quench and refresh and renew their spirits. They knew what lay ahead may define them.

They looked at one another differently now; they had seen inside one another where secrets had festered. Yolanda's little game did not bring forth the inner world of them all: Luke held on to whatever was beyond his Third Window; Lonnie announced his kinky, silly organ donation plan; Susan recalled the innocent incident when her snowball disrupted a funeral procession; Coach Mac shared big moment when he saw a TV star in an airport; Faceman Blazer with his Beach Boy good looks revealed that he was once offered $300 to do it with an older woman; and unwelcomed Vic failed to demonstrate his prowess with his story about choking a coon.

However, others opened their hearts: Pauline revealed how her rigid biblical indoctrination led to the unsightly burn scars on her arm; Dorsey couldn't shake how his mother wished he'd been someone else; Arnie confounded everyone with his eerie gift of always knowing the time; preacher man Odell told the story of how the Lord saved him from drowning while the love of his life admitted that she no longer believed; Cate regurgitated the rage that a rape left in her; JaMar exuded bitterness over a system that imprisoned his brother unjustifiably; Jimmie and her mother lived with a lie about the suicide in their family.

Despite the rivalries and annoyances, their connections had been genuine and meaningful. But through the Third Window exercise, their bonds were intrinsic and would not escape their memory. They would do more for one another, stand up for one another without hesitation, and take more chances to promote their principles.

The GSU Homecoming tradition called for the Harvest Day Sing-a-Thon competition to occur before the Friday night pep rally and bonfire. Since 1950, the Kappa Deltas had owned the sing-off. This year's routine would be the 17th in a row for the KD Ladies. They gained their edge through the volunteer services of Gracie Tisdale, a devoted alumnus who prepared an always fresh and creative musical arrangement. Now a middle school music teacher in Memphis, in recent years she had prepared medleys of railroad, Broadway, and river tunes, generally to accompany prissy little dance steps and big finales like *Chattanooga Choo Choo*, *I Got Rhythm*, and *Moon River* in four-part harmony.

Committee Chairman Dean Ewing, student reps Buddy Baxter and Eleanor Eaton, and three faculty members came up with the Homecoming theme, "Let Patriotism Prevail." The idea was for this to counter GSU's growing reputation as a Midwest hub of student unrest and to showcase their wholesome students belting out hits of clean cut acts like the New Christy Minstrels and Bobby Goldsboro. Popular music could be approved if it were something like the Turtles singing *So Happy Together* or Herman's Hermits' *Mrs. Brown You've Got a Lovely Daughter*. The KDs had submitted their playlist: a medley of *Yankee Doodle, You're a Grand Ol' Flag, When Johnny Comes Marching Home,* and *This is My*

241

Country – an arrangement consistent with the theme that, once again, made the KDs the favorite.

The Harvest Day Sing occurred in the Vachel Greathouse Theater, an aging 400-seat facility named for one of GSUs eminent founders. The sing-off always attracted an overflow crowd, but there would be no consideration of moving it to a larger hall: tradition trumped practicality. The judges, eager and conscientious on the front row, awaited this demonstration of what was right with the youth of America.

This year's competition featured four fraternities and six sororities. The frats generally delegated this duty to their pledges. To disguise any semblance of talent, they outwardly did not take the event seriously. Sororities, on the other hand, went all out: some went so far as to establish mandatory rehearsals over a month or more. None had the extra touch of a KD Gracie Tisdale production, however. The five other sororities tried to overcome their lack of talent with skimpy costumes and winks at the judges. They were cute, they had nice butts, but they were no threat to the KDs.

242

Shortly into the KDs opening number, Dylan's *Blowin' in the Wind,* the confused judges fumbled through their playlist. The patriotic numbers the girls turned in apparently had been substituted surreptitiously with songs of protest. They followed with Phil Ochs' *I Ain't a Marchin' Anymore*, during which they shed the red, white and blue outfits with tie-dyed t-shirts, bellbottom jeans and headbands. As they sang, slides of the war and protests were projected on a large screen behind them. To the roar of the crowd, they followed with Pete Seeger's *Where Have All the Flowers Gone*, and the Beatles recent release, *All You Need is Love* that had the entire audience singing along. Dean Ewing entered through the rear door as the KDs took their bows and scattered off in different directions. Before the dean could round up the culprits, the girls were out of sight and ready to celebrate this most memorable Harvest Day sing. They knew in advance that this would be the year they forfeited a cheap plaque to make a statement.

The other Friday activities included the faculty tug of war, receptions for alumni by decade, and recognition of the fraternity and sorority with the house decoration that best reflected the year's theme. The Phi Mu's won the sorority award with their fireworks display that was coordinated with blaring John Philip Sousa marches. The Sigma Chi's took top honors in the fraternity division with their (unloaded) grenade tossing demonstration in the side yard of their tired Tudor house. This was meant as social commentary, but the judges saw it as a tribute to our brave boys in battle.

The bon fire was lit on the quadrangle at sunset, and it roared and cooked the crowd until the nine o'clock pep rally. It wasn't long into the program when it was clear that, this year, traditional cheers and testimonials from football players and coaches would be replaced with the anti-war sentiment that was now a dominant force on campus.

The rent-a-cops that Dean Ewing hired to keep order were more closely aligned with the protestors than the administration suspected. Security looked the other way as they smelled the pot but didn't see it. They didn't really care what kind of beverage was inside the paper bags. They couldn't see any harm that a couple was getting it on behind some shrubery.

What was left of the charred effigies of Johnson and McNamara framed the podium. Pregnant Pauline assumed the emcee role and looked like a mix of an unkempt Janis Joplin and a girthy Mama Cass. Susan read an essay by fellow Kentuckian and Trappist monk Thomas Merton from Gethsemani. Blazer got folks worked up with some Ginsberg. And JaMar read "*We Real Cool*" by Gwendolyn Brooks:

> *The Pool Players*
> *Seven at the Golden Shovel*
> *We real cool. We*
> *Left school. We*
> *Lurk late. We*
> *Strike straight. We*
> *Sing sin. We*
> *Thin gin. We*
> *Jazz June. We*
> *Die soon.*

The crowd roared despite the interruptions of the harsh, squealing p.a. system. The rally could be heard across campus. The beat of the music, into the town. Those that couldn't be there wished they were.

Alumni in town for the homecoming traditions recognized the place, but not whatever else it was that had transformed the GSU party school culture they remembered. There were rumors of a sit-in or a takeover of Peacock Hall or a bombing of the ROTC building, but Renwick's team identified all the threats and barricaded any access.

After her greeting, Pauline handed over the microphone to Dorsey. That simple gesture of confidence locked in his devotion to her and their friends and signaled to those who had derided him that he was capable and confident and cool as anybody. He introduced the special surprise guest of the evening: star of the TV series A Man from U.N.C.L.E. – Napoleon Solo himself, Robert Vaughn. Vaughn was the first major actor to come out publicly against the war. He had become increasingly active in rallies and demonstrations and public appearances. His grasp of the history of conflict in Vietnam lifted his credibility and star power. He was firm, impressive, and convincing. Newspapers, area television, and the wire services covered the event and took part in a news conference

246

following Vaughn's speech. Coverage of protest events trumped the coverage of Homecoming activities included in press packets that Buddy had prepared.

A National Guardsman, learning that Luke was a veteran, delivered a note to him who promptly handed it to Pauline. Her face lit up and she handed the note to Susan who whispered the news to JaMar and Luke. Pauline waited for quiet. President Renwick, his wife Barb, Dean Ewing and Buddy watched nearby.

"I have some great news! Some terrific news! I have a telegram here from a former member of Will Yoder's platoon, Corporal Sal Rinaldo from Queens, New York. Listen up please! I have a message about Will!" Pauline held the note up high. The crowd settled. She started to speak into the microphone but a jolt of feedback yanked her away. She tried again: "I have a note from one of our soldiers in Vietnam. He sends us word that he saw Big Will in a prison camp in the Pu Loung Valley. Will's alive — you hear that everybody — he's alive, but he's a P.O.W." Cheers and mumbles reverberated from the crowd. Pauline fought off tears and spoke slowly with an unsteady voice. "So while we hate to think... we hate to think what he may be going through, it's good to know that Will is alive and there's still a chance to bring him and all the troops home and not in a box...IF WE JUST END THIS GODDAMN WAR! RIGHT? ARE YOU WITH ME! ARE YOU WITH ME!" The crowd erupted in support and the band cranked it up.

GSU President Renwick and his wife, Barb, sat up in bed, exhausted from all the Homecoming activities, anxious over the unrest that was increasingly difficult to control. Barb sipped a cocktail while she read another cover story in Life magazine about the escalation of the war. Harlan finished his cigarette and felt the need -- for the first time in a long time -- to confide in her, to draw on her judgment, to allow him in to enter her intuitions.

"They're good kids, honey."

"I know, I know," Harlan said. "But they're taking all this too far. We've got a reputation... "

"...as a party school. You know that," she said.

"Well this is a fine way to reverse that image," he said.

"I think it's the disgruntled veterans that are causing the problems," she said.

"Maybe, he said. "But that Cody girl seems to be the instigator. She's a pal of that Kentucky girl, daughter of the horse breeder. He's been on my list of donor prospects. I know that he's extremely upset with his daughter's involvement in all these protests. It's not my style to be adversarial, but maybe that's the only thing that will get the attention of our leaders. You know, if I were their age, facing the draft and friends killed or reported missing, I'm not so sure that I wouldn't be out there protesting with them."

It was hardly daybreak, and President Renwick was already pacing about in his office, on his third cup of coffee. Dean Ewing and Buddy Baxter were on duty, responsive to his unpredictable directives. Renwick had had enough; yesterday had been another long and disruptive day. He was tired and aggravated. He was sure he could document enough threats to the social order, illegal substances, and behaviors beyond community standards of decency to at least have the leaders distracted through Homecoming weekend.

"You know Barb told me that it could backfire." Ewing nodded his support. He would have agreed no matter what the president said.

"I've gone out of my way to be patient with these people. We've given them every opportunity to do their thing without condescension, disruption or censorship. Buddy, you know where they are, I presume. Down by the river?"

"I'll check sir."

"Where else could they be?"

"I'll ask around."

"I have some leverage with the one who runs the Greek shop," Dean Ewing said.

"Take a few Guardsmen with you and put an end to this."

Barb Renwick drove by Blazer's shop but the lights were off and Dean Ewing's car was parked in back by the loading dock. She hoped to catch Blazer before Ewing arrived. She parked out of Ewing's range but close enough to be within eyeshot of the store.

"You know I'm no rat," Blazer said.

"I've been good to you and you know it."

"Don't act like you haven't benefited from our little enterprise – *sir*."

"Just tell me where they are, or at least the Cody girl. The group will fall apart without her."

"I uh… wouldn't underestimate us, uh…them."

"Let me remind you: you know I can get you out of the draft and into law school. Your dream of a life in politics won't matter much if you leave your guts in some rice paddy."

"So I'm set if I just tell you where you can find Pauline Cody?"

"You got it. No serious charges. We just want an orderly, uplifting Homecoming Day – wholesome stuff: a parade, ball game, a few parties, the Box Tops concert, you know."

"And if I refuse?"

"We'll go after all of you. And you'll be indicted for possession, cultivating, selling…"

"I can implicate you," Blazer said.

Ewing chuckled. "I've made friends for 20 years here at the college and this little town that surrounds it — plenty of friends who owe me a favor or two."

Barb Renwick hated to think what was going on in the back room of the store. She pulled her car up to the front door, got out and knocked on the window until Blazer came out without turning on the lights. Dean Ewing stood behind him.

"What's going on, guys." Barb asked.

"Just some last minute purchases for Homecoming," Ewing said. "And as directed, we'll have the Guard on standby."

Barb was tacitly disappointed.

"Just following orders, Mrs. Renwick," the dean said. "Your husband is just looking out for this institution."

"The peace group has a right to assemble and speak out, she said."

"Of course. But they don't have a right to disrupt," Ewing said. "They're down by the river, aren't they? Roosevelt's Landing, they call it -- where they all go tubing and do who knows what. I bet that's where they are."

"No, apparently they found a better place a few miles south of town. The rapids are better there," Blazer said.

Blazer proceeded to write down directions for the dean to this newly discovered camp 10-12 miles from campus and Teddy's Landing. He took a guardsman with him.

Dean Ewing was to take State Road 52 south toward the state line, look for a deer crossing sign and a salvage yard, turn right on a dirt road toward the river, then veer off where there's a house in which the basement was all that had been built. Sometimes there's a wire across the road with a "No Trespassing" sign suspended from it. Blazer said that, a few years ago, a boy on a three-wheeler was killed when he didn't see the wire across the road and it caught him in the throat at the Adams apple. He choked on his own blood.

Ewing followed the road another half-mile past an abandoned truck to a dead end. No river. No sign of a fire pit or inner tubes. No sign of STAND or Pauline Cody. Dean Ewing realized he had been duped.

"That son of a bitch," Dean said. "The hell with them."

Dean drove over the "No Trespassing" sign and back to campus. He had to hustle to make it to a donor's reception, anxious to make a good impression.

Pauline and her entourage had crashed at JaMar Brown's place: they shared two mattresses, a couch, the filthy floor and tile steps, two sleeping bags and anywhere else they could curl up. It was typically a chore for Pauline to wake up this bunch, but last night insomnia pestered them all like excited children on Christmas Eve.

The political statements inserted during yesterday's Harvest Day Sing and later at the pep rally were to be capped off during Saturday activities of Homecoming weekend. STAND assembled at Vest Plaza, hidden below a knoll within eyeshot of the parade route – an ideal staging spot. They were there early enough in the chilly morning that their conversations produced foggy puffs that rose above the knoll like Native American smoke signals.

The first units of the Homecoming parade were pom-pom girls who carried a wide banner displaying the grasshopper logo and this year's theme, "Let Patriotism Prevail." Baton twirlers pranced alongside the banner, followed by Hoppy, the Grasshopper mascot, Uncle Sam on stilts, Shriner clowns driving go-carts and unicycles in figure eight patterns, an honor guard and the GSU marching band. This year's grand marshal followed, and fitting to the theme, it was Phyllis Schlafly, conservative leader and fiery supporter of Barry Goldwater in the 1964 presidential campaign. She sat atop the back seat of a long Oldsmobile convertible between President and Mrs. Renwick. A scratchy amplified "*My Country 'Tis of Thee*" by Pat Boone accompanied their waving.

President Renwick soaked in the festivities: the cadence of the marching band, the crowd three-and-four deep cheering and waving small American flags that had been distributed by the American Legion at the request of Dean Ewing, the clear undisturbed sky, the autumn day's invigorating crispness that could make one lightheaded. The administration's concerns about unruly radicals seizing the moment slipped from worry since Renwick gave the order to the National Guard to apprehend the kingpin Cody girl and her inner circle. Now Renwick knew it would be a great day.

The units ahead of the parade marshal broke off from view on the downhill curve along Bluff Circle Drive. The marching band sounded puny when the horns and drums were out of sight and pointed in the opposite direction. The convertible abruptly stopped. Delays were to be expected along parade routes, particularly when large floats maneuvered around tight curves. But as the delay prolonged and they sat awkwardly atop the convertible, the Renwick's and their celebrity guest ran out of people to wave to along the parade route. When the crowd shifted toward some sort of commotion ahead, President Renwick pivoted out of the back seat and marched with increasing furor around the downhill curve in the road and through the band to see that the pom-pom girls had come upon something they were reluctant to traverse. Scattered bodies -- STAND supporters -- wearing military fatigues were strung about the street, still, as if they were victims in a battle. There were dozens of bodies, twisted in different configurations and piles, intensified with moaning and artificial blood to depict the dead and wounded of the war. Other students and sympathizers along the route held up banners updating the body count to date — - 19,288 — and other banners and chants demanding leaders bring our troops — and Will — back home.

Renwick barked out orders for the parade units to continue. "KEEP GOING! RUN OVER THEM IF YOU HAVE TO! THEY'LL GET OUT OF THE WAY! THEY'RE ALL GONNA BE ARRESTED! THEY'LL ALL BE EXPELLED, GODDAMMIT!" He grabbed the drum major's whistle and blew it frantically. He waved in security personnel but it was difficult for them to weave through the crowd and the chaos to get to the protestors. The faux dead seemed immovable like rocky outcrops in a battlefield. Marching band members crumbled out of formation and bumped into one another. Melodies collapsed like the dissonance of a middle school band without sheet music. Those playing trumpets fell out of place with the trombones and tubas and piccolos. Band members couldn't play to avoid stepping on or tripping over their fellow students and friends. The National Guard marched in, but at this point stood by as to intimidate. The bodies filled the road and

257

did not budge, and the narrow, blocked street made it difficult for a paddy wagon to park closely enough for security to drag dead weight protestors into the vehicle.

The local police and security guards under contract pulled out billy clubs and started confronting the demonstrators. The Guard interpreted that as a signal for them to take charge. Members of the marching band regrouped along the sidelines, watching it all unfold, terrified by the one-sided enforcement that awaited the passive, unarmed students.

A smoke bomb went off, igniting chaos. The smacks and yelps carried up the hill where Mrs. Renwick and Mrs. Schlafly remained in the convertible, still smiling and waving, but suspecting trouble. They wanted nothing of this confrontation. From the student union building, Buddy Baxter could see the commotion; he could feel a rumble beneath his feet. His trot down the hill toward the scene turned into a sprint as he feared what he might discover.

The weaponless demonstrators curled into balls or crawled away. Neither option enabled them to escape the security personnel and National Guard. It was increasingly chaotic and frightening. A series of pops went off nearby. It wasn't clear if that meant bullets, firecrackers or other noisemakers. One group threw rocks at the Guardsmen who were ready to respond with attack dogs and high pressure fire hoses.

Pauline and her disciples sat in a circle, legs crossed and heads down. Yolanda lifted her legs, fearing a German Shepherd was about to clamp down on her ankle. Odell mumbled prayers. Immobilized by tear gas, he fought through the choking and burning eyes and tackled the dog that promptly turned on him and away from Yolanda. Arnie cried out because he didn't understand why these people did not want to help bring Will Yoder home. Coach Mac pulled the injured off the road, wrapped wounds and applied pressure to stop a stranger's bleeding. Lonnie's guitar was pelted and its strings exploded in disarray. He buckled over after he was kneed in the groin. Cate was slapped and her camouflaged shirt was ripped off her neck – retrieving memories of the rape she could never escape. JaMar was knocked down by an intense shock from a large electrical prong which trailed him as he scooted away from the sting and the gibes: "Take that, boy!" a deputy said. "How ya like that, boy?" Jimmie, disoriented, and unlike herself, was not able to take charge. Susan hid behind a tree out of site and Pauline ordered her to stay there.

Buddy Baxter stood on a bench along the parade route, horrified at what was happening. Nothing like this was to happen. Nothing like this. He saw President Renwick push his way through the chaos, ordering commands that could not be heard. Buddy started to follow him but then hesitated, stopped, and stepped backwards away from all that was going on, not knowing who the enemy was.

Enraged by the audacity of these hoodlums, Renwick yanked a billy club off a policeman's belt and commenced flailing it as television crews from Carbondale and Rollo captured it on film. He swung wildly at Pauline and missed her chin so closely that she could feel the wind and hear the swat of the club. He continued flailing, chopping, not knowing who or what he struck. It was all one-sided. Blows to necks and shoulders. Teeth bloodied. Eyes that would soon be swollen shut. Cries out that the beaten couldn't hold in.

Pauline leaned back to dodge a mighty swing, but in so doing, the billy club landed squarely across Blazer's face, collapsing it. He fell face down, out cold instantly, blood oozing out of his ears and nose. His Beach Boy blonde hair, mixed with splattered bright blood from the blows, produced an orange tonic in his hair that already caked where there would be cracks in his temple and cheekbones. Pauline dropped to her knees to assist him when they were trampled. Somebody's boot kicked her in the ribs, then the pelvis, then the back, then the abdomen. She turned and looked up to see Renwick, face and eyes red with rage. She wouldn't yield to the pain as she wrapped her arms over her womb to shield the blunt force trauma that could have already started hemorrhaging within her. No one could hear her cry out, "No, please, don't... don't hurt my... It's... it's... Will's baby! She was kicked again. Renwick was in the face of any demonstrator he could find. "I want you people OUT OF HERE!" he screamed. "OUT OF HERE!"

261

The protestors, including some who needed medical attention, were pushed into paddy wagons. The seriously injured somehow by somebody were lifted into ambulances and station wagons and were on their way to Our Lady of Something-or-Another Hospital in Mount Vernon. Hundreds of others ran away, dozens were strung about, too hurt to move. Someone saw Arnie on the bottom of a pile, trampled, smothered. Luke turned him over, his face caked with dust, his mouth open. Luke breathed into him and pounded his fist to Arnie's chest, crying and screaming at him to "goddamnit c'mon now and BREATHE!" But Arnie did not respond. Vic just then arrived and pushed his way through the crowd, summoning Susan who was nowhere to be found.

President Renwick canceled the football game, Box Tops concert and remaining Homecoming activities. The injured waited their turn to receive care. Those who were empathetic gathered up signs and banners that had not been torn apart. Students who were not involved stayed around the site, wondering what they could or should do. Trash was picked up and the parade route was hosed down. A somber tone hovered over the site. Phyllis Schlafly took the opportunity to castigate the protesters for the media.

Not until late afternoon did President Renwick share a statement. Dean Ewing helped him craft it. The event, as tragic as it was, was not a national event that attracted national coverage. However, local, regional and state media brought attention to it, just not the type of attention they ever expected or hoped would come out of Grant State.

President Renwick spoke atop the hill on the steps of Peacock Hall:

"The *riot* was instigated by outside agitators and a handful of misguided students, violent radicals, and peace and love freaks who tried to use our time-honored traditions here at Grant State to spread their propaganda. We also have evidence that reveals a plot to take over the administration building and, fortunately, our security officers were able to disarm a bomb that had been planted near the ROTC building. As you know, we have a zero tolerance policy with regard to any disruptive demonstrations on or

affecting this center of learning." Dean
Ewing whispered in the president's ear
and then Renwick continued. "And we...
certainly all of us are devastated to learn of
the loss of one of our longtime beloved
employees, Arnie Latham, who apparently
was caught in the cross fire and was
trampled by the mob. Arnie was a fixture
on the GSU campus for many years, a
simple man, a groundskeeper, a faithful
volunteer at Grasshopper basketball
games. What a tragedy. We express our
condolences to his family."

"Arnie had no family," clarified
Barb, the president's wife." We, this
university, was his family."

More journalists reported the
incident, with images of students being
pushed back, of clubs raised and dogs
sent through the crowds with enough leash
to reach the limbs of assigned targets, but
news reports failed to make reference to
President Renwick's role nor did any
footage include him slinging a billy club.
The administration's damage control
worked; their influence paid off; Renwick
and Ewing skirted the truth.

In the interim without Pauline, there
was no one to serve as spokesperson for

STAND, no clear successor, merely chaos without a defined purpose and no back-up plan. Once stitched up and treated for dog bites, Odell and Yolanda were released from the hospital. Blazer would be there indefinitely, in and out of consciousness with fleeting memories of what happened. A group drove up to the Mt. Vernon hospital to visit and talk about Arnie and worry together about Pauline and Blazer. No one would look at Blazer the same way again. Even nurses cringed when they peeled back the bandages to check on him. An eye was gone and the Faceman could no longer be recognized. His jaw and temple were caved in. Bandages encircled his head and piles of bruises would remain purple and green for weeks. His wounds were too sensitive to touch or clean. He faced multiple surgeries and a face with a permanent look of a palsy. His political future was over, his friends assessed.

Susan never thought it necessary to let Vic know she was okay. She was at Pauline's bedside in the hospital, and others were in and out as allowed. It was a double room with crucifixes above each bed and wallpaper of leaping sheep and a noisy fan in the window that only seemed to suck in hot air out. The other bed was occupied by a woman in labor with her third child. A middle-aged doctor, somber with a gentle countenance, someone Pauline did not remember meeting, arrived and pulled the curtain. Pauline, disoriented, pulled herself up in the bed, assuming he was there for a reason.

"Miss Cody, I'm Doctor Farrell, again. How are you feeling?" Pauline blew up her bangs. She wondered if this was another one of her dreams.

"I've been taking care of you. You took some hard blows that were not good for you – or your baby."

"What do you mean?"

"I'm afraid there was a good bit of internal bleeding and there may have been some cranial damage. We had to proceed with the delivery. We weren't sure we could save your baby." Pauline's pulse raced and Susan squeezed her clammy hands. "You lost a lot of blood."

"He's a little fighter."

"What? What do you mean? He?"

"Yes, Miss Cody. I'd like to introduce you to your baby boy."

266

The nurse was already attached to the baby and his curly red hair that peeked out from a bandage that wrapped a wound. She peeled back the blanket to expose its face, round as a saucer. She awarded the child to her mother.

"Oh, oh..." Pauline melted and could immediately pick out Will's features. Tears trickled off her cheeks. In an instance, her world had changed. Her priorities had changed. "Oh... he's beautiful. He's so beautiful. A miracle." Pauline wiggled her pinky finger into the baby's palm and the baby squeezed it. "Would you look at those hands," she said while sniffling. "Will has big hands. He could palm a basketball when he was 12 years old. We might have us a ballplayer here, you think Sue?"

"I think you're right," Susan said. "You're surely right."

Susan spent the night in Pauline's room. Embraced by the sheer joy of her baby's birth, Pauline was oblivious to the injuries she sustained during the parade. The next morning, she wanted the full briefing. She learned of Arnie's death, and was devastated and immediately filled with guilt. She was not open to other explanations. She knew that Arnie would have been far removed from danger had she not drawn him into the cause. "Poor ol' Arnie. He was so confused when things got out of control. He was there to help Will is all," Susan said.

Pauline asked about the others, wondering who was hurt and what other tragedies may have occurred because of her big idea to make a political statement.

Susan told her about Blazer, her good-looking pal, who may be disfigured.

"And Yolanda and Odell, they both had some nasty dog bites, but they'll be okay."

"Good God," she said. "JaMar?"

"I saw what they did to him," Susan said. "It was terrible. They shocked him. They mocked him."

"Where is he now?"

"Not sure."

"Coach Mac has already resigned over all this. No telling how many students he bandaged up."

"I thought I saw Renwick," Pauline said.

"Oh yeah, he was in the middle of it," Susan said.

"Lonnie, Cate all right?" Pauline asked.

"Banged up pretty good," Susan said. "Cate's reliving the rape."

"My God."

"Lonnie got kicked... you know, down there — hard. May not be the same ladies man..."

"That's the least of my concerns."

As far as I know, Luke's okay."

"And Jimmie, Jimmie Kim?"

"Jimmie could only take so much. She jumped on the back of a guardsman and yanked off his helmet, but then they turned the high pressure hose on her."

"Shit."

Pauline questioned her relevance. She wondered if it was time to admit that she and her friends had not helped the cause of peace. Just who were they kidding?

"And Dorsey? How's Dorsey?"

"Don't know." No one could recall seeing him.

Susan saw Vic outside Pauline's room.

"Need to talk to you," he said.

She stepped outside the room into the hallway. "I need to be with Pauline," Susan said. "That's where I need to be."

"Sorry about your friends. But you need to go with me to apologize to the President. He knows you weren't behind this."

"What do you mean, I wasn't behind this. We were all part of it. We had no weapons. It was the Guard and the security people who lost their cool and turned it into a brawl. It wasn't us."

"Well that's not the way the reports are coming in."

"Don't let this screw up your future, Susan. Come with me now and let's straighten this out. You know I'm leaving for the base on Tuesday."

Susan shut the door and went back into Pauline's room.

Pauline asked Susan about Dorsey. She remembered that he made a run to the grocery before the parade started to get more bandage wraps and tomato sauce for those who were to play the part of the dead or wounded in the war.

Susan said, "Remember our pals from Sigma Nu who put Dorsey through the banana-in-the-commode-game trick?

270

...when he escaped out of the living room window in his tighty-whitey underpants?... Well, the morning of the parade, three of those ass holes saw Dorsey leaving the store... and they ended up taking him out in the middle of nowhere and dumped him on some unmarked county road. He had to find his way back to campus. By the time he got back, he missed the worst of it.

"Such jerks," Pauline said.

Susan stayed at Yolanda's off-campus apartment, upstairs in the tutor home owned by Ellen Berman, GSU's librarian, away from the news people and protestors who were more fired up than ever. Local police were already referring to Arnie's death as accidental, spurred on by the protestors, but some tough talkers who took part in the demonstration wanted someone to be held accountable for Arnie's death and the injuries to dozens of students, particularly Dave Blazer who may have to live with a battered, monstrous face. Pauline didn't feel like a leader; she wanted nothing but time away from it for now, a chance to recover from the trauma and what went wrong. She needed time to bond with her child. She

271

whispered and hummed songs to Little Will. She told him all about his daddy's legacy, his goodness, and things he could look forward to when his daddy returns. Pauline turned even more to prayer, pleading for Will's release and safety. Without him, she felt ill-prepared to take on the parenting tasks ahead.

At Shoals Fieldhouse, a memorial service for Arnie attracted a pile of flowers, photos, an autographed basketball, his St. Louis Cardinal cap and other items to memorialize this lovable figure on campus. Arnie had no enemies, no family, no minister, no pals from the lodge. His life was simple and surprising: he loved GSU basketball and Will Yoder; he loved to fish; he loved Pauline and anyone trying to bring Will home; he loved to beautify and nurture the grounds around campus. But he did not love — and, in fact, resisted — revealing his bizarre capacity to know the time, anytime.

Coach Mac rounded up his players to share stories about Arnie. "At every timeout, Arnie would pat our players on the back and mop up the greasy sweat when they fell on the court. What was there not to love about this lovable man,"

272

said the coach with a patchy voice. "Arnie found a good life here on this bluff, at this campus, in this community. He deserved better than to leave us when he did, how he did."

All the GSU basketball team shared touching and funny anecdotes about Arnie, but no one — the speakers or the audience — was in a mood for levity. They were angry, fed up. Good ol' Arnie should not be dead.

Ms. Berman insisted on watching the baby so Pauline could attend Arnie's funeral in the gymnasium. There were a few seats available on the floor, but she and Susan sat alone in the second level that offered only wooden bleachers painted years ago. Pauline was there but just barely; she carried too much of a sense that she was responsible for all that happened. A few morose hymns on tape and slow organ favorites were followed by Cate and Lonnie's rendition of Janis Ian's *Society's Child* and the verse that stayed with those who knew Arnie:

> *When she wouldn't let you inside*
> *When she turned and said*
> *But honey, he's not our kind*

She said I can't see you anymore, baby

Can't see you anymore.

STAND's inner circle was together under one of the backboards — Arnie's vantage point during home games — when Luke noticed that Pauline and Susan sat above them alone on the upper level. Luke led the others up from their seats so they would all be together — deeper back in that section where it was dark, like disciples hiding after the crucifixion, frightened and needing comfort and inspiration and hope.

Barb Renwick was there, exuding a scornful demeanor, as if she wanted nothing to do with the two evil men she sat between: her husband and Dean Ewing. She strained to see who was in the group in the bleachers above her, and noticed that Dave Blazer was not among them. She heard that he was injured and that it might take awhile for him to bounce back. She didn't know that his face would have to be reconstructed and that he would frighten children. She recalled their occasional flirtations and fought off the urge to fantasize. Tributes to Arnie were interrupted by harsh feedback from a sound system that no one seemed to be able to operate. President Renwick checked his watch; his wife noticed and sighed.

Dorsey was inclined to explain his absence to Pauline but he didn't want to admit that he'd once again been a victim of hazing from frat boys. He may have been outnumbered three-to-one, but he didn't want to admit that, once again, he'd been teased and taunted. Next time they confronted him or tried to intimidate or rattle him, he would be ready. He was occupied by thoughts of revenge and various scenarios of how he would find satisfaction.

It was only natural that they convene and debrief at Teddy's Landing. Possum Run River was unusually high and smooth, high enough over the pointed rocks to be deceiving and dangerous. Crippled autumn leaves clasped on to branches that hovered above the river. When they snapped and floated down and landed on the moving water, they would ride the current like a parade of tiny gondolas. The fire felt good in the dampness; the aroma

275

had a luring essence. Before long Renwick would have the landing closed off. But he had no authority. It would be abandoned, leaving behind living and non-living relics to decay over decades. The landing would still be governed by the ancient birch with its mighty trunk of mossy-green patches, circles of bark that spread like age spots. Messages in the bark could not leave; they stayed back to age with the tree.

Scattered about were fat configured logs, rubber inner tubes tied to shrubs, dented beer cans, and the four windows with Roman numerals in them that Yolanda sketched in the dirt to extract secret stories from most everyone.

Teddy's Landing was the place where they had shared their theories and frustrations and unsettled moments, where they had feuded and made music and grew closer by sharing and disclosing. Most had injuries from the Homecoming bludgeoning, but given Arnie's fate and what Blazer the Faceman would be facing, there was no complaining as they hobbled down the dirt path to visit their sacred place.

There was, though, a good bit of second guessing:

"Well what the hell do we do now?"

"I've been expelled, now I'm looking at the draft, man!"

"No shit."

"You and me both."

"You knew the consequences."

"Should've thought of that first."

"No matter, you'll always be proud of being on the right side on this one."

"Yeah, good fucking consolation."

"What happened, anyway? This was gonna be a nonviolent protest?"

"What do we do now, great leader?"

"Yeah. What do we do now?"

"Stop everybody. STOP! Let's think things through," Pauline said. Their bruised leader still ached all over; her side throbbed with pain. But the pain did not consume her; she had other priorities: She sat on a log and made her breast available to Little Will, warm within a bundle of blankets.

Many had already lost faith. They feared their futures were ruined, that their connection to this protest that had gone awry would be a permanent stain on their record. They were sure that no other schools would admit them, no one would

277

hire them, no one would be sent funds from home. Before Pauline could advance a revised game plan, they started to gather things and split. Pauline stepped up.

"Hold on! Hold on now goddamnit!" she grimaced. "Nobody's going anywhere. Let's… let's talk about this, lay out some options."

Her faithful hung on, and the sounds of the woods and the water grew tamer, as if a beaver dam barricaded Possum Run River and muffled the rumble of the currents. No one offered comfort. No one ordered encouragement. No one wanted to talk about issues or policies. No one shared funny stories. No one could take away much from the four windows that Yolanda had scribbled in the dirt. They knew it was inevitable that they would go their separate ways.

"You'll not abandon the cause," Jimmie Kim pointed her remark to Pauline. "None of us will — right?" Jimmie asked. No one responded.

"This war's a long way from being over. Remember the veterans group that marched in front of Peacock Hall — where we first met Luke, you know, when the asshole Pikes passed the football to snub

278

the marchers — well they're going to Birmingham for a rally in a couple of weeks and then there's one down at Florida State. They've asked us to go along," Susan said.

"See? We can keep this alive," Jimmie said. "Luke, you'll be going."

Luke never said much so he was hard to gauge. "Hand me those two-by-fours stacked by the shed there, will you Cate?" He yanked out a few nails. "Might as well find some use for this lumber."

"So you going back to Alabama?" Jimmie asked.

"Think I'll start setting up my shop soon. Have a building lined up over in Carbondale that might work, at least to get me started. Cabinets, trim work. Might even see if I can make a few baseball bats with that good ash I came upon," Luke said.

Luke had been the only member of the group that did not participate in the Third Window exercise. He held on to his feelings and was self-conscious about the post-traumatic stress symptoms that he concealed: the flashbacks, sleeplessness, emotional numbness, feelings of guilt from what he did in the war and what others did that he didn't reveal.

Susan picked up a board and tossed it in his pile. She noticed Luke, strong and hard with raised scars like cattle that had been branded. Their eyes met and they both wished something had come of knowing one another earlier. But there were distractions with her protective boyfriend Vic and those he arranged to watch over Susan while he was away. Luke knew he would not be comfortable with a society girl like Susan so he never pursued her. Now that they would be moving on, he wished he'd done more to hint of his yearning.

"So you're going?" Jimmie asked Pauline again.

"I've been thinking that maybe I should go visit Will's parents in Indiana."

"That'd be real nice," Susan said. "They're Mennonites, you know."

Pauline nodded.

"Don't expect to be welcomed into the family," Yolanda said.

"But they have a right to know, don't you think?" Jimmie asked. "I'm glad you're going."

The grounds were soggy but JaMar managed to light a fire and Odell helped him arrange some logs in a semi-circle. Luke lit a joint and passed it around.

"Whatcha gonna do, Dorsey?" Susan asked.

He shrugged.

"This has been a good thing for you, hasn't it? A good experience? You were my first recruit," Pauline said.

He nodded. "Can't believe that Arnie's gone and that Blazer is hurt like he is, and that you're there with Will's baby... You know, it wasn't supposed to end this way. Just can't believe it's coming to an end. College was never much for me until we took up the cause," Dorsey said.

"You still have your job at Long John's," Odell said.

"Yeah."

"Well that's something," Odell said. "Pray and the Lord will open up doors – for all of us."

"Are you all sure we can't just keep things going? You guys are... you're my only friends. We can't quit. We can't just quit. You know we still get signals now and then about somebody seeing a soldier that fits Will's description — you know, being tall and all — in some village or camp, helping the wounded," Dorsey said. "Let's find a way to go over there and find him, bring him home."

"That'd be cool," said Lonnie.

"State Department won't approve it. You know that. We've tried," Susan said.

"Not like we can rent a private jet," Lonnie said.

"Well I'll never give up," said Dorsey.

Pauline teared up.

"No and we won't either, Dorse. We won't either," she said.

"Promise?"

"Promise."

Coach Mac Shoals resigned before President Renwick had the privilege of firing him for participating in STAND's illicit activities. Renwick had always resented how the coach was revered on campus and in the media, whereas he struggled with one public relations faux pas after another. The coach took Arnie's death hard. He would miss — and never get over — his loyal pal. "I think I'll just get me a little trailer and park it on Oswego Lake in northern Indiana. All I need is my lawn chair and my lucky basketball net.

Once in a while maybe I'll take in a pick-up game there in Chesney Buck Park in Minnow where I first saw Will play."

"I think I'll just go home for awhile, work out some things with my folks," Susan said. "They just bought a new stallion, could probably use some help on the farm. And Vic said he would write every chance he gets."

"Cate and I have a few gigs lined up around Chicago, said Lonnie. Then we'll scoot on up to a folk festival in Milwaukee. We may need a new look, new style. After Milwaukee, we'll think about what we're gonna do. Gotta stay ahead of the draft board, so I'll just be a short hop to Canada from there, you know, if that option makes the most sense."

"I appreciate you filling me in," Cate said sarcastically.

"You know I always take care of you, doll baby," Lonnie said.

"I don't need to go to Canada. What if I don't want to go to Canada?"

"You can't live without me, and you know it — for better, for worse, right?"

"Take up for yourself," Jimmie said to Cate. "Once a skirt chaser, always a skirt chaser." Jimmie was increasingly turned off by Lonnie and couldn't believe she'd had a fling with him. "I've had it with men."

Jimmie skimmed a few rocks across the river. "You know, being rich by 30 is not as much a priority for me as it once was."

"Really?" Susan asked.

"But you have so many great ideas," Cate said.

"I think you're onto something with that Olympic board game," Dorsey said. "You're just ahead of your time, Jimmie. That's all."

"How about *you*, Brother Odell?

He avoided looking at Yolanda. "I, uh... I may not be ready, but maybe there's a little country church someplace where I can get a start pastoring."

"You'll be a big hit," Yolanda said.

"You could bring your sinners right down here. This little river is just right for baptizing," Luke said.

"I've decided to turn over this decision to the Lord. I'll just put my future in his hands."

"Well remember us when you come into your kingdom, will you there Rev?" Lonnie said.

Yolanda took a stick and retraced the Roman numerals inside the boxes in the dirt in front of the beech tree.

"So how about you — oh wise one who draws in the dirt?" JaMar asked Yolanda.

"I like teaching, but I'm not sure how I'm going to finish school now. I like leading discussion groups, maybe I can do some of that kind of work."

"That touchy-feely shit? Luke asked.

"Maybe. I don't know. Just an option. Motivational speaking, life planning, time management... I'm sure it's hard to break into a field like that."

Yolanda clapped her hands and ordered: "Speaking of touchy-feely shit, everybody come here. Gather round. Everybody. Come closer, now."

"Group hug. One last time," Pauline said.

They squeezed together. "You know, Reverend," Lonnie teased Odell. "Having sex standing up can lead to dancing."

"We've been together for just a few months, but I believe these memories will last a lifetime," said Pauline.

"They'll stay with me," Susan said.

"Maybe," Luke said. "Tragedies stay with you."

"So do good times," said Dorsey.

"You've all shared in the birth of our son," Pauline said.

"We've shared intimate things about ourselves," Yolanda said.

"What, you act like we're never going to see one another again," Dorsey said.

"What do you expect? We form a commune?" JaMar said.

"Who you kidding? In a few years, we'll not even remember names when we bump into one another in an airport," Lonnie said.

"Will too," Cate said.

"You're the best friends I've ever had." Dorsey said.

"Closest, for sure," Susan said.

"Well we can make it a point to stay in touch, to keep up with one another," Pauline said. "I love you, each and every one of you."

"We were part of a noble cause," Susan said. "Blazer will bounce back. And Pauline's baby – won't it be a wonderful surprise for Will when he comes home. Won't he be some kind of dad?"

There was a pause. A moment of silence that did not need to be requested.

Pauline hugged Susan. Some cried. Others wanted to.

Lonnie strummed softly before starting to sing. The others joined in:

> *How many times must a man look up*
> *Before he can see the sky?*
> *How many tears must he have shed*
> *Before he can hear the people cry*
> *How many wars will take till he learns*
> *that too many people have died*
> *the answer my friend is blowin' in the*

wind

> *the answer is blowin' in the wind*

The night before Dave Blazer's first surgery, Pauline and most of her followers bargained their way into his hospital room to express their love and encouragement. Blazer uttered responses that sounded like an unskilled ventriloquist.

"You hang in there now," said Pauline.

Blazer tried to respond, but couldn't. His mouth would not move.

"I'm praying for you," Odell said.

"Just a bump in the road. You'll bounce back. I believe in you," Lonnie said.

"I'll place my bets on you," Susan said.

Privately, based on his current condition, Blazer's friends were not optimistic.

Yolanda added: "We'll save you a spot down along the river. Renwick can't keep us out."

JaMar had not come up for air since retreating to his place that doubled as a studio. His art, his talent, was defining him and enabling him to express his views and experiences. He was immersed in his work, and while the event at GSU were still fresh in his mind, he was inspired to capture the terror and angst on the faces of those beaten during the demonstration. They were all large charcoals, some as large as a wall, each highlighting weapons used against the students: billy clubs, high-pressure hoses, electrical prongs, attack dogs, and boots kicking and stomping on bodies under piles.

"Powerful work, Patty," Pauline said. "Good God. These are frightening. You're really capturing the horror of that day."

"My way to tell the story."

Pauline looked about at his other pieces mounted on the wall or stacked on the floor. "You really are good, you know it?"

JaMar appreciated the comment, but he didn't respond.

Pauline continued. "So what's next? You hanging around these parts or moving on?"

He kept drawing. Charcoal had smeared on his forearm and shirt. "I'm thinking of dying my skin to white and traveling around the country to see how people relate to a white man. *White Like Me* – that's my working title. What do you think?"

"Great idea, but it could be dangerous." Pauline said. She knew he was being sarcastic and making reference to the book, *Black Like Me* -- the story of a white man who altered his skin color to pass as a Negro to gain a greater sense of what black Americans go through.

He pulled out an abstract charcoal sketch from a stack of drawings.

289

"Here you go," he said.

"I can't take this. You could bring a nice price for this."

"On the house." JaMar released one of his rare smiles.

An Indiana storm idled in the western sky, granting good folks like Ruth and Abram Yoder more time to rock in cane chairs on the front porch of their neat and clean clapboard home. Part of Ruth's routine was to open windows so the curtains could wave at the day. Early potted mums, weeks away from color, framed the steps to welcome friends and neighbors. Hanging ferns twisted with the gusts of wind that were not yet threatening. The barn served as a stable for plug horses Minnie and Dolly, a hayloft, and a corner for Abram's projects. Friends and neighbors would bring him things to fix, knowing he would not charge them.

A crooked basketball rim was mounted on the side above the barn's wide gate. There was no backboard; the side of the barn served that purpose. The land around the goal was worn bare.

They figured the pond would surely freeze over again come winter, but this autumn was warmer than usual. When cold weather storms finally invade, they bring on gray overcasts and snow that might not melt until April. Until then, the abundant golden clusters of Sugar Maples adorned the flat fields and fence rows of the farms of this Amish and Mennonite culture. Until the snows come, the fallen leaves form brilliant skirts around the trees that pad and feed the circumference of the roots.

Ruth wore a bonnet and a long, loose dress; Abram, a firm straw hat and suspenders. With chores, a sponge bath and dinner settling in, Abram resumed his current whittling project while slowly rocking on the front porch. Ruth was making progress on a quilt for a niece who would marry in June. Their 34 years together enabled them to communicate more through body language than small talk. They stopped following the news since most of it focused on The War.

Given the breastfeeding and burping routine, Pauline relied on Susan to drive the ten hour trip that took twelve. Pauline was nervous about all this. They crossed the county line and passed Chesney Buck Park in the tiny town of

Minnow, Indiana. A quarter mile north of the town they saw the mailbox labeled "A. Yoder." The car dawdled along the grass and gravel lane, past a small family cemetery and a water well rimmed with black-eyed susans that were yielding to the season. Auntie Sue -- a nickname Susan suggested the baby adopt -- stayed in the car with the baby while Pauline approached the porch. Abram stood without greeting or welcoming the strangers. He was taller than ever, ruler of this land. Ruth stayed seated. As Pauline got closer, she could see that their faces were stern and worn with worry. She introduced herself.

"Afternoon," Pauline said. "Pauline. Pauline Cody."

"Afternoon," said Abram.
"Missed the storm," Pauline said.
"Yah, so far. But we need the rain," he said.

Pauline found him intimidating, a man of few words. Stern, but with a rhythm in his words that she found appealing. He sounded a lot like Will, without his humor and good nature. Pauline admired a row of lilies along a brick path and a wildflower garden that wrapped around one side of the house.

"Lovely." Pauline was not one to be touched by such things, but this setting was idyllic and caught her attention.

"The good Lord provides the seeds and saplings; the least we can do is plant them." said Abram.

"I'm a friend of Will's."

Ruth set down her quilt.

"How do you know our son? Ruth asked.

"From that college, I suppose?"Abram suggested.

"Yes sir," Pauline said.

"Long drive from that college," Abram said.

"Yes, it was."

"Do you have news about our son?" Abram asked. "Did the military send you?"

"No. And as far as we know, there is still nothing new about his status. He was reported missing and then we learned that he was in a prison camp."

"We heard that news, yes," Abram said.

"With his special skills as a medic, he should be protected. The enemy will need him."

"The enemy, you say. And what enemy is that? Those Asian people are not *my* family's enemy. Will broke every tenet of our community and our tradition. Serving as a medic does not justify his involvement in a war. God said 'Thou shalt not kill.' "

"Will is not there to kill anybody, but to rescue and heal."

"He's among those who *do* kill, and do it proudly. Keeping score of body counts... Will may be a hero to the American government, or to his friends and fans, but he has turned his back on his family and faith."

Ruth noticed Susan in the car and was suspicious. She moved closer and confirmed that Susan was in the car holding a baby.

"Your friend's?" she asked Pauline. "Your friend's baby?"

"No," Pauline said.

Ruth cleaned her glasses and took off her apron. "Why did you come all this way?"

Susan handed the child over to Ruth.

"I thought you might like to meet... your grandson," Pauline said.

Ruth gazed at the baby, and melted. Abram took a deep breath and looked the other way.

"His name is Will, Will Junior. We call him Little Will. I know it's a shock and we thought about contacting you first…"

"What, are you here for money? Is that what this is all about?" Abram asked.

"No, of course not," Pauline said.

"Then you are here to tell me that I have a son who shirked his responsibility and abandoned a girl he got in trouble?"

"No, he doesn't know."

"What kind of son have we reared, mother?"Abram said to his wife.

Ruth babbled and the baby cooed.

"And our letters, they've never reached Will," Susan added, "so there was no way to let him know about his son."

"We should have kept our Will on the farm. He could have lived an honorable life. There is always a need for good men in good trades," Abram said.

"You may be disappointed in him, but Will was — *is* — a young man that everyone at Grant State loved and admired. You raised him well. He loved you and wanted you to be proud of him.

Ruth wiped her tears with her apron.

"He would never embrace violence. He could have been rich by now, playing professional basketball, a celebrity, but he turned away from that temptation. He felt like he should do his part and help the wounded and injured, that's all — you know, all the young men who were drafted and didn't benefit from a college deferment like he did."

"Our son chose to be of this world. Look where that path in life took him: to secular professors, a carefree college life. Now a child conceived out of wedlock, conceived in sin. Are you a Christian, Miss Cody?"

"It depends on how that's defined. I'm certainly not the Christian my mother wanted me to be. But if it's any consolation to you, Mr. Yoder, since Will has been missing, Susan and I and many other GSU students at GSU have dedicated ourselves to help end the war and bring our troops home. And we've been persecuted for taking a stand."

"We will only end wars when no one is willing to fight," Abram said.

Abram wanted nothing of the child. The news struck him harshly and he would need time to think through how he and the

Mrs. would deal with this unsettling circumstance and the reaction within their Mennonite community. But when he saw Ruth's countenance while she held and rocked the child and hummed him lullabies, Abram knew there would be no qualms about this child being welcomed in their home. With each passing of days and weeks and months without news of their wayward son, the Yoder's hope was like a wound that would not heal. And without expressing it, the Yoder's also knew the child would be a salve to help soothe their grieving. It may have been too much too soon to stay over at the Yoder home, but they all endured the awkward visit and learned more about one another. The baby slept soundly as the homeplace exuded warmth and belonging. Ruth brought out lemonade and leftover corn fritters. Abram lit a pipe and rocked in his chair. The recurring squeaks from the chair were like an old friend talking back, setting him straight.

The storm veered off north of them, pushed along by an orange glow, leaving a sunset to savor. They watched it together. They watched it ease into the night.

It made no difference to Pauline. The announcement from the military, the letter to Abram and Ruth Yoder from President Reagan, the family and friends who concluded that this would be the end of it — none of that mattered to Pauline. When it came to declaring that the father of her child was unaccounted for and that the search for him would be suspended — to her, it was more of the same bureaucratic run-around. No explanation was credible until there were verifiable remains or Will found his way back home. Nothing else would be a resolution; nothing else would satisfy her.

Saigon fell just four years before, but Defense Department officials were already trying to close the book on this ugly chapter in American warfare. More than 50,000 U.S. troops had been killed, and perhaps millions of Vietnamese, Cambodians and Laotians. More than 1,300 P.O.W.'s were still missing and 1,200 bodies of those reportedly killed had not been recovered.

For twelve exhaustive, exasperating years, Will had been another one of those missing GIs. Officials speculated that he may have spent most of that time in a P.O.W. camp. Few of the kept would choose to live out that time in such a place; death would be relief were it not for the satisfaction it gave the keepers. Friends and family tried not to think about what Will may have endured: slow torture, repeated beatings, garbage scraps for food, sleep deprivation, time in the hole. They wondered how many times a gun had been put to Will's head as enemy soldiers screamed threats he didn't understand.

Will's believers hoped — but they increasingly doubted — that his skills and value as a medic may have gained him some sort of special accommodation. They avoided thinking about the atrocities he must have witnessed and what it may have done to him. If Will survived, would he be traumatized for life, infected or crippled, jaded or indifferent? Would he have had a breaking point and done anything to survive? Could a gentle giant like "Big Red" have turned into a monster? Would he be the same person? What — or whom -- would he remember?

Since Secretary of State Henry Kissinger and Le Duc Tho negotiated the 1973 Paris Peace Accords, there had been spotty releases of missing soldiers and prisoner exchanges and inconsistent rumors of a red-haired prisoner who loomed over the rest. Pauline followed up on every lead. She pleaded with military experts. She hired psychics. She spent every cent she could save. She refused to hold a memorial service.

Beyond her relentless efforts to rescue Will through these years, Pauline lost interest in public affairs and her flair for activism dried up like the wilted garden that her ol' man Hump would never get around to watering. Unlike the rest of the nation, the Watergate scandal had not captivated her and she grew evermore cynical of politicians, generals and the media. In her partying days, she would have been on the front row for all three days at Woodstock; now she doesn't even listen to the soundtrack. She didn't watch much television and she was stern in the programs she allowed for Little Will. She didn't like the way the *Dukes of Hazzard* mocked a rural culture that was not so much different than the way things were in Bobcat where she grew up and never expected to return. Even though it was a comedy, *MASH* was off limits; the topic was just too close to home and too hard to make light of. But once Little Will finished his homework, she'd let him tune into *Different Strokes*, the *Bad News Bears* and a new all-sports channel, *ESPN*. When she said no, Little Will was not one to whine or lock horns with his mom. He had his dad's gentle genes and did what he could to make things easier on the two of them. He studied extra hard to make her proud and never stopped to wonder why it took him longer with reading and figuring. Pauline never told him about the injury they both suffered when he was still in her womb and how the doctors said it could set his mind back. Pauline didn't buy it. No one would overestimate her kid. Did they know his father? Little Will had his dad's determination genes.

This little family — mother and boy, Pauline and Little Will — found a way to make their own way. They moved to Paducah when the boy was just a toddler. She got on at the Union Carbide plant as a receptionist and file clerk while she looked for something better. Three years later she and Little Will up and moved to Cape Girardeau when Pauline was pissed off from being passed over for a City of

Paducah parks management job whose duties resembled a class she took at GSU. A member of the selection committee discovered that Pauline had a past as an anti-war rabble-rouser at Grant State and that's all it took. This was not the first time Pauline had been nipped when employers discovered who she was.

She finally caved in to mother-in-law Rhonda who set her up with a well-established Mary Kay distributorship in Cape Girardeau. It had been Norma Dean Fleming's district, but she retired, bought a camper, latched it on to her long pink Cadillac and set off to Panama City to find a new man.

At the Cape, Pauline and Little Will lived in a gray two-bedroom duplex with burgundy shutters and a mailbox that matched. They lived on Dunklin Street, a quiet cul-de-sac near the campus of Southeast Missouri State — a longtime rival of GSU. Little Will enjoyed his bicycle, and a cul-de-sac left his mother with a higher sense of safety. However, the thin paneled walls of the duplex did not absorb the unrestrained moaning and pounding of the newlyweds next door — so much so that Pauline switched bedrooms with Little Will

after their first few nights when he asked
questions she was not prepared to answer.
Her fortuitous eavesdropping brought
back memories of the time -- the one and
only time -- when she was with Will and
how they were so nervous and excited, not
knowing that the two had created one, a
new life that would be, for Pauline, a
bundle of joy that would give meaning to
her life.

The Mary Kay work came easy to
Pauline. She knew how to motivate an
audience from her days as an activist. Her
schedule was flexible enough that she
never missed Little Will's school plays,
parent-teacher conferences, soccer or
basketball games. But she didn't get
caught up in the Mary Kay hokey culture;
to her, it was a job. Her life was her son
and the hope that lay dormant in her heart.

It had been 12 years since Pauline
and her roommate were in the Huddle
House and heard the news about Will.
Pauline still confided in Susan, her
steadfast friend, as they tracked the
government's occasional news or
speculation about injured or dead soldiers
still being found in Vietnam.

Pauline's phone was mounted in the kitchen next to a bulletin board and refrigerator that showcased the mainstays in her life: a newspaper sports clipping of their hero, Will "Big Red," Little Will's school pictures, her sister Jesse and her family, a Bob Dylan poster, a watercolor of the Kappa Delta house, and leaders of STAND posing by the statue of George Graham Vest and his dog, Ol' Drum.

Pauline caught up with Susan over the phone. Pauline pecked on the wall, a signal for Will to turn down the music.

"Sorry," Pauline apologized to Susan for the noise. "He's a big Doobie Brothers fan. Great kid, he really is. But you're right, he's getting to that age when he really needs a father. Uh huh. I know. I know. Yeah, but I'm just not sure if I'm ready for the dating scene. And it would seem like I'd given up hope, that I had concluded that we're never going to find him. You know I'll never give up, but that's what he'd think. You know, it's as real to me as ever: I still imagine Will's expression when he meets his son for the first time."

Susan could sense it, once again. Pauline's slurred speech was a hint. The

304

stress of these twelve years. The encouraging news. The inconclusive reports. The miscues. Raising a boy. Lonely nights. She reverted to the party girl of old, but not the carousing party girl of old. Pauline was more of a homebody now, but she was still prone to the bottle. As Pauline and Susan chatted over the phone, Susan knew the sounds of ice cubes landing in a glass and the trickle of bourbon as it was poured.

"Hey, on the helicopter request: looks like Vic's gonna come through for us after all," Susan said.

"No (hiccup) shit?" Pauline replied.

"No shit. He still has a couple of authorizations to secure in Defense, but he's ready to finalize it," Susan said.

"By God, your old man there, maybe he's not such a (hiccup) prick after all," Pauline teased.

"You've never given Vic the benefit of the doubt on anything, you know that," Susan said. "He said he could probably get a Huey Cobra."

"That'll work! Now he knows that I have to go with him — right?"

"Yeah. He was reluctant; then he agreed. He found someone who really knows the region well. He'll be a great resource."

"Remember I've been over there four times already, twice when we hit bad weather," Pauline said.

"Not everyone wants to take the risks that you do," Susan said.

"So there's a catch. I knew it," Pauline said.

"Vic's media consultant wants some of this footage for his next round of campaign ads. His constituency and donors were strong supporters of the war, you know. Looking for a P.O.W. is a politically popular thing to do. But you'll need to be out of the camera's range -- understand? " Susan said.

"Yeah sure. He can marry you and he can't even be seen in a picture with me?" Pauline said.

"You were the leader, remember? You did the interviews, news conferences. You spoke at the rallies. I just tagged along," Susan said.

"Enough that you got expelled like the rest of us," Pauline said.

"The media *has* been easy on me. And that's fine with me," Susan said.

"So your role these days?" Pauline asked.

"Well the wives, we sit there at the head table and eat our rubber chicken dinners and when they introduce Congressman Victor Devillez and his *lovely* wife, we smile and make everyone believe that we're so delighted to be there and so very proud of our husbands," Susan said.

"So you're not?" Pauline said.

"He's a better man than you've ever given him credit for. He was largely elected on his war record. But he works very hard. We don't agree on everything, but he wants to make a difference, and he believes in America," Susan said.

"Yeah, love it or leave it," Pauline said.

"These consultants. They've painted Vic as this brave, tough veteran with a family legacy of combat, family man, man of faith, and a farmer who is one with the soil. He is much of that, but hell, it was *my* family's money that got him elected. When he talks about working on the farm, he's referring to the stud farm in the heart of bluegrass thoroughbred country. Not like he's digging potatoes or plucking off sucker worms from tobacco leaves. I don't know why they can't just shoot straight with the public rather than try and make candidates into something they're not," Susan said. "They tell him to stick to their strategy if he wants to keep winning."

"Well tell the Congressman that I appreciate his help with the copter and all the approvals and arrangements," Pauline said. "Will's still living, I just know it."

Pauline finished her drink. It didn't hit the spot, but she thought that maybe the next one would.

Pauline was at that place again, back in the soupy creek amidst the jungle fog. The snakes were now her pets, wrapped around her neck and shoulders, licking her ears and cheeks with flickering clandestine tongues. Old Drum barked as the Doobie Brothers played through the stout bamboo.

Will's large mop of red hair had grown long to hide his face and ears. He was skin and bones, and there were large dark circles under his eyes. He could walk and dribble on water, but he kept dribbling off his feet and Vic would yell, "Out of bounds! Out of bounds!" Will held a pistol to his temple and pulled the trigger, over and

over. It made a firing noise but the bullet
exited the other side of his head without
effect. He howled and recited a line with the
rhythm of a teasing child: "Star fucker, star
fucker... yooou are a star fucker!" Will
pranced right out of the prison camp and
stood along a highway, littered by
abandoned artillery and dead bodies. He
held up a make-shift poster that a hitchhiker
would use: "Minnow, Indiana or Bust."

Little Will stood by his mother's bed
and shook the covers until she woke,
disoriented from another dream. She
sweated and panted, scaring her son
before regained her bearings. She had no
interest in holding on to or making any
sense of the nightmare.

"Just a dream, mom. Go back to
bed," Little Will said.

Congressman Victor Devillez called
it "Operation Big Red." He lined up a
helicopter pilot who had made a dozen or
more similar runs through regions along
North Vietnam's Red River in the Lao Cai
Province where several enemy prison
camps had been located. Now abandoned
for several years, it was difficult to
decipher clues about the direction either

side took once the gates were opened. While he zoomed in low and hovered, the pilot pointed at landmarks and sites where he'd been told of executions and bodies burned.

The crew and Pauline studied the aerial photographs from previous rescue endeavors. The last trip — which occurred after U.S. and North Vietnamese diplomats reached a peace agreement — documented that fighting was still occurring in remote areas and work camps where communication systems had been obliterated.

Meanwhile, the film crew captured landscapes, remnants of camps, the devastation of villages and the countryside, signs of death. The Congressman spoke into the camera comfortably, describing a valley where his Delta Company 4 was ambushed by a Vietcong offensive that resulted in a significant loss of life, including the death of Staff Sergeant McDougal from Wisconsin who pulled Devillez from a ravine just before they were hit by mortar fire.

"Excuse me, Congressman. Can we stay focused on our mission here?" Pauline asked.

Pauline had tracked the battles of the war and theorized that Will's unit was captured near Khe Sanh in connection with Operation NIAGRA orchestrated by Westmorland and named for the series of cascading shells that characterized the American attack. Village witnesses were inconsistent in their versions of what happened; some made reference to a system of caves in the area that were enemy battle stations as well as a temporary holding cell for prisoners that, for whatever reason, were not killed immediately as most were. As the war's end was apparent, the enemy's extensive trench system doubled as a mass burial site.

They set up camp and interviewed villagers, former North Vietnamese soldiers, and former paid agents who were willing to speculate on Will's whereabouts for a fee. Pauline looked away as backhoes dug up bodies already decomposed beyond recognition that were still due a proper funeral and resting place back home. No one acknowledged it — particularly Pauline — but they were thinking that Will's unusual height might stand out in a pile of bodies. Pauline knew

311

that his remains could be among the unearthed, but she held on to an innate sense that Will was safe somewhere, wandering, confused but still searching, still determined to find the path back home and to the son who to Will would be a stranger.

Back in D.C. before the debriefing, Congressman Devillez introduced Pauline to his well-groomed, attractive and articulate staff. This is "a friend, a sorority sister, of Mrs. Devillez from our college days," he told them. He felt no need to acknowledge the role that Pauline and Susan had in the 1967 incident at Grant State. The activism of that time had been a source of intense aggravation to Vic; more than a decade later, it still lingered. His favors for Pauline were less about their longtime acquaintance and more about the intervention and persistence of his wife, Susan.

His office featured photographs of the Congressman shaking hands with those he held up as gutsy, determined champions: former Vice President Spiro Agnew, Olympic swimmer Mark Spitz, and Kentucky Derby winning jockey Angel Cordero, Jr. atop the renowned

312

thoroughbred, Seattle Slew. On his desk next to photos of his family was a shot of the Congressman and farm manager Luis standing next to Battle Bound, Strathmore Farm's effective stallion and the largest source of the family's business revenue.

His office was handsome but hardly the plush décor that characterized the offices of his colleagues with more seniority. Sprinkled among his knick knacks were Grant State University memorabilia and an exhibit of his military gear from Vietnam — a popular talking point with visitors from his district. The film crew continued compiling footage for the campaign. They captured images of the Congressman pointing to a large map of Southeast Asia on a table once owned by General Omar Bradley. He moved pieces of miniature airplanes, tanks and troops; clearly he enjoyed military strategy.

Pauline couldn't restrain herself. "Beg your pardon, Congressman, but war is not a board game. For God's sake."

Their aversion to one another had long settled in.

Since he was old enough to climb trees, a few weeks of Little Will's summers were spent with his Grandma and Grandpa Yoder in Indiana. Pauline was expected at the annual Mary Kay convention and, following that, she was persuaded by her former college roommate, Susan Strathmore, to join her for their yearly "girls getaway." The gals would go off to the Big Apple or Chicago or a beach somewhere and demonstrate that they still had some Grant State party juice left in them. Pauline put on a good front, but her thoughts were always with Will, wondering and worrying if he was lost or had been found, dead or discovered and given new life after a release. Susan knew that the pain and pressure of the ordeal had stayed with her friend, now going on twelve years. She heard Pauline crying in a restroom stall and in the opposite hotel twin bed after the lights went out. She drank more than ever. Since college, Pauline had gained five pounds per year and lost her shape and — she was sure — her desirability. Depression seeped within her. Little Will was the light of her life but she worried

314

how she might handle things if he turned out to be an unruly adolescent.

Little Will became a popular fixture in Minnow. The town was a quick bike ride from the Yoder farm. He knew the names of the barber, the fellow that ran the bait shop and the postmaster. Everyone knew of the boy. They looked past the circumstances of how he came to be with a profound sense of pride that Will Yoder's boy was among them, along with the spirit of his father.

However, the town of Minnow struggled. Attitudes changed. Upbeat comradery that characterized the Klaassen's morning coffee club veered off into political divisiveness. The Lions Club theme song, "Can You Hear Those Lions Roar," that traditionally opened every meeting, attracted lackluster participation, and Chesney Buck Park was unfunded and neglected since Will Yoder left Minnow and Grant State for Vietnam. The park's basketball court was neglected, there were patchy gaps of concrete and the rim dangled from the backboard. Consequently, Little Will turned to his vivid imagination, playing against imaginary opponents.

Abram mounted a new backboard and rim to the barn above the open door of the stable. As a bonus, he poured a concrete pad for a court to surprise Little Will for his birthday.

Other than a go-cart or BB gun, for Little Will, this was about as good as it gets. They marked off the lines for out-of-bounds, the foul line and three point arc (a distance kids his age could not reach). The Yoder Court was an immediate gathering spot that attracted those with a wide range of skill and knowledge of the game. Abram posted the "Rules for Use" on the barn: Thou shall not curse; Thou shall not hang from the rim or net; Thou shall keep your shirt on; Thou shall not tease or torment; Thou shall not "hog the ball" or "show off," etc. Despite Abram's regulations, the Yoder Court quickly was a busy, popular place, the talk of their little town, and something Will would have treasured.

Abram continued to mellow through his years. He had long since warmed up to the boy, setting aside the moral ambiguity surrounding his conception. When Little Will wasn't around, Abram could still be stern and grumpy, and quick to complain about joint pains he refused to medicate. Ruth coordinated their lives and found respite by participating in travel group outings sponsored by their church. Abram preferred to stay home on the farm, but he went along so Ruth wouldn't worry about him.

Little Will brought out the best in them and reminded them so of their son Will when he was a youngster. They came to respect and enjoy the company of Pauline and the challenges she faced raising her son alone. The Yoders would no doubt have had a different view if they knew about her drinking.

During Little Will's many visits, Abram taught his grandson how to work the land and care for tools. They planted gardens on the right cycles. They gathered from the ground bruised wormy apples that Ruth could cook and not waste. They pruned the grape harbor. They dug a water well. They turned to nature's remedies to fight off pests and predators. In the winter Abram and Will would find a sugar maple on the sunny side of an upward slope and draw the sap for another season of syrup to go with Ruth's hotcakes.

Abram introduced the boy to carpentry and took him to the Herschberger barn raising. He showed him the best wood for whittling. They repaired fences and built a weathervane.

Little Will was right there and up close when Abram delivered a foal birthed by their slow gray freckly plug horse, Daisy. They milked cows and goats, sheared sheep and kept a couple of border collies for herding.

The aroma of Grandma Ruth's meals wafted over the cornfield and down by the smoke house as a signal that dinner or supper was ready. No hollering or bell ringing was necessary. Food was only from the farm and seconds were seldom allowed. Desserts were limited to Sundays. A stack of fresh baked sliced bread and butter was available when Little Will needed to top off a meal.

Pauline improved as a cook, but with her spasmodic routine selling Mary Kay products and recruiting others from whom she earned a cut, meals were typically on the go and Little Will never complained. Abram and Ruth admired Pauline's drive, but they questioned her priorities. Ruth made sure that Pauline knew when Little Will was growing out of his shoes or when he had a doctor or dentist appointment. Ruth would go ahead and knit Little Will a new sock cap or ear muffs, and sometimes Pauline wouldn't even notice.

Though Abram mounted the basketball goal on the barn, and poured the concrete for the court, he still had mixed emotions about sports. He remembered how it brought on so much notoriety and glamour to his son, a worldly game with worldly temptations when, as Mennonites, they were to set aside the world and its worldly ways. Were it not for basketball and college, Will would have stayed at the farm and used the skills his father taught him. He would not have made the same circle of friends and would have stayed clear of anything to do with the wars created by nations. Abram knew that their son would not have enlisted, would not have been missing, would not have been a prisoner. He would be alive and working the land and building useful things and watching sunsets and giving honor to his God and Savior. But Ruth reminded him that the course their son took also brought Little Will into the world

319

and into their lives, a blessing they cherished and would forever give thanks. Surely, they concluded, what had transpired must be part of the Lord's plan.

Pauline never expected to stay with Mary Kay this long; the thought of plucking her eyebrows and caking her face with cosmetics was something she never valued growing up and through her college years as a makeshift leader in GSU's counterculture. To her, the Mary Kay life was a living, a way to keep Little Will in coats and shoes that fit. She managed to pay her bills, put food on the table and re-stock beer and bourbon. At sales meetings and rallies, Pauline played along with the hokey exercises and chants to promote enthusiasm among the neophyte distributors. She got along, but there was nothing extra for Little Will's college fund and a Mary Kay pink Cadillac was not parked out back. She drove a Volkswagon van adorned with bumper stickers that supported George McGovern for President and Greenpeace. Her rear windshield featured her catchphrase: "*I Will Survive*" — Gloria Gaynor (and me). She could turn the Mary Kay script on automatic pilot, but Pauline's mind was focused on two things: the kid and the kid's father who she needed for child rearing, for financial support, for conversation, and for intimacy — deep-seated wants and needs Pauline had not experienced since Will left for the war.

Once again, a helicopter search quashed her hopes. The efforts of her best friend's husband and his entourage were appreciated, but Pauline would have stayed home had she known that the ulterior motive was largely political.

She had left Little Will with Abram and Ruth; now they faced the long drive back to Cape Girardeau where Little Will had homework and a science project and Pauline had a long list of sales calls to make.

Little Will gazed at the flat farmland along the road toward home. "Mom, do you think we'll ever find him?"

"Yes, I do."

"I do too."

"We have to believe. We'll just keep on looking. Your Dad is big and strong. If anybody could make it through that awful war, it'd be your Daddy."

Little Will pulled out an Etch-a-Sketch that Pauline picked up to help pass the time on the road.

"Mom, you know the problem with this thing.?"

"No, what?"

"When you're really careful and draw something that turns out just right, there's no way to hang on to it. It's gone with just a shake and you can't ever get it back."

"That's the way it is with a lot of things."

"Will, honey, how would you feel about me going on a date sometime?" He shrugged to reflect an indifference to the idea. She knew his body language and never brought it up again.

They pulled in their Cape Girardeau driveway at 9:20 p.m. and expected it to be a late night. Pauline looked forward to a shot or two of bourbon. She left the engine running and they stayed in the parked car so they could sing and laugh along with the latest Rod Stewart hit:

If you want my body and you think I'm sexy
Come on sugar let me *know*

If you really need me just reach out
and   *touch me*
Come on honey tell me so...

As Pauline picked up the peanuts and wrappers off the floor of her van, it occurred to her that Grace Mae would have been furious if she allowed a child of hers to listen to, let alone sing along with, such a disgusting, suggestive tune.

Pauline juxtaposed the religious practices of her parents against those of the Yoder's: Grace Mae's explosive evangelical zeal and Hump's casual tendency to do whatever to get along, against the strict but wholesome spiritual grounding of Abram and Ruth.

Pauline's stepmother Rhonda had become a devoted cable television viewer of the PTL Club, starring Jim and Tammy Bakker. She and Hump trusted that their $1,000 lifetime membership would beef up their odds for success through its prosperity theology and Heritage USA theme park. Hump went along with breadwinner Rhonda and was just fine with the new routine of fulfilling their church-going obligation by watching TV and eating sweet rolls.

323

There were no thousand dollar
checks sent to Pauline in Cape Girardeau,
however. Since Rhonda and Hump
married, she had bought and sold several
Mary Kay distributorships, requiring
moves to Marion, Mt. Vernon and Webster
Grove. Pauline was no longer under
Rhonda's Mary Kay purview so neither had
much of a reason to call one another.
Rhonda knew that Pauline's heart was not
in the Mary Kay way and Hump never quite
took to the illegitimate grandson.
Christmas gifts and birthday cards arrived
sporadically.

Hump's other daughter, Jesse, was a
quiet payroll clerk at Carson Newman
College in Tennessee. She married a
skinny fellow who worked in student
housing who Hump never liked because
he didn't know how to drive a straight shift
and he didn't have the first day of deer
season circled on his calendar on his
refrigerator.

Rhonda would report that her
prodigal daughter, Lisa, lived in Panama
City, but she wasn't really sure.

Consequently, when it came to
family, Pauline and Little Will were drawn
to the Yoders and their tranquil place near

Minnow, Indiana. Invitations to gather in
Bobcat with the Cody side of the family
were few and hollow. But as Little Will was
more involved with soccer and scouting
and the Mineral and Rock Club, and as
Pauline had to hustle to hold on to her
client base, weekend and holiday trips to
Minnow to visit with Grandma and
Grandpa Yoder were more difficult to
arrange. Moreover, so many of Will's
activities were after school and in the
evenings, so Pauline was increasingly
alone — alone to concoct various exotic
cocktails she remembered from college,
or just alone with her Makers Mark which
was just fine on its own.

A few suitors signaled romantic
interest in Pauline, but she didn't return
the gesture. One had been a protestor in
the 60s, but he was more of an intellectual
than she could handle. One came on too
strong by sticking his tongue half-way
down her throat at her front door after he
gave her a ride home from a Mary Kay
mentor meeting when her battery died
and couldn't be jumped. First and
foremost, Pauline had a kid to raise and
any philandering she might indulge in
would be seen as inappropriate even

though she and Will were not official —
and "hell…" Pauline would remind herself,
"When he comes back — *if* he comes back
— he may not want anything to do with me,
he may not even know me or remember
me." Just the same, Little Will didn't see it
that way. His father was alive and on his
way home and his mom and dad would get
married as soon as he returned and they
would, finally, be like a real family.

It was all Pauline could do to hang
on to hope. The rumors, the speculation,
the sightings. The false alarms. The
moments of despair. Thoughts of ending it
all. She checked the fine print of her
insurance policy and there was indeed a
suicide clause; there would be money
there for Little Will's college.

She wanted it all to go away. She
didn't want to hear any more. She
wondered if she was being punished for
her cavalier romp in the hay with Will
twelve years ago. Her mother had taught
her that things of the flesh were not
recreational, but to propagate the species.
"Maybe, Lord, this is your way of
punishing me for bringing a child into this
world out of wedlock."

But then her son would do something funny, or precious, or remarkable. She would standby his happening. She would not entertain the notion that he was not a special gift to the world.

The envelope and letterhead were of high quality stock connoting importance. Pauline had never been on the Grant State mailing list and came close to tossing it along with other junk mail. But it looked and felt official with its full-color GSU seal and waving American flag postage stamp. Pauline read it in a whisper.

Dear Ms. Cody,
On October 27, 1979 Grant State University will honor 1967 alumnus Will Yoder with the unveiling of a statue on the new Freedom Plaza located near the campus Memorial Gardens atop the bluff on which our beautiful and historic campus is perched. Commissioned by the Bluff City American Legion, Sculptor Raymond Anders depicts Yoder's athletic and military prowess — in particular, his service to his country as a volunteer medic

and later as a prisoner during the Vietnam War.

We invite you to attend the dedication ceremony that will be held in conjunction with the university's annual Homecoming festivities.

11:30 Sculpture Site

(In case of rain, the ceremony will occur in Peacock Hall.)

Yours truly,

Buddy Baxter
Assistant Dean of Student Affairs

"Buddy Baxter! Dean? Holy crap!" Pauline said as she laughed out loud.

A hand-written note was added to the letter: "Let's bury the hatchet. Hope you can make it! – Buddy"

Pauline phoned Susan immediately.

"Did you get that invitation from Buddy Baxter?

"Yeah. Did you know about the statue of Will?"

"No."

"I just don't want people to think that this means he's been given up for dead," Pauline said." There's still, what, a thousand still missing in action?"

"Bury the hatchet. Easy for him to say."

"Dean Baxter. Good God. Can you believe that shit? The little fucking brown-noser."

"Yeah, but if he had anything to do with inviting us, I'm sure he's had some critics. Good of him to put this together, I guess."

"How many of our STAND group do you think they found?"

"I don't know where anybody is except Luke. He's still in Carbondale, I guess. And he won't come."

"You know Faceman Blazer won't show with all that he's been through."

"Lonnie and Cate went to Canada."

"Yeah, but he's had that amnesty option for couple of years. Maybe they've come back."

They bantered about and wondered who received the same invitation and who would make the trip. They swapped memories — fun, gratifying and tragic.

Pauline's first inclination was to skip the ceremony and all the Homecoming brouhaha. No doubt Little Will had some kind of activity scheduled that day — that could be her excuse — and Pauline knew she would be bombarded by questions and speculations about Will, such as: *Don't you think it's time to pronounce him dead so that everybody could move on?*

"However," Pauline said to Susan, "How many kids can say that a statue has been made of them, or of their father? Little Will needs to be there when it's unveiled, don't you think?"

"Maybe so. Guess we should go. For my boy's sake."

The new La Quinta Hotel was built near campus on property that had been the Sigma Nu and ATO houses, fraternities that had calmed down since the `60s and relocated to Fraternity Row. Buddy organized a separate reception at the hotel for the 1967 anti-war activists, a group he posited would have a special interest in the sculpture since the response to Will Yoder's capture in Vietnam sparked the movement at Grant State.

Buddy had also been there during the Homecoming parade that year when things got ugly. He knew the protestors didn't cause the violence, panic or stampede that killed Arnie Latham and injured many others. Buddy convinced himself that, as a student intern, there was nothing he could really do, but now he wished he had spoken up in defense of the students and acknowledged the role of then-President Harlan Renwick.

The welcoming event was held by the La Quinta indoor pool that smelled like chlorine and ranch dressing. The moisture in the air made the finger sandwiches soggy. As Pauline entered, Dorsey Sugg was the first person she sighted. Chubbier than she remembered, wearing unbecoming tiny tight swim trunks with a lightning bolt across the crotch and sporting a mustache that no longer looked stylish, he pounced off the diving board, erupting cannonballs toward a crowd that was not in the mood to get wet and be left with polka-dotted clothing. They shifted out of range to the bar where a cassette tape deck played music of their time: the Beatles, Aretha Franklin and Otis Redding led the playlist. Dorsey strutted about with his air guitar, pretending to be Jimi Hendrix when his raw overdrive kicked in.

Buddy prepared a special guide to the weekend activities: the time and location of receptions, brunches, award ceremonies, pep rally/bonfire, an Earth, Wind and Fire concert. The Fall Harvest Sing had been held on Friday afternoon and, once again, the KDs took top honors with a sweet medley of tunes from the Carpenters: *Close to You, We've Only Just Begun, Kind of Hush* and *Muscrat Love* — a far cry from the peace theme of their '67 Fall Sing. The weekend schedule also included the unveiling of the sculpture, the Faculty Tug-of-War, Homecoming Parade, football game versus Austin Peay University and a special show at Dooley's --- still open after all these years but with its fourth owner.

Pauline brought along Little Will so he could see the statue unveiled and dedicated. A life-size sculpture, it was the first time Little Will had a sense of his father's size and strength. Despite their misgivings, grandparents Abram and Ruth came along to attend the ceremony and watch Little Will while Pauline mingled with old friends. Little Will was perfectly happy spending time in the pool and watching TV in the room.

Susan and Pauline talked routinely but they had not seen one another for more than a year. Susan was trim and radiant as ever. Hair pulled back and wearing a conservative suit, she was a stark contrast to Pauline's disco look featuring a paisley silk blouse and a bright orange tube top. Susan worried about her old friend. Dark circles sagged from her sad eyes. Her flushed skin was ruby red, blotchy and scaly. Wrinkles had taken root prematurely.

"Honey, you okay? You look stressed," Susan said. "How you and the bottle getting along?"

"I'm all right. It's some new medicine I'm on," Pauline said.

"You can't keep worrying about Will," Susan said.

"Drives me crazy. Up and down. He's spotted somewhere, then they say it's a false alarm. I get excited, then they tell me he's probably dead. God dammit I've about had it!"

Dorsey lost his balance and slapped the water with a loud belly flop.

"Dorsey!" Pauline screamed. "Somebody give that man a dose of self esteem, will you, so he won't have to be the center of attention."

"Whose idea was it to bring him into our group anyway?" Susan said, teasing and suggesting Pauline.

"How you been, Pauline?" asked Congressman Victor Devillez. "Don't tell me: you're mayor of Bobcat."

"We live in Cape Girardeau. I'm in sales."

Grayer and more distinguished since she saw him last, Vic wore a three-piece suit with a tie matched by his handkerchief. A watch dangled from his pocket.

"How are things in the arena?" Pauline asked.

"Nothing that a new president can't fix," Vic said. "Carter will be a one termer. Any more leads on Will come your way?"

"You'd have heard from me if any reports came in. Thanks again for the use of the helicopter."

"Yeah, well maybe we'll have better luck next time. I have my best man on it, monitoring every report."

"Thanks."

"Hope you didn't mind us shooting a little campaign footage while we had the aircraft."

"No, as long as I'm not in your ad."
Vic forced a smile and Pauline pretended
she was kidding.

The music grew louder or maybe it
was the increased crowd volume after
everyone had a few drinks. Jimmie Kim
tapped Pauline on her shoulder.

"Jin Ae? Jimmi Kim! How the hell are
you? You look great!" They embraced and
squealed. "Where the hell are you, now?"

"Chicago."

"No shit. Working on that second
million, I bet."

Jimmie ushered them both around to
meet her girlfriend.

"This is Brandi." A tall, thin beauty
with long auburn hair, she was a stunning
complement to the short and stocky
Jimmie and her shag cut that resembled
that of activist Jane Fonda.

"Hmm. Well, so…are you two… you
know…" Pauline said, suspecting the
obvious.

Susan joined them and introduced
herself.

"I have different priorities now,"
Jimmie said. "In career, in relationships.
Did a stint in the Peace Corps. That's
where we met. Ethiopia."

335

"Really! Hot damn! Well that's...
incredible," Pauline said and Susan
concurred.

"I learned that my ambitions were
an attempt to compensate for my father's
failures, and that if I didn't stop bouncing
from one stressful start-up to another, I
would end up like him. Now I'm a *social*
entrepreneur. We install clean water wells
in remote areas. Africa and South America
mainly. Brandi's a first-rate plumber,"
Jimmie said.

"Well that's... wonderful! Plumber,
you say?" Everyone knew what Susan was
thinking; never had they seen a plumber
look like that. "Wow! Really proud of you,
Jimmie," Susan said.

"Could use your help. Your family
foundation. Heard you set one up after you
sold the horse farm," Jimmie said.

"That's right. While I can't speak for
the trustees, you know I'll do what I can,"
Susan said.

"Thanks," said Jimmie.

"You'll do well at whatever you do,"
Pauline said. "You're such an idea person.
I always thought your Olympic board
game would sell."

Dorsey made another splash and it rained down on them. He hopped out of the pool, dripping, and joined them. He pointed a finger to his cheek, signaling to Susan that he would like a kiss. She moved forward to satisfy him but, at the last moment, he turned quickly to face her before she could turn her lips away and escape his kiss on the mouth. She laughed, then swatted and shooed him away.

Luke James handed Dave Blazer a beer. Luke tried not to gape at his old friend's prosthetic eye and caved in jaw that required him to speak out of the opposite side of his mouth. Luke wore a flannel shirt, khaki's and Chuck Taylor tennis shoes to go with his laid back nature. Dave still had the same Beach Boy look less the injury.

"I stopped after the fourth surgery. Said the hell with it," Dave said. "The Faceman, they used to call me." He chuckled. "Who the hell named me that anyway... ah, t'was the troublemaker Pauline, I do believe. No, I'm not much of a chick magnet anymore but at least I'm not scaring off little kids like I was before the operations. You still have your little shop in Carbondale?"

"Yeah, I borrow the money, assume all the risk, work harder and longer hours and pay myself less than my employees... get the idea?"

"Yeah."

"But, no, I've always liked working for myself. I can take off when I want — about every six-seven years," Luke said. "My wife used my work as an excuse to divorce me. But there were other... complications. We adopted and she took the kid."

"Sorry, man. Still build cabinets?" Dave asked.

"Yep. And we do some hutches, dinner and rocking chairs, a little bit of this and that. I tried making baseball bats but the competition from aluminum did us in," Luke said.

Congressman Devillez worked his way into the huddle. Yolanda was as striking as ever: her immense afro, African garb, tall and thin like a starlet. "So, how many of these former agitators are still fighting for their cause?" Vic asked.

"Some are," Susan said.

"Maybe we'll conduct a poll," Vic said.

"Vic, no. No poll. Please," Susan said.

"Yolanda here just ran a marathon," Pauline said.

"Well that will advance social justice," Vic said.

"She's is a wonderful marriage counselor," Susan said.

"So you're married?" Vic asked.

"That's not a requisite, but yes, to a music publisher," Yolanda said.

"That get him into Woodstock?" Vic asked.

"What is it with you tonight, Vic?" Susan asked.

"Just wondering what kind of impact, if any, came about from all you do-gooders from the 60s? And all the touchy-feely bullshit, really brought you people together, heh? Hell, most of you haven't even spoken since you split, or should I say, since you were kicked out of GSU," Vic said.

Luke and the Congressman eyed one another. Both remembered their encounter in front of Peacock Hall when Vic took on the protesting Vietnam Veterans, when he and Luke had words. They kept their distance from that point on.

When he heard that Vic was running for Congress, Luke sent him a $200 campaign contribution.

Reverend Odell Calhoun sipped on his Coca Cola and showed photos of his four children to Dave Blazer, his old roommate.

"God has a reason behind everything, Dave," the Reverend said.

"Sure, preach. I guess a decade or more in a God-forsaken P.O.W. camp was a loving God's plan for Will Yoder? Was my disfigurement God's way of humbling me? Hell, I'd have been governor if it hadn't been for that," Blazer said.

"But now you can use your political skills, your savvy, in ways to help more good people get into office. Your job now as a strategist can be a noble profession." Odell said.

"I'm glad you see it that way," Reverend. Brother Odell had not changed – in looks or in temperament. He had always appreciated Dave's practical advice about his preaching style, but he had to tolerate his shenanigans when they shared the mobile home in college. Then and since then, Odell gave Dave the benefit of the doubt.

340

Odell had scooted up the growing independent Christian church ladder then veered off with 20 devoted families to purchase and renovate a former Service Merchandise store into a church of 2,300 members and an annual budget of $4.3 million.

He saw his former girlfriend across the pool. Odell's wife, a church organist, was home with their four children and busy planning special Advent activities. Yolanda's husband had no interest in the reunion and had an album deadline to deal with over the weekend. Odell extended his hand and Yolanda pulled him closer for a gentle embrace. She wanted to know all about his family. As he gazed at her ravishing beauty, he felt himself growing hard and his heartbeat throbbing. He couldn't control a fantasy that she would follow him back to his hotel room. He decided to have a glass of wine after all.

The '79 pep rally concluded about the time the '67 event was warming up. Twelve years later, the rally was limited to corny chants for the grasshopper football team and tailgaters already staking their claims on locations

341

for Homecoming Saturday. Cheerleading had evolved into a sport of its own. Nowhere was anyone left with a sense that GSU was a bastion of social or political expression. Partying was apparent, of course, and it was hard not to notice rowdiness, but there was not a sense that a particular voice should characterize the emerging generation. President Jimmy Carter and Secretary Cyrus Vance were not burned in effigy. Hollywood actors were not brought in to leave students with a sense that this was a special time and challenge. The `79 pep rally was just about building enthusiasm for a football game. Pauline believed that her people were proud that their time at GSU was more than that. She believed that they would hold on to their memories and always stand for justice and peace.

Not that Pauline and her old pals were too mature to tie one on. The pep rally and tailgating was all they needed to get things going. Pauline checked on Little Will and the Yoders before she started downing the vodka tonics. That brought back memories of keggers, mixers, streaking and tubing. Thoughts of those good times kept her mind off Will when that was all most people wanted to talk about. She had nothing to report, nothing to predict about the father of her child, and whether Will was wandering in a jungle, shacked up with a prostitute in Hanoi, still captive and confused, or rotting in some mass grave.

About the only thing they noticed that was different about Dooley's were the neon lights in the windows that now promoted Coors Light instead of Sterling Big Mouths. Twelve years ago, Coors was hard to find and Sterling was cheap with a regional fan base. The darkness inside and out hid the bar's chipping paint that had been ignored by the series of owners that gave it a go every few years. The overflow Homecoming crowd softened any threatening regulars who played serious pool and pinball. Dorsey pushed two long tables together and ordered three pitchers of Stroh's to get things started. Around the room, the laughter and greetings from former chums already made it difficult to talk. Pauline and Susan had still not touched base with everyone from their `67 core group. Besides Dorsey, Luke showed up at Dooley's, as did Susan and the Congressman, Jimmie and her girlfriend, the altered face of Dave Blazer and Yolanda. Brother Odell went back to the hotel; being seen at such a place with a gorgeous woman was not worth the risk. Jimmie noticed that the area where the poets used to gather in the back of the bar now had foosball machines and darts. They learned that Coach Shoals was in a nursing home in Indiana.

It must have been the new owner, thrilled with the infusion of Homecoming business, who stood on stage and tapped on the microphone.

"How ya'll doing TONIGHT!" A roar verified their mood. "We're delighted that you chose our little club here to be part of your Homecoming weekend at GSU — as you know, a campus with a longstanding reputation as a PARTY SCHOOL — YEAH, RIGHT ON!" The crowd roared again. "Tonight we present to you a couple that is no stranger to Dooley's. They've appeared on college campuses from coast-to-coast, at folk festivals, singing their own music, and now as remarkably life-like impersonators of one of the most popular and successful acts of our time. You'll recognize the sound. Join with me in welcoming to Dooley's, "Parsley-Sage!"

The crowd applauded, but then they would have clapped for anything. The duo kicked in with a robust bongo beat followed by familiar and harmonious lyrics:

Celia, you're breakin' my heart
You're shakin' my confidence daily
Oh Cecelia, I'm down on my knees
I'm begging you please to come
home
Come on home..

The crowd knew every word. The duo finished one number and didn't need to introduce the next one. This was music and themes that were cherished by both students and alumni in the audience. They eased from "*Sounds of Silence*" to "*Scarborough Fair*" to "*The Only Living Boy in New York.*" So many favorites: "*The 59th Street Bridge Song*" ("*Feelin' Groovy*"), "*April Come She Will*," "*A Dangling Conversation*," and more. The choruses lifted the crowd's volume: "…and they walked off to look for America" "… *I am a rock, I am an island…*" They closed with a tune fitting for Homecoming, "*Old Friends*," and performed a "Mrs. Robinson" encore and then one of the singers — the one portraying Paul Simon — concluded, "Sweet. Thank you, good people. Let's remember the wisdom in those words."

"Son of a bitch! Does that sound familiar? That's them! I knew it! It's Cate and Lonnie!" said Blazer. "These Simon and Garfunkel impersonators are Cate and Lonnie Youngman!"

"What?" Pauline asked.

"I'll be," said Susan.

"That was Cate singing the Art Garfunkel high harmony," Dorsey said.

"She looked like a man," Jimmie said.

I didn't recognize her either with that big "fro," Susan said. "Her hair was always long and straight."

Cate and Lonnie knew their old friends would be there and they were glad they surprised them. They had come back from Canada when amnesty took effect in `77 and they'd had a great response with this new act. Cate's voice worked perfectly for the Garfunkel high note harmony.

It was hard to talk amidst the ruckus of the bar. Buddy Baxter, sitting on the other side of the room, ordered another pitcher for the group. They had a full agenda for Saturday, but they stayed up like kids at a sleepover to learn of new jobs and appealing places to live if they ever considered relocating. They compared changes in hair and weight, shared photos of kids, teased, flirted, complained and imparted all the answers. For Pauline, however, the conversations always came back to Will. Although well-intentioned, this did not ease her pain. She needed to get back to the hotel. No one could talk her out of driving and no one would ride with her.

After an indulgent shower and more makeup than she was used to, Pauline looked surprisingly fresh after three hours sleep. Last night's clothes that were tossed in the hotel room corner reeked of smoke and alcohol. Grandma Ruth and Grandpa Abram Yoder waited in the lobby and looked conspicuous in their traditional Mennonite attire. Little Will appeared pensive about the day ahead: the dedication of the statue, all the talk about his dad, the way in which people were sure to make over him.

The new GSU President, Dr. Felix Culpepper, kicked off the Saturday activities with a Hall of Achievers brunch that was held under a tent in the front lawn of Peacock Hall within eyeshot of the statue of Will — still covered with cloth — on the new Freedom Plaza near Memorial Gardens atop the bluff where one could see where the boundaries of four states come together.

Following an eloquent introduction, Dr. Culpepper introduced honorees who stepped out from behind a partition as a GSU string ensemble enhanced the elegance of the ceremony. The first honoree was a chemical engineer with Monsanto who earned his baccalaureate degree at GSU and now worked in upper management in St. Louis. He had also been a district governor of the Rotary Club.

Next was a GSU student who didn't quite graduate but had earned a stellar reputation as a photojournalist. He traveled with Rosalyn Carter during the 1976 presidential campaign. The defining piece of work in his portfolio was a photo that captured Mrs. Carter's expression when she learned that her husband admitted to a Playboy magazine interviewer that he lusted after other women.

The third honoree looked familiar to Pauline and friends: a young black professional with a short flattop and pinstriped suit.

"And finally, we are pleased to induct into the university's Hall of Achievement a young man who is on the cutting edge of housing policy in this nation," said the president. "Director of the Greater Atlanta Rent Control Alliance, his agency strives to keep housing affordable and to reduce displacement of low-income and elderly residents. Ladies and gentlemen, Mr. JaMar Brown."

Pauline and her entourage were stunned, and then...well, delighted. They joined in hearty applause for their old friend and colleague whom they had not seen in a dozen years. Without his immense afro, dark sunglasses and jewelry, the new JaMar was easy to overlook. He had just arrived in a charter plane and planned to at least join Pauline and the others for the unveiling of the Will Yoder statue. Pauline and the former activists surrounded JaMar as they strolled over to the site of the statue.

"Well, well!" said Vic.

"Congressman," JaMar replied.

"We didn't recognize you! We didn't know about all this." said Pauline.

"My man, JaMar Brown! You been doing some shit," Dorsey said.

"That really is wonderful, all your success, JaMar," Susan said.

"I thought you wanted to be an artist?" Luke asked.

"More important for me to stand up to the man, if you know what I mean. You dudes taught me that," JaMar said.

Buddy Baxter, now part of the GSU senior staff, coordinated the event. The Board of Regents, families of honorees, media, friends and former teammates of Will Yoder were there for the unveiling. As they strolled to the site, Buddy pointed out various campus improvements, new and renovated buildings and new academic programs that were to be expanded or relocated. Buddy's love of GSU was genuine and obvious. He hoped to live out his career at the university.

It was sunny, brisk and fall foliage was at its peak. Leaves had been raked. Things looked tidy. The marching band could be heard tuning up down the bluff in the quadrangle. It reminded Pauline of that

350

October morning in 1967 when everything went wrong. She had not planned to ever step foot on the campus again; nor had any of the others. But this was not about Pauline or her views. It was not about her followers. It was not about The War. It was about a young man who served so that someone else might not have to. It was about a young man who gave up a glamorous, affluent lifestyle to help treat, heal and save victims of war.

At a distance, Pauline could see Vest Plaza where they had staged the `67 demonstration, with its statue of Senator George Graham Vest and his trusty dog, Old Drum, still on guard after several decades. She looked around and could see that almost all the former STAND leaders were there, less Arnie. Several brought along spouses and makeovers, shared successes and new directions. A caregiver from a local nursing home rolled the feeble Coach Mac Shoals up a sidewalk in a wheelchair. There was something gratifying about being together again. Some missed this place and cherished the memories — despite the tragedy of `67. Others would never forgive, forget or acknowledge that a few good words and

351

an attractive addition to the campus would in some ways even things out for all that Will, his friends and his family had been through.

Before Buddy introduced President Culpepper, he appropriately acknowledged that Congressman and GSU alumnus Victor Devillez, and his lovely wife Susan, had joined them for the ceremony. The Congressman was invited to say a few words; he managed to work in a reference to his service in Vietnam and how he had always been one of the military's strongest supporters in the House of Representatives."

"Ladies and gentlemen, friends, alumni, members of our Grant State family," said President Culpepper. "Today we honor in perpetuity a remarkable young man. A hero. A young man who placed others ahead of himself. A young man who demonstrated excellence and commitment as a star athlete, student, soldier and leader. A great young man, a hero, who embraced what few of us can live up to: 'There is no greater love than to lay down one's life for another.' "

Little Will tugged on his mother's suit, "Mom, he makes it sound like Dad's already dead."

They stood politely through the kind words, the overblown and inappropriate points, until the fabric was drawn off the sculpture. It was a life-size bronze relief featuring three panels representing three phases of Will's life: Will shooting a basketball, treating an injured soldier and standing behind a barbed wire fence. When the work of art was revealed, the audience responded with reverent applause and the media swarmed in with cameras and questions for sculptor Raymond Anders, President Culpepper and the Yoder family. The reception went on a good while. A young GSU staff member who knew little about Will Yoder looked at his watch. Former teammates shared Will's record stats and gracious sportsmanship. Coach Shoals entertained the crowd with animated and exaggerated stories; he still used his basketball net as a prop.

"And you must be Little Will." President Culpepper petted the boy's red hair after the ceremony. "Keep growing, lad. Grow as tall as your father and keep working on that jump shot. Maybe you'll follow in his footsteps and play for the Grasshoppers some day."

Little Will shrugged, took his mother's wrist and pulled her away.

Pauline, her family and friends strolled about campus. They looked at the buildings and grounds, fraternity and sorority house decorations and the tailgaters lighting their charcoals. Little Will enjoyed the faculty tug-of-war, particularly when several ended up in a mud pit. While that important battle took place, Luke James pulled aside some of the Pikes (brothers of Pi Kappa Alpha) while he carried two rolled up pieces of cloth.

A good hour before the Homecoming Parade was to start, viewers were already claiming their spots along the Bluff Circle Drive route. This year's Grand Marshal was the actor Joe Conley who played storekeeper Ike Godsey on *"The Walton's."* Other special guests joined President Culpepper and his wife in the viewing stand: rookie Missouri Congressman Richard Gephardt and Mrs. Harlan Renwick, widow of GSU's former president, who stood next to Buddy.

The prancing pom-pom girls carried the banner to announce the parade. There were sad looking Shriner clowns on tilted three-wheelers squeezing earsplitting horns, sparkling baton twirlers and a wobbly Uncle Sam on stilts. The popular Grasshopper Marching Band was followed by entries and floats from GSU clubs and organizations, fraternities and sororities, community groups and commercial enterprises that relied on student business.

The Pike fire engine was a campus relic that the brothers used more as a conversation piece to lure chicks than as a means of transportation. The vehicle was a regular feature in the Homecoming Parade. The brothers typically passed out small megaphones stamped with a Pike logo that doubled as a funnel for chugging contests. As their big red machine rolled by dignitaries and judges, Buddy was struck by the thought that something covert could be planned, that Pauline and her group could be planning another unauthorized demonstration that would, once again, damage GSU's reputation or even lead to violence.

This time, Luke made arrangements for Pauline, Susan, Little Will, even Grandma and Grandpa Yoder and others from the 1967 peace group to ride the Pike fire engine on the parade route. They stopped in front of the reviewing stand with President Culpepper and other dignitaries.

But rather than carry out something subversive, this laid-back and unifying entry rolled down the hill past where the riot had occurred more than a decade ago. This time, it was the music of John Lennon that came forth from the fire engine:

All we are saying...is give peace a chance

All we are saying...is give peace a chance

All we are saying... is give peace a chance

All we are saying... is give peace a chance

All we are saying... is give peace a chance

They hung two banners from the Pike's fire engine to face each side of the street:

STudent Alliance for a Nonviolent
Democracy STAND 1967
Remembers Arnie Latham and prays
for   there turn of Will Yoder
U.S. Troops Killed in Vietnam 58,269
U.S. Troops Injured 153,303
U.S. Troops Still Missing 1,664

Alarmed, looking about for the
reaction of dignitaries, parade goers and
the media, before he had time to think
about what to do, Buddy was relieved to
see President and Mrs. Culpepper singing
along with John Lennon's voice and people
on both sides of the parade route. Mrs.
Renwick smiled and sang. Mrs.
Culpepper's personal guests joined in.
Congressman Devillez did as well. The
music's gentle pace and enduring lesson
wafted over the crowd. Mrs. Renwick
tapped Buddy on the knee to assure him
that everything would be okay.

As the reassembled STAND group
caught up on news and shared stories,
most knew that, a few months after the '67
tragedy, GSU President Dr. Harlan
Renwick was cleared of any wrongdoing in
connection with the demonstration that

resulted in Arnie's death. Subsequently, Renwick took a non-pay voluntary leave of absence and immersed himself in learning more about warfare and social unrest. He convened meetings and organized panels of college presidents, elected officials, military leaders and students with perspectives ranging from the indifferent to the radical, the dove to the hawk. Renwick's involvement was intensified when the son of his wife's sister came home from Vietnam... in a box.

A short time later, Dean Ewing was charged with growing a marijuana crop that was hidden behind an abandoned body shop and a shabby mobile home rented to Dave and Odell. Ewing was linked to a partnership with The Greek Shoppe, a retail outlet known to not only sell fraternity and sorority gifts but drug paraphernalia as well. Ewing claimed he knew nothing of the side enterprise and pointed to a former student partner, David Blazer, as the culprit. But the judge was sympathetic to Blazer, who was beaten and disfigured in the '67 protest, and Blazer had covered his tracks and could not be linked to the allegations. Ewing escaped with probation, retired, and has since relocated.

Pauline and her entourage left the '79 Homecoming game at halftime with Grant State down 17 - 3 to Austin Peay. They wanted time to visit Arnie's grave before it turned dark. In `67, they had all pitched in and paid for the funeral and burial over four installments. Not all the donors had the means but they all fulfilled their pledge. They selected Saint Christopher Cemetery, an old one near Arnie's regular fishing spot below the bluff along Possum Run River, accessed by a single lane bridge where there was once a store and a mine.

It was a rugged, lovely spot. It had been chilly enough that the woodland canopy had lost most of its foliage. Sweaters felt good. A swirling wind welcomed them and the creatures alerted one another of the intruders. Grave markers went back 150 years. They explored about, sharing the interesting names, dates and epitaphs on the markers. Odell ran his fingers over the letters that would dissolve over time.

They noticed several prominent tombstones connected to a family that apparently owned a distillery for several generations. There was someone whose epitaph told the story of a man who hung himself on Christmas Day after his wife left him. Babies were marked by tiny graves without head stones and were clustered within a deteriorated fence with chipped stone angels at the entrance.

Dorsey led them to Arnie's grave. It was in a corner and the marker was already inflicted with a rash of moss. A root had tilted it. Pauline yanked out weeds that covered the words. Odell patted the stone as if it were Arnie's shoulder.

"I loved this old fellow," Cate said.

"What's not to love," said Blazer.

"I like the inscription we came up with." Susan read it aloud:

Arnold "Arnie" Louis Latham
Jan. 4, 1931 - Oct. 21, 1967
A kind man who lived
humbly,
died for peace,
and always knew the time.

The moon gave them all the light there was. Through the years, the trail to Teddy's Landing had shifted and flooded, leaving driftwood and prickly shrubs to high step and slash through.

"Where...uh, where the hell did this big stone come from?" Pauline grunted, "...uh, sucker won't budge...like a stubborn mule."

"Good God," Dorsey said.

"Can we get through?" Jimmie asked.

"Outcrop above must have eroded," Luke said.

"If there's someone sitting on the other side of this big rock in a long white robe then, then Brother Odell, you can take it from there."

Skinny Yolanda slipped through a crevice and noticed the water level. "Look how low the river is."

"Be no tubing tonight, folks. I'd slice my big ass on the rocks," Pauline said.

"Here. Grab hold. I'll help you through," Blazer said as they lined up to follow.

It had been twelve years, but they were back at the Landing. Their hangout. Their hideout. The place where they kicked back, got drunk and high. A place where they shared their dreams and secrets.

"Look, some of the logs are still here," Susan said.

There were rusty beer cans in a pile along with flat inner tubes still tied to a shrub. They tossed the invading driftwood and lifted the better logs back into a semi-circle configuration where they belonged. Luke built a fire in front of the birch tree that had lost much of its graffiti to peeling bark. Lonnie had his guitar. Odell lugged in a couple of coolers and pretended he didn't know what was in them. Dorsey brought a jumbo box of fish and hush puppies from Long John Silvers. Cate put on some tunes in her boombox. They were set.

"I have fond memories of this place," Susan said.

"Is this where your friends hung out?" Brandi asked Jimmie, her partner. "Cool place."

"Reverend, toss me a brewski, would you?" Blazer asked.

"Hey there, Dorsey! I see where you delivered on the loaves and the fishes. You the miracle man! Hell, we'll never run out of food, now," Luke said and Odell chuckled.

"We got everything we need here," Lonnie said.

"Build me a little shack over there along the river and I might just move in here," Dorsey said."

"Mr. Brown, do you have a lovely daughter?" Pauline asked of JaMar.

"Two. Seven and five," said JaMar.

"Never figured you for a family man," Pauline said. "And so clean cut, now, with your professional, establishment attire. You use an afro wig for special occasions?

"Yeah, gotta scare off the whiteys now and then. Just working from within the system these days, that's all. But I'm no Uncle Tom, you understand," JaMar stressed.

Lonnie turned down the boombox and tinkered with his guitar and then he and Cate eased into a *"Red Rubber Ball"* by *The Cyrkle*.

"Now that's right up our alley. Powerful. A hard hitting protest song if I ever heard one," Pauline said sarcastically, but it didn't stop everyone from joining in the chorus:

Yes, it's gonna be all right
Yes, the worst is over now
The mornin' sun is shinin' bright
A red rubber ball

Pauline observed that, as they took their seats on the logs, they sat exactly where she remembered them sitting twelve years ago. Luke passed around a joint.

"What can we plan here tonight? Anything we can disrupt? Occupy?" Pauline joked.

"It's almost my bedtime," Blazer said.

"We gotta long drive ahead of us tomorrow," Lonnie said.

"Has everybody given me their address and phone number?" Susan asked.

"I thought the parade went well. Thanks, Luke, for putting that together with the Pikes," Pauline said.

"Yeah, great banners," Dorsey said.

"I teared up when everybody sang along," Jimmie said.

"That simple tune and message from Lennon — what a difference that's made," Susan said. "There's still a place to speak out for peace."

364

"More important than ever," Yolanda said.

"You really think it matters?" Vic asked.

"Sure. Gotta believe it does," Yolanda said.

"So… we just negotiated Salt II with Brezhnev. You think he would have given a shit if GSU students were marching in front of Peacock Hall?" Vic said.

"If it's part of a larger contingency -- yes," Yolanda said.

"You're not saying that the movement didn't make a difference," Susan said.

"I don't believe there has been a U.S. soldier killed in Vietnam since, what, `75 -- four years ago?" Vic said.

"I'm just glad it's over," Susan said.

"Surely we've learned something from it all," Cate said.

"That the people won't stand for an immoral war?" Lonnie said.

"Maybe the war would've ended sooner if there had been unity at home," Vic said.

"What? We should have supported more killing?" JaMar asked.

365

"North Vietnam hung on because they knew our leaders were scared of a revolution," Dorsey said.

"Bullshit. We were never close to a revolution," Vic said. "North Vietnam lost the war — January 1973. They finally gave up. Paris Peace Accords — remember?"

"But then the South fell, what, two years later?" Lonnie asked.

"Yeah, after the attack in the Central Highlands," Vic said.

"We had a report once about Will being in the Central Highlands," Pauline added.

"South Vietnam was never sustainable without us," Jimmie said.

"Well you can't tell me that the marches and protests didn't make a difference. *We* made a difference," Susan said.

"Our problem is that we seem to partner with the wrong regime," Yolanda said.

"Like the Somoza dictator down in Nicaragua. He's been booted out, and now the Sandinistas are in power. They any better?" Luke asked.

"This new guy in Iraq — Saddam Hussein — they say he's brutal," Vic said.

366

"We can't be friends with everybody, and we can't expect other countries to be perfect allies and just photocopy our constitution," Luke said.

"And we can't prepare for every attack or regime change. We're more vulnerable than people think," Vic said.

"What do we do if one of our embassies was taken over by radical extremists?" Pauline asked.

"That's not gonna happen," Vic said.

"What if it does? What do we do?" Blazer asked.

"Bring in more troops and hope they don't kill the hostages," Dorsey said.

"Economic sanctions," JaMar said.

"Negotiate," Yolanda said.

"Prisoner exchange," Blazer said.

"It's complicated," Susan said.

"Bewildering," Yolanda said.

"Frightening." Jimmie said.

Yolanda picked up a stick and started drawing boxes in the dusty surface. Dorsey pulled out a few beers from the coolers and tossed them about.

Jimmie wrapped her arm around Brandi. "Guys, we were hoping to recruit a few demonstrators for a gay

367

rights march coming up in D.C. Don't tell me you guys are burnt out?"

"I'll try and go," Susan said. Vic made a his face to indicate disapproval. "Me too,"Yolanda said. "I'll go."

"Well, you're all welcome. Hope you can make it. It'll be like the old days," Jimmie said.

Several of the guys slipped off to piss behind a shrub. It was more problematic for the gals since the shoddy restroom they pieced together twelve years ago had been lost to the wind and elements. Yolanda leaned over to look at the quick rippling water that was so clear she could see minnows dart around the rocks lit only by the moon and the campfire.

Pauline didn't want their last night at the Landing to be a debate on policy and activism, although it was interesting to her how views had shifted since they had gone their separate ways. Some were more informed than others. Some had become jaded. Some had other priorities. Pauline was of the latter: Little Will was her priority now and she figured she was doing all right as a parent for her boy to be turning out so well. She wanted to bring him out, stand him in front of everyone and brag about his sweetness and diligence, activities and promise — despite her lingering concern that he may have slowness issues from the blow she took at the demonstration when she was carrying him.

"Let's, uh... switch gears," Pauline said. "I'm sure many of you haven't had the chance to catch up on what everybody's been doing in the last 12 years or so. So who'd like to...uh, who'd like to start? JaMar? This morning, we learned about the great stuff you've been doing in Atlanta."

"We're making a dent, yeah, but it's always an uphill battle. When you bury yourself in your work, there can be consequences. I was married, two kids. We split and she met this guy who took her out more. They have the boys in Minneapolis. So I don't see them much."

"You get drafted?" Yolanda asked. "Yeah, but I joined the reserves. Basic training and then a weekend a month for six years. Beats jungle duty," JaMar said.

Yolanda stood next to where the four windows were drawn in the dirt. She repeated the exercise and put four boxes and Roman numerals in the dirt with a stick. "Anybody remember? ...when we went through our own Third Window, when we shared things about ourselves that nobody else knew? Anyone remember what JaMar shared with us back in `67?"

"Yeah, he told us about a brother we didn't know he had," Dorsey said.

"That's right," Pauline said.

"And that he was serving time," Blazer said.

"Unjustly," Lonnie said. "Your brother... still in jail?"

"He was out, then he was back in, now he's out again. He'll finish community college next year. Kid got screwed big time, wants to move on," JaMar said.

"So anything else from your Third Window you would be willing to share?" Pauline asked JaMar?

"Now why would I do that? I don't hardly know you people. Haven't seen or kept up with you in more than a decade. Hell, you didn't even recognize me at the ceremony this morning. Why should I spill my guts?"

"Don't have to," Pauline said. "Sometimes it's just good to get shit out."

JaMar picked up the stick Yolanda used to draw in the dirt. He traced it over the numerals already there and took a deep breath. "After we all got expelled in `67, I moved to Atlanta to find some work and to take a couple of courses at Morehouse College. I was angry and bitter about what all had happened to us. I guess you could say that I was on the brink. Then this pissant bigot comes along named Lester Maddox, Governor of Georgia. When Dr. King was shot, Maddox — that mother fuckin' Maddox — denied him the honor of lying in state in the capitol. The niggers were taking over, you see. Then the asshole endorsed Wallace, George Wallace, for President, who was doing everything he could to keep Negroes out of public schools. One setback after another. So when I learned that Lester Maddox was scheduled to receive an honorary degree — Doctor of Laws, imagine that — from Bob Jones University in Greenville, South Carolina, I decided to go to the ceremony. But I went with a pistol in my coat pocket. I was gonna kill the bastard."

"My God, JaMar," Yolanda said. "What happened?"

371

"I had the courage. I didn't care about the consequences."

"But you backed off," Jimmie said.

"It just struck me that he would win — the bastard would win — if I made a martyr out of him. He got his plaque and I left as he started his rant," JaMar said.

Yolanda sighed in relief. "Thank God you didn't go through with it, JaMar."

"For sure," Blazer said.

"Glad nobody saw that gun on you," Luke said.

"Thanks for sharing, JaMar. Really, thanks," Yolanda said.

Yolanda noticed Odell gazing at her. He tried to be discreet, but wasn't. She knew that things would never have worked out between them, but there were traits she cherished about Odell that she knew her husband would never have.

"So, uh... who would like to go next?" Yolanda asked.

There were no volunteers.

"Lonnie. Lonnie Youngman, aka Paul Simon," Yolanda said.

"Glad everybody liked our new act. It's been good to us," Lonnie said.

"So how was Canada?"Blazer asked.

"Cool... make that cold."Cate said.

"We were in Winnipeg mostly," Lonnie said. "Real nice people. Made us feel welcome."

"But it's always good to come home," Cate said.

"Still can't believe that Carter issued that unconditional amnesty," Vic said.

"Needed to put the war behind us," Luke said.

"It was an insult to our brave veterans," Vic said.

"Guys, it's a done deal. The war's over," Susan said.

"Cate, how about you? I know everyone remembers how you had the courage to tell us about the... the *attack*, you know. You doing okay, hon?" Pauline asked.

"The memories come back now and then. The rage."

"Well, tell us about your life on the road?" Yolanda asked.

"Me and you and a dog named Boo," Lonnie said.

"It's not as glamorous as it sounds," Cate said.

Lonnie strung his guitar and sang a verse:

373

*"Each town looks the same to me...
the movies and the factories..."*

"I know that song," Dorsey claimed:
"*Homeward Bound*."

"Anything else about yourself that
no one else knows?" Yolanda asked.

"Well, since I've been playing the
part of a man, I've had this embarrassing
habit of scratching my crotch," Cate said.

As they laughed she pointed to
Lonnie for him to take his turn.

"Everyone remembers what
Lonnie's big secret was the first time we
played this game. Remember? He had a
special stipulation on his organ donation
plan."

"Oh yeah!"

"Who'd want that old thing,
anyway?" Blazer said.

"Ah, but a skilled, experienced,
handsome and ample organ it is," Lonnie
said.

"Not that ample," Cate said.

"Okay, okay... you boys and your
penises. What about present day, Lonnie? I
know you like to be center stage. Anything
buried deep within you that you've never
told anybody?" Yolanda asked.

374

"Well this might surprise you. I'm sure you'll wonder how in the world I've been able to keep this from Cate all these years. Maybe I shouldn't..." Lonnie said.

"No, really. C'mon Lon," Yolanda said.

He paused and turned serious, but the others felt another wisecrack coming on. Cate rested her chin on her two index fingers.

"I've kept something secret all my life. It's not anything I'm proud of, but I know it wasn't really my fault." Lonnie's eyes started to water. Cate had never seen him like this but she wasn't convinced that he was sincere.

"I can't read."

Pauline's first instinct kicked in. "Well, that's not so uncommon. Lots of musicians learned by ear and can't read a bit of music: Stevie Wonder, Ray Charles, BB King..."

"No, I mean I can't read. Period."

"What?" Yolanda said.

"I've bluffed my way through it all my life. Used all kinds of gimmicks."

"I'll be damned," Pauline said.

"It's okay, man," JaMar said.

"Takes courage to admit something like that. Proud of you," Luke said.

"You have some kind of problem — dyslexia or something?" Dorsey asked.

"I don't know. Never had it checked. Oh, I can write my name and I've learned what some signs mean, but that's about it," Lonnie said.

Cate was stunned that she could have been fooled for so long. She wrapped herself around him then he reached for his guitar, its strings the only alphabet he could use. He strummed and sang and everyone joined in *"With a Little Help from My Friends"* to offer a break before the next heady report or revelation. None of them expected their chums to remember what they had shared in `67 or open up again in this extemporaneous exercise a dozen years later. But it was, for the most part, working.

From behind, when his wrinkled eye socket and dented, patched face were out of view, Dave Blazer looked like the same Faceman with Beach Boy hair and good looks that was to facilitate his run up the public life ladder. Now, as difficult as it was to talk and as easy as it was to jolt people who first came upon him, he had worked his way into the Washington scene as a political strategist. He had, in fact, advised Victor Devillez in his Congressional race to use his war record in Vietnam as his central campaign thrust.

"So, Mr. Dave Blazer, we know you live in Washington," Yolanda said.

"Virginia, actually. Close enough," Blazer said.

"You're not married."

"I'm on the lookout for a sweet, stacked, blind girl."

"You were excused from the draft, I presume."

"Yeah, those who are missing an eye are generally scratched off the list. What a deal, huh?"

"Is there anything from your third window that you would like to share?"

"Well it's kind of embarrassing," he teased, "but I, uh... no, I can't divulge this..."

"Oh, come on. You'll probably never see any of us again anyway."

"Well, I have this intense fantasy for — I've never told anybody this and you won't believe me — but I have this thing for Helen Reddy."

"Helen Reddy?"

377

"That's right. *I am woman hear me roar*... God, that Aussie accent. Drives me WILD!"

"Helen Reddy, you say."

"That's right."

"Helen Reddy."

"That's right."

"Well you did take a pretty good blow to the head back in `67." Even Blazer laughed at that one.

Blazer put his arm around his old roommate and burped.

"We want to give everybody a chance, now, so who's next?"Yolanda said. "Brother Odell Calhoun, how about you? You've sure seen a lot of changes in your life. What success you've had. You'll be on TV before long, saving souls...

"... and raking in the big bucks," Blazer said.

"Tell us about your family," Pauline said.

"Well, I married a pretty lady I met at church camp when I was 24. We were chaperones at Lake Chippewa in Arkansas. A few years later we were re-acquainted at seminary. Mary Leigh worked in financial aid for a few years but

378

has stayed home since the children came along."

"Two?"Pauline asked.

"Four. Two of each." Odell said.

"You all live where now?" Pauline asked.

"Hopkinsville. Hopkinsville, Kentucky," he said.

"Big church?" she asked.

"We've been blessed," he said.

"Is there anything you would be willing to share with us, Odell? Something about yourself you've never shared with anyone?" she asked.

"I think it's the Catholics who confess their secrets," he said.

"Oh you can share anything – just something that no one knows about you, or something that happened to you? I still remember your story about nearly drowning," Pauline said.

"That wasn't a story," Odell said.

"But the voice guided you to safety," Pauline said.

Odell connected with Yolanda and lost his train of thought. She knew, of course she knew, that Odell had a thing for her since they first met in '67, sensed his yearning and hoped he would not re-enter their times together in his remarks.

"Well I'm glad that Mary Leigh isn't with me. I probably wouldn't share this if she were here," Odell said.

"Go ahead. Spill your guts," Blazer said.

"Well... I, uh... I think I may be... I may be losing my faith," Odell said. "I was brought up to accept scripture, without question. I had a calling. I didn't need theology and fancy professors.

"You were a natural," Blazer said.

"Your roommate corrupted you is what happened," Luke said sarcastically.

Blazer gave Luke the finger.

"No, a couple of years ago, I was introduced to theological scholarship, biblical archeology, some of the works of Marcus Borg and John Shelby Spong, in particular. There's a whole community of scholars who've spent years researching and writing and putting various scriptures into the context of their time. None of that had ever been introduced to me. My faith – - or what little I have of it now — is evolving, and now I have this massive congregation and ministry that was built around traditional and literal scriptural

380

principles. Plus I have a wife and four kids to support."

"So your sweet little organist of a wife doesn't know about this?"

"No."

"Deep shit, man. Take a few hits off this joint," Lonnie said.

"Seriously, you'll never know how all that went on here was so important to me, like a   fresh summer breeze coming through my window."

Yolanda walked up to Odell, grabbed his hand, and kissed him on the cheek. "You guys continue to surprise me, Yolanda said.

"Luke, how about you? How 'bout it? Still a Saluki?" Pauline asked.

"Still have my shop in Carbondale. I get by," Luke said.

"Family?"Pauline asked.

"Divorced. No kids," Luke said.

"So you've had an exciting life, Vic said sarcastically."

"Carpe Diem," Luke said. "No really, I'm a simple, plain sort of fellow. Not famous like you, Congressman," Luke said.

"C'mon," Vic said.

"Nah. Think I'll just leave you hanging," he said as he grinned.

"You're among friends," Vic said.

Luke thought about describing his post-traumatic stress disorder: the flashbacks, the nightmares. His wife left him when he refused to continue therapy. His business failed. He drew disability.

"My third window is… uh, let's just say it's nailed shut," Luke said.

"You passed the first time we did this," Yolanda reminded him.

"And life went on. Think I'll pass," he said.

"Okay… okay, spoil sport." Pauline took a swig of bourbon.

"Who'll be next, then -- Jimmie? We know you're living in Chicago with Brandi. You've come out and we support you. And you're doing such important work bringing fresh water to the poorest of the poor," Yolanda said.

"Proud of you, Jimmie," Susan said.

"Back in `67, I know it was tough for you to tell us about your father," Yolanda said.

"It meant a lot that you would share that," Cate said.

Lonnie's ego kicked in and he hoped Jimmie would tell everyone about their little fling once upon a time.

"I was once on Salt Creek Trolley," Jimmie said.

"What the hell?" Pauline said.

"Salt Creek Trolley. I was a Cub Scout and our troop went on a field trip downtown to the studio where we watched an episode of "Our Gang" — you know, Spanky and the Little Rascals. We sat on a trolley and this chubby announcer in a conductor's suit came around to ask us questions that grown-ups thought were *so* cute. Kind of a local version of the Art Linkletter show," Jimmie said.

"What'd he ask you?" Yolanda asked.

"He wanted to know what I wanted to be when I grew up?" Jimmie said.

"And what did you say?"

"I said I was gonna be rich. He just chuckled, but it just pissed me that he didn't take me seriously. Then he asked me if my favorite food was rice. 'No, it's ice cream,' I said, like what all the other kids like. And I don't use chop sticks." Right then and there, I knew I would be dealing with prejudice throughout my life. I was different and would be treated differently," Jimmie said.

"Yeah, for us it's fried chicken and watermelon," JaMar said. "Lots of stupid-ass white people out there."

Dorsey finished chugging a beer.

"Speaking of stupid-ass white people..." Lonnie mumbled.

"I'll go next," Dorsey said.

"Catch us up on all you're been doing there, Dorse? Let's see, when you left GSU you were drafted," Yolanda said.

"Yep, served my time in Germany, got out and went on the G.I. Bill, finished my degree at Florida Atlantic in gorgeous Boca Raton. Parlayed my experience back in Bluff City in to the management trainee program with Long John Silvers and I now own 14 stores and am regional manager for 35 others. I drive a late model fire engine red Mustang convertible. I have an oceanfront condo and belong to a tennis club with lots of shapely ladies. Life is good."

"Well, well... I should say," Pauline said.

"Always knew you had it in you, Dorse," Blazer said.

384

"You could've fooled me," JaMar said.

"Way to go, man!" Lonnie said.

"And I, uh... I pulled together some guys and started a fraternity at FAU. It was for all the dorks, like me. A fraternity for those nobody else would give a bid to. No hazing. I'd had enough of that shit back at GSU. In fact, I funded a charitable foundation that tracks and discourages hazing in fraternities, military academies, where ever. Looking to get in to the school bullying thing," Dorsey said.

"Shit, Dorsey," Luke said.

"You the man," Lonnie said.

"You people are amazing," Yolanda said.

"Dorsey, I knew you'd make something of yourself," Pauline said.

The women suddenly looked at Dorsey differently. He was more attractive than they remembered and his confidence was appealing.

"Yolanda, you want a turn?" Pauline asked. "I remember last time you caught us off guard ...when you told us you were an atheist."

"Guess you still are?" Odell asked.

"I'm more of a humanist these days – an evil secular humanist," Yolanda said.

"And your husband…"

"Mike."

"You and Mike: you must like Music City."

"We do. Mike's in the music business, but there's a lot more to Nashville than that. We live near Vandy."

"Remember the demonstration we went to at Vandy?"

"Didn't Peter, Paul and Mary perform?"

"Sure did."

"So you, uh… you like counseling."

"I do."

"Have you used the, uh… Third Window thing on other groups? Clients?"

"Sometimes. Don't you guys feel a special bond with one another? Bet you've shared things here you haven't even shared with your husbands and wives – right, Vic? Odell?"

They nodded.

"So what more are you going to share with us, Yo?" Cate asked.

"Guess," Yolanda said.

"You're a Scientologist?" Blazer asked.

"Nope?"

"You had an abortion," Jimmie asked.

"Uh uh."

"You slept with Dr. King after his 'I Had a Dream' speech?" Blazer asked.

Susan slapped Blazer on the shoulder. "How dare you!"

"Just kidding," Blazer said.

"Well... recently I learned that I'm a descendent of Frederick Douglass," Yolanda said.

"Frederick Douglass? The abolitionist?" Susan asked.

"Really?" Pauline asked.

"Didn't he marry a white woman?" JaMar asked.

"His second wife was white, but I'm a descendent of his first wife, Anna Murray who was black. They had five children."

"Always knew you had good genes," Odell said.

"Yo, you might come into some money," Luke said. "Might own some land somewhere."

"Get in on some royalties." Dorsey said.

"Get real," said Yolanda.

"So... you're famous," Pauline said.

"Knock it off," Yolanda said.

Regardless of this discovery, Odell always knew that Yolanda was something special. He let his memory linger, their times together, tender times that didn't advance beyond the two of them holding hands. He snapped back into focus when Pauline called up the next participant.

"Okay... whose left? Pauline asked.

"Susan?"

"That's right."

"Susan, anything you've kept to yourself that you want to share?" Yolanda asked.

Lonnie whispered to Luke. "I'd just like to know why she married that jerk."

Jimmie recollected and teased her: "Were you ever implicated in that multi-limo pileup after you hurled a snowball that went crashing through the windshield of a funeral procession?"

"It didn't crash through any windshield. It was a toss, a gentle toss," Susan clarified.

"We're harboring a criminal. We should've turned you in long ago, you know that. It's called aiding and abetting," Blazer said.

Pauline smiled and tried to get them back on track. "So, you have this lush horse farm in the rolling hills of the Bluegrass State. You sip mint juleps all day on the front porch. Life's tough."

"It's a beautiful place, for sure, but it's a hard-nose business, too," Susan said.

"Well you look wonderful. Age has been good to you, Susan," Pauline said.

"Amen to that," Cate said.

"You always were a picture of health, trim, glowing... everybody was jealous of you," Pauline said.

"Well, something will go wrong with all of us at some point," Susan said.

"But you've always taken such incredible care of yourself," Yolanda said.

"Yeah, but there's only so much you can do," Susan said.

"What's that supposed to mean?" Pauline said.

"Some things are beyond our control, that's all," Susan said.

"Are you trying to tell us something?" Pauline knew her.

"I have a lump. On my breast," Susan said.

"What?"

Tears trickled down her cheeks and Vic was there to comfort her through her whimpering.

"The doctors are optimistic. Just had the tests. Might have to do the chemo thing," Susan said positively.

Vic dabbed her tears, then his own. He clung to Susan and covered her hands with his. "Why didn't you…"

"I didn't want you to worry. I didn't want it to ruin our weekend or this reunion. It's probably nothing – or something they can take care of easily. It's really quite routine these days," Susan said.

"It's not routine and we're going to Mayo's," Vic said.

"The doctors in Lexington can handle it, Vic. I'm fine, really," Susan said.

Vic was unhinged. His fingers shook as he lit a cigarette and took a long drag until it furrowed his forehead. At last, the group gained a sense of how much Vic did indeed care for Susan.

"Vic, I know this may not be a good time, but do you want to share anything with the group?"Yolanda asked.

"I don't think so. You ready to go, hon?"

"No, Vic. I want you to open up…
and be part of our special little
community," Susan said.

"The last time, you told us all about
the killer raccoon you strangled with your
bare hands," Luke said.

"You all stop now. Go ahead, Vic.
You can do it," Susan said.

"You can pass if you want," Yolanda
said.

"My thoughts are with my wife right
now. No time for stupid little games," Vic
said.

"It's okay, hon." Susan kissed his
hand. "We all need to open up sometimes.
I'm all right, really I am," she said. You
don't have to.

The Congressman tossed down his
cigarette, ran his hands through his hair as
he pulled his thoughts together. He sat
down on a rock, picked up a stick and
doodled in the dirt. He didn't look up.

"The bombing of Cambodia was
well underway. Ordered by Nixon. Illegal
as hell since Cambodia was a neutral
country. We did what we were told. Our
unit was to provide ground support for the
bombing raids along the border. I don't
remember exactly where we were except

that I think we were getting close to the Laos border. I'd been in combat for a few months without a scratch while I saw men killed all around me. I was issued an M-16 that had an effective range of about three football fields. So firing through that jungle I seldom could see my targets. I may have killed hundreds or a handful or none."

"I don't remember the blast or how long I was down, but I remember waking up and not being able to see. It was like I was at the movies but the screen was all white. I assumed I was dead because I couldn't hear either. But then I felt a burn in my lower left leg. My vision started to come back. I felt blood and loose skin and muscle and metal. I brought my hand up to my nose as if I could tell by the smell of the blood if it was really me who'd been hit. I realized I was lying at the bottom of a bank. The bank had been scraped of vegetation and was slick with mud. There were bodies and body parts all around in various twisted configurations. Some were from my unit. Most were enemy troops. It looked like everyone but me was dead. It started to rain and I opened my mouth to catch some drops on my tongue."

"My M-16 was near me but the clip was missing. I attached my bayonet and started poking around on our guys to see if anyone was alive. When I concluded that they were all killed, I started poking around on the enemy and a couple of villagers who had also been blown to bits."

"As I poked around on this one enemy soldier, suddenly he sprang up, scared the shit out of me and knocked the rifle out of my hands. He pounced on me and we wrestled in the mud, punching and biting and gouging. I guess I forgot about my injury. He was quick but he was so light that I could throw him off of me. I grabbed my rifle with the bayonet and I pinned him down."

"Then I had a good look at him. He was a kid, a goddamn kid, maybe 14. At first he looked terrified, then when he knew I could overpower him he shouted at me and spit in my face, probably to tell me how he was proud to die for his cause. I put the bayonet to his neck and he stopped resisting while he waited for me to end his life."

"It's okay, Vic. It's okay, honey," Susan said.

393

"You didn't have any choice. It was you or him," Luke said.

"War's hell, man. You did what you had to do," Blazer said.

"I couldn't help but think this was all such a waste. He had a family somewhere that he'd never see again. Who knows what that kid could have been someday — a teacher or a farmer or a poet. But he would never have that chance. I thought about how unfair it was. I reared back to ram the knife through his throat..."

"You don't have to relive this, Congressman," Luke said respectfully. "Really, we understand that you had to..."

"It's okay Vic. We're not going to judge you," Odell said.

"No, don't you understand... I couldn't do it. I pulled back the bayonet and jerked my head as a signal from him to get going. He seemed perplexed at first, then he scooted up the slimy bank to the top, where he stood up and smirked as if to reinforce what he had heard about Americans: that we were gutless cowards. And then he turned to run and was immediately taken out by at least a half-dozen rounds from somewhere."

"So just like that he was dead and I'm flown to a MASH unit where I get stitched up. Later they tried to rebuild my knee but they didn't have much to work with. So I'm discharged and get a Purple Heart that later becomes the theme of my campaign for Congress. Some war hero, huh? I let my buddies down. I let my family down and didn't live up to my legacy. I let my country down. I let myself down."

"No you didn't, Vic," said Susan.

"I think you showed compassion when few men would," Yolanda, said.

"Proud of you, man," Dorsey said and Luke and Blazer nodded, then all the others nodded.

Susan comforted her husband and felt closer to him than ever. Pauline invited everyone to gather around for a group hug. JaMar started humming and everyone joined in: *"All we are saying... is give peace a chance..."*

They must have sung Lennon's verse thirty times with no intention of stopping when the Congressman's beeper went off. He backed out of the singing pack, retrieved his mobile phone and returned the call.

"Devillez." After a pause: "Uh huh. You sure." Another pause: "Well let me break it to the mother of the boy... yes, I understand. Okay." Another pause: "Thanks. Let me know if you have anything else."

The singing broke up when Vic took the call. They knew this could be significant.

"I just received a call from my chief of staff. I've had him monitoring the releases of the POW's. He has some reliable sources in Defense and the State Department." He paused and looked at Pauline. His face turned soft. He didn't have to say anything; they knew it must be news about Will.

"A mass grave has been unearthed," Vic said. It was near the Laos border, not far from a camp at Dien Chau. We had checked that area before but didn't know of this grave. The bodies were badly decomposed, so they've been there a while. But several still had their dog tags on, and one was of a William Yoder."

"You sure? They've made mistakes before."

"The body was of a tall man and there were others in his unit buried there.

They'll check the dental records as soon as they can, but this is probably it, I'm afraid. Real sorry, Pauline. You've done everything you could do. But now, after twelve years, at least you can finally bring some closure to this."

Pauline broke loose of Susan's embrace. Drunk, frantic and full of angst, she mumbled, cussed and struggled to run across the rough terrain, around the large stone that came loose and blocked the entrance to Teddy's Landing and up the lane to where she had parked her VW van. She climbed over the rock and into the darkness. The others shouted and urged her to return.

"Don't let her drive!"

Dorsey, Jimmie and Luke went after her, but she had a head start and they could hear the ignition turnover before the van came into view. The headlights bounced and bobbed along the rough road as she drove out of site. The rest of the group ran up the lane and got in their cars to catch up with her.

Her first thought was just to drive. And drive. Drive to lose those who may be following her. She sobbed and didn't want any more comforting. She wanted to find a bar or a church, whichever came first. She wanted to talk to Will and tell him she tried to bring him home. She wanted to tell him about his fine son.

Her drive was interrupted by spasmodic images from her dreams — the haunted visions from the jungle. She crossed over medians and bumped off of guard rails. She cussed at Will and cussed at God. She felt the presence of her mother, sitting in the passenger side, scolding her and reciting the books of the Bible while a lit candle first dripped hot wax and then caught her arm on fire.

She found herself driving up Bluff Circle Drive toward Peacock Hall when the van veered off the road and grated to a stop among thorny shrubs. She stumbled out of the van and stood wobbling in front of the freshly unveiled sacred sculpture of Will. She stroked the bronze statue, wishing it would come alive. She peered into the three faces: the athlete, the soldier and the prisoner. She cried. She sobbed. She stepped back, walked around behind the sculpture and stood atop a low limestone wall, closer to the sky and the spirits that were assigned to her. Below, the lights of Bluff City wrapped around the

398

campus. She remembered the stories of those — perhaps distraught or broken-hearted — who leapt to their death from this ledge. Temptation rushed through her in a panic. It was time to end the pain and join whatever awaited. She prayed for forgiveness. She was ready to do it: to leap.

But then she thought of Little Will who was already without one parent. The fine boy who was better than she deserved and who might need extra care. She was ashamed. She would not give up. She had been a leader. She would not go out like this.

Pauline stumbled back to her van and drove down the bluff, but the booze still impaired her driving. She weaved and as she downshifted, her foot slipped off the clutch and the van bucked, the engine shut down and the steering wheel was hard to turn. She overcompensated and lost control, bumped over a sidewalk and collided with an old oak that stood its ground. Pauline was flung forward through the windshield and the glass slashed her head and neck. She landed on the university lawn.

After the first steady rain, Pauline's blood could no longer be seen on the lawn; it had already seeped into the soil to forever link her with Grant State University, to forever draw from its chemistry. The stain was gone, but the memories of a rowdy young woman from Bobcat, Illinois were not diluted. She had advanced above the person she was to learn and lead others and affect social change. She and her followers had grown closer and enduring by opening themselves up to the fresh breeze beyond their Third Window.

Spring 1981

Pauline and Arnie were gone. Coach Shoals was losing his faculties. Luke was one step ahead of the collection agencies. That left nine of Pauline's disciples who for the most part kept up with one another. They never forgot Little Will's birthdays even though the boy had only vague recollections of who they were. They never stopped mourning or comforting one another. They held on to memories. They got on with their lives.

Jimmie and her partner Brandi continued their fresh water project, but they were forced to devote more and more time to fundraising. They planned to slow down and spend more time at home when their adoption was finalized. Their baby was infected with a new virus called HIV, but that did not change their plans.

Dorsey increased his portfolio of Long John Silvers restaurants to 29 in seven states. He no longer managed any stores. In Boca Raton, he pursued a celebrity who developed a successful cosmetics line. Dorsey invited all his STAND colleagues from GSU to his wedding to be held on his fiance's yacht. His foundation has been responsible for anti-hazing policies in organizations and institutions across the country.

No one heard much from Luke. Several phone calls to him indicated that the number had been disconnected. Susan contacted Buddy Baxter at GSU to see if the school had a forwarding address. Buddy was not optimistic since Luke, like the others, had been expelled in 1967.

Coach Shoals passed away in a northern Indiana nursing home not far from Minnow due to complications from pneumonia. After considerable public outcry largely organized by Dave Blazer, GSU announced that it would call off plans to name a new facility the Quad-State Coal Arena, after the St. Louis-based company. Instead, Blazer organized a counter campaign to keep the name Mac Shoals Fieldhouse after the legendary basketball coach, despite the fact that the GSU Board of Regents terminated his contract after he participated in the 1967 incident.

JaMar left his position with the Greater Atlanta Rent Control Alliance for a position at the federal Department of Housing and Urban Development. He was in high demand as a consultant and was an artist of growing notability. His charcoal portraits were recently featured in the Newmann Gallery on Washington D.C.'s DuPont Circle.

Lonnie and Cate continued to live life on the road, performing at clubs and festivals. The couple has cut three albums and was developing their own sounds after having been Simon and Garfunkle impersonators for many years. Lonnie made great progress with literacy training and recently passed his GED exam.

Yolanda had opportunities to grow her counseling practice, but she and her husband enjoyed their discretionary time that allowed them to travel to see performances of her husband's prospective clients. She occasionally facilitated marriage enrichment weekends, and she almost always incorporates the Third Window exercise.

With both of their spouses absent during the `79 reunion, Odell and Yolanda were tempted but did not succumb to an adventure into adultery. On several occasions, Yolanda had engaged in affairs without guilt or significance, but Odell stayed true to his wife, the organist, and they had two more children and one foster child. Running a mega-church and caring for a large family did not leave time for the theological exploration that Odell found intriguing. Given his circumstances, it was best not to rock the boat, so he stuck with the prosperity theology formula that had served him well.

Dave Blazer -- aka "The Faceman"-- had grown indifferent to the reactions that came forth from his facial injuries. His looks didn't seem to stand in the way of his effectiveness as a prominent D.C. political

403

strategist. He subsidized a paramour to meet his needs and sneaked away to attend every Helen Reddy concert he could.

By the summer of 1981, Susan Devillez's cancer was in remission and doctors at the Mayo Clinic were still optimistic. Strathmore Farm's new stallion, Thunder Gulf, was promising but not yet proven. Acknowledged as one of the more consistent Congressional hawks, Victor Devillez was re-elected to another term and was named to the House Rules and Armed Services Committees. During a fundraiser in Arlington, Congressman Devillez was pulled aside by a top aide.

"Have you talked to Brewster?"

"No, why? Where is he?

"He's at the office. Just had a call from Defense. Still trying to tie-up some loose ends   on this latest recovered batch of POWs. Another mass grave."

"God almighty. Okay. Let's get on it. Really need to bring some closure to this -- for the family's sake."

"For sure, but Congressman, on the Yoder file, there's a problem."

"What? What kind of problem?"

"Apparently dog tags were issued for a William *O*. Yoder and that's what we thought we took off the body. Turns out that all the dried blood and twisted metal made it hard to read the name and serial number. When we analyzed it again, we could see that the tags actually belonged to a William *D*. Yoder. *That's* who is lying in that mass grave. The "O" and the "D" looked so much alike, that…"

"Which means that the medic is alive."

"At least he wasn't buried in that trough."

"Good God."

"So what do we do?"

"Let's sit on it for now. I don't want to give any false hope to that family. They've suffered enough as it is."

Five Months Later

Life went on. Abram and Ruth resumed their routine of not doing much of anything. Growing old was part of it, but the deep-seated source of their pain and despair were the relentless images of their son -- at times dead, at times living -- leaving with them the wounds of war and more than a decade of mourning, depleting them of energy, determination and hope.

Abram gradually got around to doing things that needed to be done around the farm: mending fences, pruning grapes, weeding the garden, training Little Will if he agrees to a simple life. Once the boy whipped through homework and his chores, he and his buddies would gather at the barn and shoot hoops with friends until darkness sent them home. He improved his game, but given his average height and undeveloped skills, it was apparent that Little Will would not be a standout.

Ruth tried hard to stay positive about her son; Abram kept his bitterness inside. They spent a good bit of their time on the front porch rocking or swinging and not saying much. They were increasingly indifferent toward government, it's reports, policies, effectiveness and projections. Outreach volunteers from their Mennonite community made regular visits that were not particularly appreciated. There only source of joy was there hope for Will to come home. This gave Ruth the strength she needed to fight off cancer for Abram to endure Parkinson's

406

disease and the occasional falls that went with it.

Ruth noticed the ferns hanging from their front porch ceiling, twisting with the wind.

"Storm shifting this way, maybe?" Ruth said.

"Maybe," Abram said. "Supposed to veer off and miss us."

"Ferns won't stay green much longer," Ruth said. "Look how the wind is twisting them one way, then the other. And the wind chimes, they're acting up again."

"Sugar Maples...prettiest I've ever seen."fgn cv Ruth said.

"Maybe. Maybe so," said Abram.

"Fetch me some sap?"

"Let's give it a few weeks."

They could hear a bouncing ball out of sight behind the stable.

"Hear that?" Ruth said.

"Loves that game," Abram said.

"You know we're lucky. He never fusses about his homework. Good about his chores. Makes his bed. Can recite every book of the Bible," Ruth said.

"He's a good boy," Abram said..

"He loves that court you built for him," said Ruth.

They could hear him dribble, then heave up a shot accompanied by a high pitched, excited announcer's voice:

"And there's six seconds on the clock. Hufnagel passes to Warren. Warren to Yoder.   He's double-teamed! He fakes, drives, shoots – it's in! Will Yoder, Junior makes an incredible shot at the buzzer! The Hoppers win! The Hoppers win!"

Ruth and Abram grinned at one another as they eavesdropped on their grandson's imagination. They would have never wanted the boy to be separated from his mother, but after Pauline's death, their place in Indiana seemed like the best for young Will, and they took him in without hesitation despite town gossip about illegitimacy. Hump and Rhonda, Little Will's other grandfather and his step grandmother, came for short visits in the summers and sometimes in winter if the snow was not too deep for the long drive.

Little Will had been a blessing to Abram and Ruth, giving special meaning to their later years. In their nightly prayers, they gave thanks and prayed quietly and relentlessly that their only son would return and care for the child that he did not know existed, to have a meaningful and rewarding role in his life. In the meantime, little Will benefited from the strict, steady nurturing of his grandparents. And as best they could tell, the boy was developing well enough mentally and physically that they no longer worried about the blow that his mother took when he was still in her womb, a blow that some said could have injured his brain and hampered his development.

The aroma of fresh baked corn muffins wafted out the window. Abram whittled a piece of soft wood that would become a form yet to be determined. Ruth knitted a scarf for the church bazaar. Wind chimes seemed to be calling chaotically.

Thick ivy weaved through the fencerow along the road leading to the Yoder farm, blocking the view of the road from the porch. They could hear a car turning, then mumbling on to the lane toward the house. Abram stood up, straightened his hat, lifted his chin with its wiry white beard as his way of acknowledging that strangers were approaching. Ruth removed her apron and held on to Abram's arm. A long black official-looking car stopped at the small family cemetery enclosed by a well-maintained picket fence.

Every headstone was labeled "Yoder", except for the one entitled

PAULINE CODY
for Peace
Born April 4, 1946
Died October 18, 1977

Two men and a woman parked the car and approached the house cautiously. The men were in uniform, freshly pressed. One was short and fit; the other, taller than the bearded old man Abram. The Tall One used a cane and shuffled with the help of the other man to steady him. The Tall One was gaunt, taciturn. His approach lit an endless fuse that ignited in Abram and Ruth whenever a rumor surfaced about Will's fate.

Was this the day the army would make it official, that he had been killed in combat or by friendly fire, taken prisoner, tortured or damaged to the point of uselessness and despair? Could he have survived the decade or more of incarceration? Had he been a prisoner all this time?

The Tall One removed his garrison cap, revealing a head of freshly trimmed red hair. Ruth could feel her heart pounding and Abram prayed that it be true. If it were so, he imagined how much of him under that military suit was battered and yet to heal. Ruth and Abram stepped cautiously down the front steps to bring their dream into focus.

Could it be? Ruth held her hands over her mouth, then gently placed her hands against his face. Abram wanted to believe, but this man, despite his height, looked to be half the weight that he remembered and twice the age he would be.

"This is our son, Abram." She stroked his face. "This is our son. This is our son."

She touched a scar on his neck. "Dear Lord... Will, oh Will, what have they done to you."

Tears brought a sparkle to their eyes. Ruth and Abram and Susan and Vic surrounded the worn, battered man. The Tall One leaned on his cane and showed no expression. Little Will came out from behind a shrub, dribbling his ball with delight. He stopped and passed the ball to the Tall One, but the ball bounced off his chest and he made no effort to catch it.

THE END

Made in the USA
Las Vegas, NV
21 February 2022

44335605R00246